Something New at the Borrow a Bookshop

Kiley Dunbar is Scottish and lives in England with her husband, two kids and Amos the Bedlington Terrier. She writes around her work at a University in the North of England where she lectures in English Literature and creative writing. She is proud to be a member of the Romantic Novelists' Association and a graduate of their New Writers' Scheme.

Also by Kiley Dunbar

Christmas at Frozen Falls

Kelsey Anderson

One Summer's Night
One Winter's Night

Port Willow Bay

Summer at the Highland Coral Beach
Matchmaking at Port Willow

The Borrow a Bookshop

The Borrow a Bookshop Holiday
Christmas at the Borrow a Bookshop
Something New at the Borrow a Bookshop

KILEY DUNBAR

Something New
at the
Borrow *a*
Bookshop

hera

First published in the United Kingdom in 2023 by

Hera Books
Unit 9 (Canelo), 5th Floor
Cargo Works, 1–2 Hatfields
London SE1 9PG
United Kingdom

A CIP catalogue record for this book is available from the British Library.

Print ISBN 978 1 80436 223 5
Ebook ISBN 978 1 80436 222 8

Look for more great books at www.herabooks.com

Printed and bound in Great Britain by Clays Ltd, Elcograf S.p.A.

1

Something old,
Something new,
Some place borrowed,
Someone blue…

WEBSITE UNDER CONSTRUCTION

Borrow-A-Bookshop has undergone extensive restoration to bring it back to its former cosy glory after Clove Lore's devastating flood last winter.

We will be open once more to book lovers in early September, following installation of our new shop technology (including our fancy new website, stock system and online shop) – the final stage in our recovery.

We can't wait to welcome back all those holidaymakers who are ready to live out their dreams of running their very own bookstore and café in our historic Devonshire harbour village. The waiting list (currently thirty-three months long) will also re-open soon.

Thank you so much for the kind donations that have flooded in from all across the world to help support our renovation. We feel very loved.

The Borrow-A-Bookshop Community Charity
Bookings Manager: Jude Crawley, MA
Jowan de Marisco Clove-Congreve (Charity Director)

Chapter One

A summer-warmed breeze blew Down-along, making the sails on the little girl's paper windmill spin fast upon their pin.

'Careful, Rads!' her mum warned. 'Nobody said anything about it being this steep.'

Accustomed to her mum worrying that she was inches away from a tragic accident at any given moment, Radia made an exaggerated show of shuffling extra carefully down the cobbled slope, dragging a tattered toy fox at her feet.

Happy tourists tramped past them, gripping onto gate posts and garden railings for dear life and exclaiming to one another that it was set to be another scorcher today. Some trundled cases, heading for the Siren's Tail and a few nights' dinner, bed and breakfast by the Atlantic. Others carried crabbing nets and buckets, looking forward to dropping bait over the sea wall all afternoon.

'Can we get an ice cream, Mum? Please!' the child asked in an urgent tone, having spotted the bright flag of Mrs Crocombe's Ice Cream Cottage lifting gently against the blue sky.

There was a decent queue outside. That meant the ice cream must be good. But her mother was looking at the GPS on her phone and turning this way and that.

'Let me concentrate, it must be here somewhere,' she replied, pushing up black-rimmed specs that had slipped in the heat.

'There's only up or down,' the girl reminded her. 'I'm looking for it with *my actual eyes*,' she said, pointedly, glancing at her mum's phone, which hadn't helped them one bit all the way here.

Joyce Foley (Joy for short) had joked with her daughter in the back of the taxi that the Google Maps photography robot must have driven right into the sea somewhere south of Minehead because this little bit of Devon didn't seem to be charted on her device. Overhearing, the driver had raised an eyebrow in the rear-view mirror and muttered something about 'London *grockels*', which only the little girl thought was funny. She'd told him, 'We aren't really from London. We aren't from anywhere at all.' Joy had stayed very quiet at that.

'Is this it?' asked Radia, plainly, pointing to a turning off the slope, between two dazzlingly white, freshly painted cottages.

'Hah! I suppose it must be.'

The sounds of drilling and hammering resounded within the buildings on either side as they passed between them. Evidently the work of restoring Clove Lore continued even eight months after the infamous flood.

Joy dragged the case along behind them and Radia, used to carrying her life on her back, stoically shouldered her furry, bear-face rucksack, which was so stuffed to bursting with her treasures its zip had broken on the journey here.

They made their way through the passage, past the old sleds leaning against the recently repointed masonry.

Entering a peaceful little square, Radia stumbled on the cobbles, which were freshly laid out in swirling patterns like a mermaid's scales set in sandy-coloured concrete.

The smell of paint, which was strong throughout the whole village, was especially potent here. It mixed with the rising scents of cut grass, sweltering seaweed and something good cooking way down at the pub on the harbour wall.

Joy stopped in her tracks to take in the squat little bookshop, from its stone steps to its conical roof, squint like a wizard's hat. 'Well, this really is different,' she said under her breath.

'Bookshop! Bookshop!' Radia cried, running around the palm tree in the centre of the square, the cracks in its big terracotta planter visibly repaired with silvery mortar.

She dodged in and out of the new sky-blue metal tables and chairs (which matched the sky-blue shop door perfectly), set out in little clusters all over the cobbles as though the owners meant this to be an outdoor café or some kind of meeting place.

Criss-crossing the square overhead were strung white bulbs. Even higher above circled the gulls, watching the latest arrivals in Clove Lore and laughing on the wing.

Joy tried not to think too much about how lovely it would be to sit there on a late summer evening drinking cold wine. She'd be far too busy for that.

'Mind the paint, I think the door's wet,' she told Radia, as she found the key in the jacket of her grey blazer, which she wore over a paler grey linen jumpsuit.

'One of the first things we'll do is install the code lock; do away with the need for keys. Far safer,' she said, as she pushed open the door.

The little girl shoved past her mum to get inside first.

'*Woah!*' Her windmill was immediately discarded on the wonky floorboards, shiny with new varnish.

Checking that the door was securely latched behind them, Joy cast her eyes around the bookshop. Empty shelves stood like sentries along the walls, interspersed here and there with brightly coloured vintage armchairs and little reading nooks. Dotted about were old vases filled with dried summer flowers in faded pastels. At the head of each shelf stack was a sign with words painted in curling gold script.

'Bi-ol-o-gee, gen-rul fiction... *children's books!*' Radia squealed in delight at discovering what would soon be the children's corner, below the spiral staircase of gleaming black iron – also freshly painted, her mum guessed from its glossy sheen.

Throwing herself across two patchwork beanbags, Radia shrieked, kicking happily. Then she lifted the lid off one of the many cardboard crates shoved under the stairs – matching the others piled all around the shop – and found to her glee that it was filled to the very top with picture books and board books and chapter books, all bright and inviting. Sitting up, she grabbed for one.

'Gently. They're not for us. They're for customers.'

'What customers?' said the girl, walking her feet all the way round to the other side of the beanbag so her back was turned on Joy. She huddled delightedly over the pop-up *Beauty and the Beast*.

Coming up to her sixth birthday, Radia was already what would be described as a 'free reader' by her teachers – if she had any teachers, that is. The fact she loved to devour books even though she'd missed her reception year was a source of pride and pain for her mum, who was now observing her child turning pages and getting lost in a solitary world of imagination.

There came no reply when Joy asked, 'Need anything, Rads?' out of the usual compulsive sense of inadequacy and guilt that made her feel rotten much of the time. But there was no point fussing right now, Radia was happily absorbed in her book.

Joy skirted around yet more boxes to make her way through a low door at the far end of the shop. It led into a bright café, all painted white, with new lace curtains at the windows, chequered tablecloths and red tomato-shaped squeezy bottles.

'OK,' she admitted with a shrug. 'This is cute.'

She wouldn't be having anything to do with the café, though, thank goodness. That sort of thing was for the real bookselling-holidaymakers who'd begin arriving again in a couple of weeks, but she still had access to the café's shiny new kitchen for their own use.

Turning for the shop once more, she made her way towards the door, to a table set out with a display of books – the only unboxed books in the whole place. A handwritten note had been left for her.

> *Dear Joyce, the village's first Digital Nomad!*
> *Welcome to Borrow-A-Bookshop. Everything is ready for your stay. The paint is (just) dry so you don't have to worry about smudges. Good luck installing all the new shop tech and cataloguing the stock! Who knows, maybe you'll enjoy a bit of bookselling too! Happy (working) holiday.*
> *Love, Magnús and Alex, the last Borrowers. X*

Joy had already figured that digital nomads were a new concept in Clove Lore. She hoped she wasn't going to attract excitement or attention from the local volunteers who she'd heard about from Jude Crawley, the friendly woman who'd sorted out her contract.

She looked again at the note. God, she *seriously* hoped nobody expected her to actually sell any of these books. It certainly wasn't a stipulation of the contract or she'd never have pitched for this job in the first place. And yet they were booked in for two weeks. The installation would likely take only nine or ten of those days. Were the locals expecting her to play shopkeeper too? Radia would love that. But the thought of making small talk with a stream of strangers made Joy sweat.

She fanned herself with the note, wondering why none of the books were shelved. Had she paid close enough attention to the contract? Did it mention putting books on bare shelves?

She'd never taken a posting quite like this before, but the English seaside setting had been too appealing to resist and, thinking of her daughter's love of books and beaches – and feeling guilty at all the dreary office blocks, warehouses and shiny, corporate 'glass box' buildings they'd schlepped through recently – she'd hurriedly sent in her tender and been handpicked for the contract.

Joy let herself be distracted from her anxieties by the books on the display table, instantly grasping the relevance of some of them: titles referencing floods. The flood was the reason she was here, after all. The reason she was being paid to stay for two weeks and build the new website, install the EPOS-linked stock system, integrate the security cameras with the shop laptop and the owner's mobile, do away with the need for easily lost door keys, and all the rest of it.

Some of the books in the display she couldn't account for quite so easily. Books about mermaid myths, Vikings and a copy of *Treasure Island* – she supposed because they were by the sea?

Her eyes fell upon a copy of *The Borrowers* with its cover showing tiny human-like people peering through a mousehole at a giant world beyond the wainscoting.

There was a notecard on top of the book, which she read aloud with a growing smile. 'This one is a gift from Borrow-A-Bookshop to our youngest Borrower yet. For Radia Pearl, happy holidays!'

'A present! For me?' The girl bounded across the room and without even checking to see what kind of story it was, clutched the book to her chest. 'I told you this one was going to be different. Like a *real* holiday!'

'No, Rads, it's just work.'

'And Mum?' she continued, disregarding the whole 'work as usual' thing. 'We'll read books and go to the beach?'

'Of course we will.'

'And maybe we can stay longer this time?'

'Just a couple of weeks, then we move on. OK? Same as the others.'

Radia, however, already sensed what her wayfaring mother was too world-weary and restless to grasp: this place was not at all like the other places. This place was special and beautiful and actually a bit magic. A whole summer of adventure and possibilities lay ahead, only they'd have to cram it all into two short weeks. There had already been *one* nice surprise: the gift of a book. What other surprises were waiting for them?

Radia's heart sang as she danced around the shop, swinging her new book and her toy fox in dizzying, giggly circles.

'Don't make yourself sick,' her mum told her, knowing she'd be ignored, which she was.

So, Joy explored further, pushing open the door at the foot of the stairs. Peering inside at the single bed, she told Radia this must be her room, which elicited no response at all. Radia had seen a lot of new bedrooms.

Making for the stairs with her suitcase, she began her climb. Once at the top, Joy set about emptying her meticulously packed belongings on the plump white bed below the window seat set into the deep stone wall.

Through the glass she glimpsed a spot of sparkling blue sea between Clove Lore's steeply stacked, higgledy-piggledy roofs and chimneys, colourful masts and flags, and the raggedy crowns of windswept palm trees that tumbled over each other all the way down to the harbourside.

OK, so it was pretty in a weathered and well-salted kind of way, and it looked for all the world like a bucket and spade, sand between your toes kind of a holiday, but this really was just another job and she wasn't going to be taken in by the village's quirky charm.

It may well look different from their usual gigs. Borrow-A-Bookshop might even *feel* hidden away and safer than many of the spots they'd stopped at, but Joy had no intention of letting her guard down. She'd done that once before and learned a hard life lesson: she and Radia were far better off alone in their safe little bubble.

She lifted her clothes from the case, all anonymous black and grey, the kind of thing you wore if you didn't want people noticing you, and nothing beachy at all.

The holidaymakers they'd passed had all been in bright sundresses and shorts. At least Radia would be properly dressed, she consoled herself with a sigh.

The sea shimmer caught her dark eyes once more and, dropping the grey pile, she let herself clamber onto the cushioned window seat, her nose at the warm glass, where she watched as the boats glided across the calm horizon.

Downstairs, Radia sang the only two lines of 'I Do Like to Be Beside the Seaside' that she knew, over and over again, throwing her fox into the air and catching him before he fell.

Hugging her arms around herself, gazing down at the deep sparkling blue, Joy couldn't help allowing her lips to curl into a sleepy smile. No, she wasn't going to let her guard down or draw attention to herself in any way, but it couldn't hurt to admire the prettiness and let the sunshine in a little.

Chapter Two

Standing by the lantern at the end of the sea wall, Monty could just make out the family boat, the *Peter's Bounty*, on the horizon, a white dot he'd recognise from any distance.

He pushed back his brown curls and brought his hand to his brow, shading his dark eyes from the fierce morning light. The hottest day of the summer so far. He knew the fish would be shoaling deeply and there'd be a good haul. A fisherman knows. Even if this fisherman was confined to the pub kitchens these days.

Sure enough, a message appeared on his phone to confirm his hunch.

> Hi bro. Prep for a good lot of whitebait, 30 servings I'd say. Nuf mackerel to last you a week, and two good fat lobsters in the pots.

'Got it. Cheers Tom,' he typed back in reply, before fixing his eyes on the horizon once more. The *Bounty* was making for the harbour already and the little chamber in Monty's heart that stood empty whenever his brother put to sea by himself began to fill with calm.

It was the same feeling he'd had as a boy, knowing his dad was out there in all weathers, risking his life daily to bring home the catch. No fisherman's family is ever truly contented until the mooring ropes are tied and the boats are again bumping at the harbour wall.

Monty had a newfound respect for his mum, who'd lived with this worry all her life until the confusion came, the slow creep of dementia. Now she lived out at Barnstaple with his older empty-nester sister and her husband.

Monty would be willing to bet that even though she'd forgotten so much, his mum could still remember the feeling of watching for the boats coming in, like all those Clove Lore wives stretching back so far in history until nothing can be recollected.

Now Monty was like them, and his heart lifted and dipped with the waves as he watched his brother captain *Peter's Bounty* towards the harbour mouth.

He checked the time on his phone. Half-nine. He'd have to get back to the kitchens. There were still ten pounds of spuds to prep, not to mention the beer batter he'd need to begin soon. But glancing back at the Siren's Tail, he found he couldn't move his feet quite yet.

Finan wouldn't miss him for another few minutes, surely? He could tell him it was a two-cigarette kind of a break after the flat-out rush of breakfast service this morning. He'd understand.

Monty just needed to get away from the drone of the industrial dishwasher for ten minutes, to inhale the sea and feel the sunshine. Still, he had no right to complain about being tired or irritated. Not when Tom had been out there all by himself hauling in the nets.

The brothers often spent the weekend evenings repairing those nets down on the beach after Monty's shifts at the Siren were over. The light summer nights had made that essential work easier, and they'd worked and joked and reminisced, passing the shuttle through the intricate web of old rope, patching holes and making good.

They'd learned the skill from their dad, who'd learned it from his dad, and so on, all the way back to a forgotten year in the eighteenth century when the family had settled in Clove Lore, attracted by the bountiful bass and mackerel at this time of year, and the winter abundance of cod, flounder and dab.

The *Peter's Bounty* had passed to them when they lost their dad a few years ago and the brothers had sunk their nets every day since, until it became apparent that, although there were still plenty of fish in the Atlantic, the prices had fallen so much that one of the twins was going to have to do something else. That person, naturally, was Monty.

More like his resourceful, wily mother than his brother, who took after their dad, Monty threw himself into adapting. He'd presented the recipes his mum had taught him years ago to Bella and Finan at the Siren's Tail when their old chef was retiring.

Within days last autumn, Monty had gone from being a fisherman of nobody-could-remember-how-many generations to a landlubber up to his elbows in peelings. It was a living. So what if this wasn't quite what he wanted?

Tom, eight minutes his junior and so always considered the baby, needed the routine of fishing. Just like their dad, Tom was regulated by the tides. 'Salt in his blood, that one,' their dad used to say, and it was true. Without the sailings, Tom would grow agitated, lost even. One time, he'd fractured his wrist on the boat and was stuck on the quayside for days; he'd not known what to do with himself, pacing about by the harbour lantern until Monty brought the *Bounty* in again.

Still, everyone had noticed how Tom was a lot calmer since meeting Lou, the local newspaper reporter, last Christmas. And yet, even with her warming his bed up at the cottage, he'd wake before his five o'clock alarm and trudge Down-along every day, as if not putting to sea on time was an impossibility.

No, Tom was the fisherman, Monty was the... well, what was he?

He looked down at his hands, clutching his phone. Where they'd been calloused and salt-rubbed like his brother's, now they were soap-softened from the kitchens. How the last few months on dry land had transformed him.

He loved to cook, that's for sure, but the Siren's chips and steaks didn't interest him. All those sausages and pies served up with gravy and the endless fried breakfasts didn't do anything for him either. There was demand for his delicious seafood, but that made up only a third of his orders in a pub where the traditional favourites still dominated the menu.

As his heart sank lower, his eyes lifted to where the *Bounty* was rounding the long protective arm of the harbour. Tom waved from the cockpit, a lit cigarette clinging to his smiling lips. Monty made for the mooring.

Even though he'd been in the kitchens since seven, his working day only really came to life when Tom dragged the boxes over the harbour side and showed him the catch, all glinting scales, shining eyes – sea-fresh and so simple. Those, he knew how to handle.

His mum's recipes, memorised years ago, always made the lunch and dinner shifts pass quicker: lobster with thermidor butter, salt-baked seabass on beds of fresh samphire, whole mackerel stuffed with lemon and herb breadcrumbs. Monty loved preparing those dishes, transporting himself from the airless heat of the pub's chrome ovens to the cosy familiarity of their cottage kitchen when his mum still lived there, the door thrown open to let in the breeze.

Only, the illusory contentedness didn't last. An indoor, overheated life was harder to adapt to than he'd anticipated, and when the orders for deep-fried frozen scampi and chips flooded in, his love of food was deadened again. He had his own kind of restlessness to deal with now.

'How do?' Tom shouted as he moored up alongside the harbour steps, cutting the engine.

'Home again?' Monty shouted back, like he always did, catching the rope his brother threw.

He tied the familiar knot and listened to Tom telling him where the best fishing had been that morning, all the while wondering what the answer was to this puzzle of feeling thwarted and landlocked.

Monty was pulled from his thoughts by the wolf whistle.

Tom, always the cheekier and bolder of the twins, was greeting his girlfriend as she approached along the harbour wall with two takeaway coffees in her hands.

'Sorry, Monty. I didn't think to get you one,' Lou told him, smiling in apology as she reached the mooring.

'No bother. I've plenty coffee at the Siren,' he replied. 'You two taking a walk? Nice day for it.'

He pictured himself at his spot by the sink, working his knife, and immediately felt churlish for being jealous of their plans.

'I'll sluice the *Bounty* down later, OK?' Tom said, striding up the stone steps and greeting Lou with a kiss. 'Bit slimy, sorry,' he told her, before stripping off his waterproof gaiters and waders and throwing them back down into the boat.

Standing there, smiling in jeans and a T-shirt, he was Monty's double. Only, anyone looking would be able to tell his heart was light like feathers while Monty's weighed him down like setting concrete.

The fishmonger's van crawled along the sea wall towards them now too, just as it did every day. Half Tom's catch went to the Siren; the rest was whisked away to cafés and restaurants inland.

'You two get going,' Monty told them. 'I'll get the crates in.'

'Cheers, Monty,' said Tom, pulling on trainers, his cheeks a ruddy pink in spite of the gentle breeze coming in off the water.

Monty saluted Tom and Lou with a pointed finger to his brow and watched as they walked off along the sea wall.

Those two were getting pretty cosy; in fact, Lou had practically moved in. Old Mrs Crocombe Up-along at the Ice Cream Cottage would be pleased. She'd had Tom in her matchmaking notebook for years with umpteen names crossed out beside his, all girls who'd come to the village for summer jobs or holidays. All, it turned out, just flings.

Monty, on the other hand? The space beside his name was blank. There'd been dates, of course. Weekend-long romances over the years when hen dos and wedding parties came in from across the country, plenty of them, but they always left and Monty was never too sad to see them go.

For a while there, at Christmas, he'd thought Coral, the police officer he'd kept company after the flood, might be sticking around for a while. But as soon as the cordon into the village was lifted, she'd gone back to the station and hadn't replied to his voicemail asking her back to the Siren's Tail for supper when she was next off duty.

That one had stung a bit, if he was honest. More so in light of his brother's newfound happiness. It was definitely harder to be alone in the world when there was a walking, talking reminder of how things could look for him, if only he could find someone willing to stick around. It was made all the worse when he'd walked in on his mirror image making out with Lou in their mum and dad's cottage up at the top of the slope. Then, after discovering them sharing a cosy bath – *why* couldn't Tom lock doors? – Monty had snapped and he'd asked Finan if he could have a back room at the pub.

He'd moved his stuff in last Valentine's Day, leaving his brother the freedom of their cottage to do whatever he wanted without fear of Monty stumbling in. Everyone was happy with the arrangement. Even if Monty had this strange new feeling in his chest; a heavy sort of ache he couldn't put a name to.

The retreating Tom and Lou were reaching the turning down onto the beach as Monty woke from his thoughts to shake the fishmonger's hand and pass comments on the weather.

He made his way down the steps and aboard the gently rocking *Bounty*. The second his feet touched the planks and the gentle roll of the waves travelled up his body he was comforted.

Three big iced crates waited for them and the sight and scent of the glistening catch settled him all the more. This was the absolute root of him, his earliest memories and his DNA. He hefted the first box into his arms with ease and stepped off the *Bounty*. He helped load the van, keeping his own crate on the harbour side, then waved the fishmonger off after they'd toted up the boat's pay for the day.

This wasn't so bad, really. Not if he could keep this new brooding side of him under control. He had a home at the Siren, didn't he? A place of his own. And at almost forty that was definitely only right and proper. He couldn't live with Tom in his pocket forever. And he had a secure job too. Far safer than fishing. And Tom kept the boat going, doing what he was programmed to do from his infancy. Yep, this was the most satisfactory outcome for everyone, and he'd just have to make the best of this new normal.

Carrying the haul to the Siren, he let himself enjoy the prospect of preparing all of this beautiful seafood. He already had the recipes in mind and he had everything he needed in his well-stocked pantry – parsley, butter, oil, chilli and ginger, and there were the breadcrumbs he'd prepped first thing too. It really wasn't all that bad, working at the pub and being alone. Not if he didn't think about it too hard.

Chapter Three

Radia had only just successfully planted her beach-toy windmill in the soil of the otherwise bare window box when her mum whipped into the little bedroom on the ground floor of the Borrow-A-Bookshop.

'Careful, Rads. You'll fall.'

Joy tugged the window closed and secured the latch, shutting the colourful foil spinner out of the five-year-old's reach.

Radia, standing on the bed with her face squished forlornly against the glass, peered down at the four-foot drop. She'd have landed on lush springy turf if she had taken a tumble. 'I never fall!' she reminded her mum, sulkily.

'There's a first time for everything,' Joy warned, bringing her breathing under control after the adrenalin spike of seeing Radia leaning out into the air. 'Right, let's see your backpack.'

Radia huffily surrendered her bag, its contents already tipped out onto the single bed: lidless felt pens, hopelessly dry; a curly *Beano*, very well-thumbed; two Sherbet Dip Dab wrappers; umpteen notebooks full of drawings and the alphabet she never tired of practising. Topping it all was her toy fox who, since his hasty procurement in the Charing Cross Hospital gift shop almost six whole years ago, had borne the name Charley.

Radia's father had named him. It had been his first and only gift for the daughter he was, apparently, satisfied to peer at only once before vanishing from their lives forever, much to Joy's numb astonishment.

Radia was too young to know the half of it. Sean's abandonment – he didn't even stick around to ask his child's name – had happened so suddenly it left the new mum winded. His disappearance had come at the end of fourteen months of increasingly suffocating control, by which time Joy didn't even have access to her own door keys. His sudden surrender of power had been so uncharacteristic and unexplained, Joy still refused to believe it wasn't all another mind game and he wasn't about to reappear at any moment, laying claim to her and their child. It was like living permanently in a movie thriller where her every move was accompanied by suspenseful violin chords.

Things had been this way for so long now that Joy was used to feeling on edge. She was in very real danger of forgetting the goal she'd set for herself back in that maternity ward: a life of unguarded peace for her and her baby.

Nowadays, all she focused on was making sure Sean never found them. Fortunately, her job helped in that regard, pin-balling them all over the globe, never staying still for more than a few weeks at most. It was what 'normal' looked like for them, and it had been working out well, so far.

'Take you for an ice cream once I've fixed this, OK? We can see what Clove Lore's like,' Joy told her, eyeing Radia with a fearful softness she sometimes worried she couldn't hide, before getting stuck into repairing the zipper on the fuzzy backpack.

'And Mum?' said Radia.

After yanking the zip back into place, Joy replaced the pliers in the tool bag that travelled everywhere with them; tools that symbolised independence more than even the well-worn wheels on her suitcase. Her dad had gifted them to her when she first moved away to uni. She'd quickly sussed there was nothing you couldn't fix with the right YouTube tutorial. Nowadays, her tools meant she never had to ask for help from anyone.

'And Mum?' Radia tried again, breaking Joy's focus.

This was how she started most sentences recently; as though she'd already made her point and wanted to add more. She'd also recently dropped 'mummy' from her vocabulary, and the first time she'd used the grown-up-sounding substitution, Joy had looked so thunderstruck she'd decided to keep it up, even if it did actually make her feel a bit funny inside when she said it. 'We'll paddle in the sea and get fish 'n' chips, yeah?'

Joy couldn't help repeating, 'Fish 'n' chips?', with a broadening smile.

'That's how it's written on the signs we saw,' Radia stated blankly, making her mum weaken even more and fold onto the bed beside her, reaching her arm around her daughter's small frame, all wile and wire.

'Well, I suppose it is.' She pulled Radia closer. Every cuddle felt like being plugged back into the grid that kept Joy's heart beating. 'Because they go together. Like us. Mummy 'n' Rads.'

But Radia's mind was already down on the shore. 'Maybe there'll be some other children to play with. Some *school* children,' she said in her best making-a-point voice, which had a curiously rootless transatlantic twang, nothing like her mum's estuary English accent.

'Let's go find out,' said Joy, standing and giving her glasses a shove back onto her nose. 'Put your jellies on.'

She hoped the challenge of buckling the pink glittery plastic shoes by herself would be enough to throw Radia off her favourite topic: school, or rather the absence of it.

Joy knew only tears and frustration accompanied these discussions, and she deflected them as best she could, usually saying things like, 'We do all right, don't we? You've got reading pretty much sussed and you can write the alphabet and spell all your tricky words, and this year we'll do more sums and computers, just you wait!'

It had worked, until recently. Until Radia figured out from watching CBeebies that kids far younger than her had been in pre-school for years, some of them since they were actual babies, and loads of other nearly-six-year-olds were in Big School. Most of them, in fact.

She'd been outraged at the discovery, and after watching every episode of *Mallory Towers* and *The Worst Witch* on iPlayer (shows she wasn't really old enough for but she'd insisted she was), she'd developed a deeply romantic notion of what school would be like if only they stayed somewhere long enough for her to actually go.

At school there were smart grey pinafore dresses for winter and floaty checks in the summer, a packed lunch in a cartoon character lunch box, and a whole day spent away from hotel rooms and B&Bs with hastily arranged, annoying childminders. If she was allowed to go to school there'd be far less hanging around in empty business premises playing Roblox on a phone screen while her mum fiddled with networks and servers, or whatever it was she was up to that day.

'And Mum? *Is* there a school here?'

'I don't know. Clove Lore's a small place, so maybe not.' Joy tucked her long darkest-brown bob neatly behind the arms of her specs while Radia blinked up at her. It was getting harder to lie undetected these days.

Joy had spotted the 'Slow: Children Crossing' sign, back up near the entrance to the visitor centre car park where the taxi dropped them with their luggage this morning, and she'd caught a glimpse of the schoolyard railings painted in primary colours when they passed the newbuilds out on the promontory above Clove Lore. Definitely a junior school. She'd never hear the end of it if Radia got wind about the place, and she couldn't blame her daughter. As usual, she blamed herself.

Itinerancy. Restlessness. The endless need to be always moving on, always expected somewhere else. This had been their life for years. The contracts kept coming, thank goodness, and yet it meant Radia had a lot to put up with, and no amount of well-organised home-schooling squeezed into the evenings, weekends and long-haul flights could make up for Radia's fantasy of kindly, adoring teachers and longed-for school pals.

'*Ta-dah!*' Radia presented her feet in the buckled-up jelly sandals, her toes wriggling. 'Let's go!' Charley was now tucked under her arm, where he always clung on trips out.

Joy was saved from mentally beating herself up about all those emails she'd received recently from the local authority back in London. Unbeknown to Radia, they still held a school place for her, deferred from last September, at the big redbrick primary at the end of the road where Joy's old flat stood empty.

Joy shook the keys in agreement and they passed through the jumble of book cartons and bare shelves on the shop floor. 'But only for an hour, OK? I have to work.'

'Yeah, yeah,' Radia said, sounding like a pre-teen and rolling her eyes while shoving her mum by the bottom through the door and into the mid-August glare.

Chapter Four

'A digital what now…?' Mrs Crocombe hovered her scoop over the cone.

'Nomad,' Joy repeated, glancing over her shoulder at the open door and hoping to get out again fast.

'Is that what they're calling it? *We* were calling you *the computer lady* at the Village Recovery Committee meetings.'

Joy gave the white-haired woman behind the counter a straight-lipped smile.

'With sprinkles too, please,' Radia told the woman firmly, obviously wanting her to stick to the task at hand.

'Ah, well, there's sprinkles *in* the ice cream already,' Mrs Crocombe replied, but Radia only looked longingly at the tub of rainbow flecks behind the curved glass counter.

'Though, of course, there's no such thing as too many sprinkles,' Mrs Crocombe added, her voice bubbling with indulgence, while plunging the ice cream into the tub and giving it a colourful coating. 'Flake?'

Mrs Crocombe knew not to ask the parents. These were things the little ones should decide for themselves. Joy opened her wallet acceptingly and Radia reached up the counter-front for her cone with wide, delighted eyes.

'We do takeaway coffees, you know, Joyce dear?' Mrs Crocombe added proudly. 'New machine.'

Joy could certainly do with a coffee. She'd spotted the espresso maker in the bookshop's own café that morning, but it had been fresh out of the box and still wrapped in its protective plastic.

'Actually, coffee would be nice. It's been a long journey,' she agreed.

Mrs Crocombe startled her by immediately calling out, '*Mr Bovis!* Coffee!'

A silent wait followed before a red-faced man shuffled through the rainbow ribbon curtain from a back room, pulling awkwardly at the sleeves of his white 'Crocombe's Ices' T-shirt, as though this was his first time ever wearing a T-shirt – especially one embroidered with a pastel-coloured ice-cream sundae.

'Bit tight, Mrs C.,' he confided, but she was too busy announcing that this was his first day in his new job.

'Far cry from being Minty's estate's man, eh, Mr Bovis?'

The man sheepishly met Joy's eyes. ''Ol-day maker?' he deflected, flipping the machine's chrome switches on then off again as though unsure how it all worked.

'Red button first, then the steam, Mr Bovis,' muttered Mrs Crocombe in what might pass for a discreet voice for her. 'This is Joyce, she's the...' Joy's brows lifted expectantly as the woman searched her memory. The relief of remembering hit her '...nomad. She's a digital nomad. The one that's doing the bookshop's... computery things.'

'Any good at coffee machines?' Bovis asked, ducking a puff of steam.

'Or Wi-Fis? We're having awful trouble with our Wi-Fis,' Mrs Crocombe added.

'I'm sure I can have a look at it before we leave, once I've got the bookshop set up,' Joy told her, biting back a sigh.

It was always like this. As soon as anyone found out what she did for a living, there was always just 'one little thing' that she could fix for them, and they were always confident it wouldn't take her long.

Radia had stopped licking her ice cream and was looking between the awkward adults. 'Mum doesn't do freebies,' she said assuredly, instantly throwing Joy into alarm.

'*Rads!*'

The little girl was indignant. 'It's true though, you're always saying it.'

''Ere we are, one flat white,' Bovis announced, rescuing them. Joy took the paper cup. 'I only knows flat white. We're doing mochas this afternoon.'

Mrs Crocombe wasn't listening. Ever since the 'no freebies' remark, she'd leaned her elbow on the counter and taken a pencil from somewhere inside her round white perm. She had a look in her eye that said, *You're a sparky pair, aren't you?* Joy instinctively didn't like it. 'Here until September, did you say?'

Joy hadn't said anything about leaving dates, so this must also be Village Recovery Committee meeting info. This woman's memory wasn't as bad as she let on.

'That's right,' Joy replied. 'We leave on the first.'

'A good long time, two weeks. All manner of things can get settled in a fortnight,' she said, her eyes narrowing upon the eldest newcomer. 'Travelling alone?'

'Always,' Radia blurted between licks of her cone.

'No, um... daddy in tow?'

And there it was. The prying. The wondering how it all worked. Joy's heart sank even though she was used to the questions.

28

Exactly how did a mother travel the world with her kid, making money as they went? What about home? What about family? What about The Poor Daddy? It made her furious. And it made her want to turn and run. Fortunately, someone new stepped inside the shop, saving her from the inquisition.

Everyone looked expectantly at the rather glamorous, haughty-looking woman with a clipboard now standing inside the doorframe. She had a look which suggested she did not have time for anyone's nonsense today.

'Mornin', Minty,' chimed Mrs Crocombe, leaving off the scent of whatever titbit of gossip she'd been chasing Joy for.

While Joy glanced at this Minty woman, who was sharply tugging her green bodywarmer down at the hem, Radia was far more absorbed in watching the red-faced man in the skinny T-shirt who was clumsily clattering cups by the coffee machine. He'd spun round and hunched over the levers as soon as the busy lady burst in and Radia noticed the tips of his ears had gone red.

'How's the wedding ice cream coming along?' Minty demanded over everyone's heads.

'You'll have to ask our little taste-tester here,' Mrs Crocombe said smilingly, looking at Radia clutching her near-empty cone.

'Wha'?' Radia gaped, suddenly aware she was being looked at by lots of people.

'You're the first customer to sample my confetti burst ice cream for Minty's new wedding business. It's my classic clotted-cream flavour with sugar sprinkles mixed in – that's the confetti bit – and a shot of sweet goosegog puree right in the middle. That's the "burst". So, *is* it good enough for a bride, Radia?'

The busy lady held her pen over her clipboard as though whatever Radia said now was a matter of the utmost importance.

Radia looked to her mum who nodded in encouragement, making her feel suddenly like a judge on a singing show.

'Well…' She took her time. 'I dunno what goosegog is… but I loved it!'

Minty immediately ticked a box with a curt nod. 'Good, good. That's another job off my list. Forty litres, in the first instance? To be stored here, yes?'

'As agreed,' Mrs Crocombe told her, wiping her cloth over the counter with a look of proud triumph before suddenly stopping to follow little Radia's line of sight. The girl was peering once more at Bovis's slumped shoulders.

'Mr Bovis?' hissed Mrs Crocombe with a fixed smile. 'Minty's come down from the Big House to see us.'

The man turned with an affected look of surprise as though he hadn't been aware of Minty's arrival until now. 'Ah! Right you are,' he puffed, the blush spreading across his neck. 'Good mornin', Mrs Clove-Congreve.'

'No need for formality, Bovis. You're not my estate's man anymore,' replied Minty, a little uneasily, even if she was standing poker straight with her nose held high.

'No, nor nothin' else neither,' he grumped under his breath, before giving a little sigh of surrender and carrying himself away through the rainbow ribbons once more.

'Ah, I see,' Minty lowered her voice. 'Still not recovered, then?'

'He'll come round,' Mrs Crocombe assured her.

Minty shrugged off Bovis's troubles and chirped, 'Righty-ho, lots to be getting on with.' She barrelled out of the shop, her face buried in her 'to do' list once more.

As soon as she was gone, Mrs Crocombe leaned conspiratorially across the counter.

'That's the lady of the manor, Araminta Clove-Congreve. Mr Bovis was her estate man for years. He was ever so… devoted.' She winked in an exaggerated way that almost made Radia's eyes pop out of her face. Lowering her voice, as though she fancied herself the very definition of discretion, she added, 'Minty recently married the man who owns your bookshop, Jowan de Marisco, only Mr Bovis can't get over his feelings. Poor fellow.'

'Oh dear,' Joy said, not for Bovis's sake, but for her own. This woman seriously loved to gossip. They'd have to avoid her as best they could this summer.

'Was he her *boyfriend*?' Radia asked, deeply invested, and making Joy fluster again.

'I haven't paid yet,' she chirped.

Mrs Crocombe didn't seem to hear. 'Oh no, it wasn't like that,' she told the little girl, adding in a low voice, 'but he loved her, all the same.' And, even more quietly, 'Broken heart's a terrible burden.'

'Right, well, it was nice to meet you,' Joy said, louder this time, holding out her Visa card.

'Cash only,' replied Mrs Crocombe, and Joy had to bite her lip.

Was the whole village like this? Still living in the nineties? Cash only and with shonky Wi-Fi, even after the refurbishments?

The ice-cream parlour certainly looked bright and fresh. Everything was brand new, except Mrs Crocombe who looked as sun-bleached as the village's mossy roof tiles and as wind-blown as the scrubby roadside gorse they'd passed on the way here.

No wonder Jowan from the bookshop charity had brought Joy in to get the place hooked up to the twenty-first century. Now that she'd met some of the bonkers village residents, with their love affairs and prying eyes, she was glad she was staying only long enough to do her job.

'She gone?' Bovis's red face peeked through the ribbons, and Joy hurriedly laid a ten-pound note on the counter, told them to keep the change, and walked straight out, hoping Radia would follow.

'Who's getting married?' Radia asked, her feet still planted firmly in front of the counter.

'Ah, one of my biggest successes!' beamed Mrs Crocombe. 'Elliot – he's our vet – and Jude, one of the young folk who borrowed the bookshop for a summer holiday a while back. T'was me got them together, in fact.' Her eyes shone.

Radia grinned back. She definitely liked Mrs Crocombe.

First of all, she made the best ice cream Radia had ever tried, even nicer than the pink stuff she'd had standing by the Grand Canal, waiting for the *traghetto* ride she'd begged her mum to take her on.

Secondly, she loved it when adults included her in whispered things, and all that talk about broken hearts had been a hundred times more interesting than anything she'd ever heard her mum saying.

Lastly, and the best reason of the lot, she looked like a cuddly, cosy type of granny, just the way Radia remembered her own grandma in London. She hadn't seen her grandma for so long – outside of a few brief FaceTime calls – her imagination had filled in the blanks until she had become half Mrs Doubtfire, half Mrs Claus.

'Radia?' her mum called from out on the slope.

'You'd better run along now, little one,' Mrs Crocombe twinkled.

The girl shuffled in her mum's footsteps as slowly as she could. Glancing back as she left the shop, Radia spied the owner of Crocombe's Ices pulling a notebook from her apron pocket, her pencil paused above the pad.

She strained her ears just long enough to pick up the words, 'Might be one for the betting book, Mr Bovis? Our nomadic thingumajig. She'll be a match for someone, I reckon. Did you happen to catch her surname?'

Chapter Five

Monty wasn't sure what was required of a best man. There hadn't been many local folks' weddings at Clove Lore in recent years. His gut response was that he wasn't up to the job. What did he know about marriage? Or the wearing of tails and top hats and shiny shoes? Did they still do that these days or was he thinking of his parents' wedding picture on the cottage mantle?

Yet, with Elliot Desvaux looming over him with a big hopeful grin and sparkling eyes like he might actually cry with pride, Monty had clasped his hand and pulled him into a hug.

'I'd love to, mate. Love to.'

Elliot's relieved laugh reverberated around the new chrome kitchen of the Siren's Tail, where Monty had everything (just about) under control ahead of lunch service. Steam rose from various pots, pastry puffed up into golden crusts in the ovens, and a big bowl of egg whites sat ready for whipping into meringues for the summer fruit Pavlovas.

Monty added, less emphatically, 'You sure you want me, though? And not a family member or a friend from…?' Monty realised he had no idea where Elliot was actually from. Somewhere posh in the south-east, that was all he knew.

'No, nobody from home,' said Elliot briskly, stepping out of the hug with one last pat on Monty's shoulder and almost backing into the big fridge.

'Got a date in mind?' asked Monty as he turned to lift the lid from a simmering pot of creamy seafood bisque, filling the air with its mouthwateringly delicious aroma.

'Uh, that's the thing.' Elliot looked like he wanted to shrink even more than he usually did when he was feeling awkward. At six-five and broadly muscled like a boxer-come-dancer, and so striking with his long sheets of black hair falling over broad shoulders, he always seemed to fill every room he entered. 'It's... soon.'

Monty paused in his stirring. This couldn't be good. He was run off his feet with shifts at the pub now the B&B guests were flooding back in, keen to get first dibs on the newly refurbished sea-view rooms. 'How soon?'

'September second.'

'Jeez! Why the rush?'

'Minty,' said Elliot, ominously.

'Got it. She's not an easy woman to say no to.'

'That's one way of putting it. When Jude told her she wanted us to have a small ceremony in the ballroom at the Big House, Minty went into overdrive. Says we're the perfect guinea pigs to test out her wedding-planning venture.'

'Ah! Sorry for you, mate.'

'I know,' Elliot agreed soberly. 'Mind you, it *is* all on the house, except our suits, and it's not like we need wedding cars or anything. There's Jude's dress, of course, but she wants to wear her mum's. It just needs altering. Minty reckons she can score all the flowers and that kind of stuff for free from her new list of wedding contacts. She's got big plans to make ours a *showcase wedding* to help attract future clients.'

'I bet she has.' Monty inhaled through gritted teeth, shaking his head at the powerhouse that was Araminta Clove-Congreve, as much of a local institution as the historic Big House and sprawling estate gardens that she oversaw up at the top of the village. She was the last in her family line and fiercely set upon keeping the place going – and nothing was going to stop her.

'I saw her on my way Down-along a minute ago,' said Elliot. 'Marching around with a clipboard. I dived into the lime kiln shed to avoid her.' He looked a little guilty at this.

'Has she given the vicar his orders?' Monty asked.

'Ah, no, he's off the hook this time. Just a celebrant for us; me and Jude aren't into that kind of thing.'

'Got it. So, I've a stag do to organise?' Monty's eyes lit up at the realisation.

'We might be short on stags. There's only you, me, your brother, Jude's dad, Izaak and Leonid, of course, and Jowan will bring Aldous…'

Monty laughed at this. It was just like Elliot to make sure he included the village's pets in his celebration. The vet did have an especially soft spot for wayward little Aldous, Jowan's toothless Bedlington Terrier.

'And what about Bovis?' Monty asked. 'Is he coming?'

'*Pfft!*' Elliot drew his neck back. 'Not if I can help it.'

Bovis had a way of spoiling big events, like the way he'd declared his undying love for Minty last Christmas in front of the entire village. She'd received his protest with stoic dignity before telling him, in private and as kindly as she could, that he'd better pull himself together and forget any feverish romantic notions the stress of the big flood might have stirred up.

'Probably a good idea if Jowan's coming. Don't want Bovis glaring daggers at his love rival all evening,' agreed Monty.

The delivery man made the kitchen doors swing open and two sacks of potatoes were shouldered onto the preparation area. 'Finan's signed for 'em,' he said before striding out once more, whistling as he went.

'Cheers mate.' This reminder of the long day's work ahead sharpened Monty's mind. 'When we doing it, then? Saturday? The twenty-sixth? That gives me a week to plan something.'

'Just a few drinks in the bar, yeah?'

'I can come up with something better than that.' No doubt Tom would have loads of stag ideas. Monty wondered if his brother might have been thinking lately about his own stag do and the thought left him dizzy, but he hid it from Elliot. 'Might ask Minty if she has any ideas,' he added with a wicked grin.

'Do it and you're fired! I'll ask Bovis to be my best man.'

The men laughed and clasped hands, pulling themselves into another back-patting hold once more.

'Better let you get on, then,' said Elliot. 'Still no second chef coming?'

'Nope,' said Monty. 'The ad's been running for weeks, but no bites. Nobody who wants a permanent dawn to dusk thing every single day of the week, anyway.' He knew there was weariness in his voice that he couldn't conceal.

Elliot only looked at his friend and nodded. Whatever he was thinking, he didn't say it, only leaving Monty with one last pat across his shoulder before stalking away through the swing doors, promising he'd help with any stag arrangements and costs.

'Not likely,' Monty called after him. 'It'll be on me *and* top secret till Saturday! Oh shit!' He turned just in time to stop the bisque bubbling over.

Elliot was gone. Eyeing the potato sacks on the counter, he lifted his paring knife with a sigh. 'Ten thousand pound of peeled spuds coming up, chef,' he said into the steamy hiss and bubble of the lonely kitchens. 'Aye, aye, Monty, carry on,' he told himself dryly.

And yet, Monty found the day had taken on a new light after Elliot's visit.

In the bar, Finan switched on the sound system and Monty caught the music, singing under his breath and working at the sink. This wasn't at all how he'd imagined his day shaping up. Out of the blue, he was suddenly going to be best man at a wedding and there was a stag party to put together, and quickly too.

Life still had some surprises in store for him, it seemed, and the knowledge that he hadn't been entirely forgotten, stuck here at the back of the Siren, made him smile and move his feet while he worked.

Chapter Six

'And Mum? Do we actually have a crabbing bucket?' Radia asked, peering over the harbour wall into the clear, reedy waves.

'Can you stand back a bit, Rads?' Joy took her daughter's hand, imagining her plummeting into the surf.

Crabbing wasn't something Joy knew much about. Her family was never one for British beach holidays, they'd always go all-inclusive in Sharm El Sheikh when she was growing up and even then they weren't the bucket and spades type. They liked things a little fancier. They'd probably be away in some exotic resort right now, come to think of it, making the most of the summer heat. She still wasn't used to it; the not knowing where they were or what they were doing. This is how it feels, Joy thought, when you're cut off.

'Mum? You're doing it again.' Radia jolted her hand.

Joy's eyes snapped to her child's. 'I'm here, I'm here. Just thinking about how we get a crabbing line. Wasn't there a convenience store in the visitor centre where the coaches were pulling up?'

'But that's miles away!'

The both looked back at the point where the entrance to the harbour turned into the path that led Up-along.

The perilously steep cobbled path they'd just come down was now obscured by the seaward-facing row of cottages and their backyards bursting with palm trees and spruces. The two rows of cottages that made up the village zigzagged and twisted all the way up the incline past the pretty cobbled side street that led off to the Borrow-A-Bookshop. Yet further up the slope, right up on the hill, the turrets of Clove Lore's Big House could be seen, the St Petroc's flag flying against the blue summer sky, dotted about this morning with puffy white clouds. The visitor centre was up there by the entrance to the estate, at least a thousand-yard climb, maybe two.

Day visitors and guests from the Siren's Tail were spilling down onto the beach. It was already a hot day before the prospect of a long climb.

'Maybe you can make a friend and play with their crabbing things?' Joy told her glum daughter, scanning the wall for a group of friendly looking kids.

A voice from behind them startled her. 'You can borrow the Siren's rods and nets, if you like?'

Turning, they saw a man dragging empty crates along the wide concrete expanse.

'Can I?' Radia called back gleefully. 'Where are they?'

Joy instinctively shrank back, thinking how it was both a curse and a blessing that her daughter, through sheer necessity, had been forced to become good at making friends wherever she found them. Unlike Joy, she hadn't a shy bone in her body.

'Rads,' she cautioned, even though she wasn't sure what exactly her objection was going to be. That this guy was a stranger? That kids can't go talking to just *anybody*, even if they are smiling in an unthreatening way and keeping their eyes on their crates, showing no desire to bother them?

She'd found over the years that some blokes, once they twigged Joy and Radia were travelling alone, wanted to pry, or buy them lunch, or to meet Joy that night for a drink. She hated it, the intrusion.

'He's busy, Rads, he's working,' was the best Joy could manage, but she already knew it wasn't going to make any difference. The promise of a morning's crabbing was on the horizon and Radia wouldn't be put off by her mum's fear of strangers.

'Wait there,' he called back, before abandoning the crates and disappearing through the pub doors, giving Radia enough time to throw her mum a warning look that said, *Don't spoil my fun, it's fine*.

He was back and striding towards them in moments, carrying a sealed Tupperware, a long pink plastic net, a homemade rod with string weighted by a stone, and a bucket printed with orange crabs all around the sides. 'Will these do?' He smiled again, directed right at Radia. Then, more warily, he lifted his eyes to Joy. 'Just drop them back inside the pub when you're done.'

'Thank you,' Joy said, fighting the stiffness in her voice. She could feel her daughter's eyes boring into her from below, wishing her mum wasn't like this.

'Do you… *uh*, know what you're doing with these?' He handed the net to Radia.

'Nope! Can you show us?' she grinned back, reaching for the rod too.

'Radia, the man's working.' Joy tried a polite smile.

'I can spare a minute,' he replied brightly, 'if that's OK with you, of course?' His brown eyes were so appealingly soft and unassuming, Joy had no choice but to relent.

The little fishing party made their way to a spot by the harbour steps, close to the *Peter's Bounty* mooring.

The man crouched at the top of the steps, telling Radia to sit down safely and to mind the mooring rings. She informed him that she never fell. Joy tried not to react.

When Joy had been precocious in public as a child, her mum would say, 'What are you like?' and chuck her chin or rub a finger under her ear. Or she'd playfully roll her eyes, all the while making a show of connecting with the other adult, the one who'd witnessed the cheekiness. Maybe they'd join in and call her a 'little madam' or some other thing and the grown-ups would smile indulgently. Joy had never done that.

That would mean establishing some kind of understanding with a stranger, allowing them into their little family bubble to observe Radia and comment on her. Nobody got to say anything about her child. Nobody had the right to. She knew it made her standoffish and she didn't mind, and Radia didn't know any differently.

Radia didn't know anything about the school gate camaraderie of mums, the blithe comments made at coffee mornings about the 'terrible twos' and the tantrums of a 'threenager', and all the other little burdens or funny moments shared.

That's why instances like this – interacting with new people – felt especially brilliant for Radia. Meanwhile, Joy could only look on, hoping it would end soon.

'Ooh, what are those?' Radia was asking, peering into the stranger's Tupperware tub as he peeled the lid off and crouched by her side.

'A handful of the morning catch for you. Whitebait. Perfect for crabbing. Can you pick one up?'

'I don't know. Can I?' Radia was asking this to herself, wondering if she had the nerve. After a few slippery attempts she had one of the stiff silver fish between her fingertips. 'Now what?'

'Tie it on the end of your string. Here, let me show you. You don't have to use fish, mind, you can use toast or bits of bacon rind, anything really. Crabs aren't fussy.'

Radia watched the man's fingers work, her eyes squinting against the sunlight.

He handed the rod back to her.

'Here, take Charley,' she told him, pulling the toy fox from under her arm and shoving it into his hands.

'Ah, Charley is it?' he asked the fox. 'Nice to meet you, I'm Monty.'

'Monty,' repeated Radia, before introducing herself. 'Radia Pearl Foley.'

Monty shook hands formally, which delighted the little girl, before he did the same to Charley's soft paw. 'Pleased to meet you, Charley. I'm Montague David Bickleigh.'

'And she's Joyce Foley,' Radia bobbed her head at her mum. '*No* middle name,' she added sagely.

Monty only smiled up at Joy, who stood with her arms limp by her side and her hands balled up like she was holding onto invisible supports. But she couldn't help smiling too. Something in his gentle way made her do it.

'Radia's a bit of a special name, isn't it?' said Monty. 'Like a ray of light?'

Joy jolted. This was all getting too close for comfort, but her daughter was already explaining, 'Mum named me after Doctor Radia Perlman.'

'Oh? I don't think I know them.'

'She's a genius,' Radia reassured him. 'She invented spreading trees inside the internet.'

'Uh, spanning-tree protocol,' her mum added reluctantly.

He shook his head. 'Yep, still no clue.'

'It's fundamental to the operation of network bridges…' she began. 'Uh, never mind.' She dismissed the words with an embarrassed sweep of her hand.

'I'll have to look her up on Wikipedia,' he said with a smile that sent Joy back into silence. 'Right, so,' he went on, bringing his hands together in a soft clap. 'Radia Pearl, you need to lower that fish into the water.'

She did as he instructed.

'And keep the line close to the wall, careful not to knock your bait off. That's it. And now…' he paused. 'You wait.'

'For a crab?'

'Yup. Once you're sure he's hanging on, pull him up slowly, don't let him fall, and then you pick him off and put him in your bucket.'

'And we *keep* him?' Radia's eyes widened.

'Not forever. When you're done you let them all go, back into the sea.'

'For another kid to catch tomorrow?'

'I suppose so, yeah.'

Radia didn't look at all sure she wanted to bother the poor crabs now, but she soon changed her mind when she felt the tug at the end of her line.

'I've got one, Mum!'

Radia forgot all about Monty now, and he backed away, leaving them to inspect the dangling green shore crab waving its claw at the end of Radia's line. Joy was rubbing Radia's back and praising her excitedly.

They'd both forgotten him. Best to slip away, leave them to it. The pub was fully booked for lunch and there was a lot to do before service began.

After he loaded his crates onto the *Peter's Bounty*, he left the sea wall, but not before stopping in the pub doorway to glance back at the little girl screeching with delight as she showed her mother the creature in her bucket.

Far along the beach, beyond the crabbers, he spotted Tom and Lou walking under the cliff line. Like the twin-tracking GPS that he was, Monty was acutely aware of his brother strolling along past the beach waterfall, arm-in-arm with his girlfriend, a trail of smoke from his cigarette behind him. Every now and again Tom threw his head back, laughing.

He remembered that Tom hadn't sluiced the boat down. Another task for Monty to add to his list of jobs that day. His brother's behaviour was getting more out of character with each loved-up day that passed. Still, Monty smiled for him, even if he did blow out a sorry sigh for himself.

A delighted shriek from Radia, now lifting a second crab, drew Monty's attention once more to the holiday-makers, just as the child's beautiful, shy mum lifted her eyes to his. He caught her startled glance and ducked sharply inside the pub.

Chapter Seven

Jude Crawley, Big House Weddings Inc.'s bride-to-be, had been on a Zoom call about the wedding with Minty Clove-Congreve for over half an hour and they still weren't finished, even though Jude had her mum and dad visiting from the Borders and she wanted to catch up with them more than anything.

Elliot emerged from their bedroom ready for his shift in his veterinary scrubs and she couldn't help getting distracted by the sight of him tying his long black hair up into a knot.

'So what do you think, Judith?' Minty repeated, snapping her out of her thoughts.

'*Hmm?* Sorry?'

'Boutonnières? Sea holly and yellow gorse?' Minty said, making Jude's mum coo in agreement as she unpacked groceries behind her at the kitchen counter. 'For the seaside theme,' Minty pressed.

'Right, yes. That sounds lovely,' Jude replied, while her dad handed her a steaming mug of tea and settled beside his daughter on the sofa.

They'd arrived by car that morning and the novelty of having them here was still very strange and fresh for everyone. What they needed was a proper catch-up.

Minty was nowhere near finished. 'And there's the freeze-dried petals for confetti, from the estate's camellia grove, yes? Tasteful. There'll be no paper confetti canons at a Big House wedding. Do you want dark pink or pale pink petals? I've a good stock of both.' Minty didn't wait for an answer, bowing her platinum-blonde twenties bob to her checklist. 'Pale pink will match the driftwood signage across the estate. *What Bride* magazine calls it shabby seaside chic, you know?'

'Ooh, lovely,' called Jude's mum, who'd been rather side-lined in Minty's planning fervour. At six-hundred miles away in the Scottish Borders, she'd been the first to concede there wasn't a lot she could do. But she was here now. 'And we've brought the ingredients for the cake,' Mrs Crawley added, coming to stand behind Jude, leaning into the camera.

Minty looked concerned. 'It's such a lot of work, making your own wedding cake. Are you sure you have time for it?'

'We're a baking family,' her dad replied, his hand on Jude's. 'Always knew I'd make my girl's wedding cake one day. Couldn't imagine her cutting into some stranger's cake on her big day.'

'Leave it to us,' Jude reassured her. 'You've got three bakers here, the one thing we can guarantee is a beautiful cake.'

Minty wrote on her pad. 'I'll have someone collect it on the eve of the wedding.'

'And you've got a seamstress booked, to take up the hem on my dress?' Mrs Crawley was looking at Jude now.

'Yep, all arranged. And Elliot's just got Monty Bickleigh to agree to be his best man, so he's sorting the stag.'

'Have you made plans for your hen party?' her mum asked.

'Just drinks and nibbles here.'

Jude didn't mind surrendering the wedding plans as long as she held the reins over the hen do. That, at least, would be low-stress and simple, just her and her favourite people, including Daniel, her best friend from back home. He was coming down by train and chaperoning Jude's grandmother, who'd insisted they get first-class tickets for the journey, saying she was too old for any kind of travel that didn't involve decent seats and free gin and tonics.

'And the naked waiter's booked?' Elliot shouted wickedly, so Minty could hear, as he grabbed his backpack and made for his fiancée to kiss her goodbye.

Everyone laughed except, conspicuously, Minty, who grimaced. She'd been invited to the hen do but said she had far too much to do at the Big House, including sorting out the florist and the balloon-arch lady.

Jude hadn't been keen on the whole balloons idea but Minty had roped the poor woman in anyway and she was coming all the way from Ilfracombe to give her a demo, so it was too late now.

'See you tonight,' Elliot told Jude and his in-laws, and was gone out the door.

'Cheerio, Elliot,' Mrs Crawley called in his wake.

'We'd better be getting on with the cake,' Mr Crawley reminded everyone. 'The oven's already coming to temp.'

'And you're going for traditional white icing?' Minty wanted to know. 'Yes? Nothing that will clash with the pastels?' She was peering at the kitchen counter behind them.

'You just leave it to us,' Mr Crawley said as gently as he could, his Borders accent helping to soften the urgency as he rose and made his way to the kitchen to wash his hands.

'Very well. I'll finalise the table plans and send them over to you,' Minty told Jude.

'Table plans? There's no need. It's just a buffet. Our friends can choose where they sit.'

Minty only blinked.

Behind her, Jude heard her dad reorganising the oven shelves to accommodate the cake pans. 'Better go,' she told the screen, apologetically.

Minty ended the call, saying she had to get to the Siren anyway to make sure the champagne was on its way up to the Big House cellars, like Finan and Bella had promised.

'You mean Prosecco?' Jude said, alarmed, worrying about the budget, but Minty's screen went blank.

'She's quite the organiser,' Mr Crawley said, tying his apron, which read *Crawley and Son, Bakers* across the pocket. He'd brought three of them from home.

'Hmm, it's possible a person can be *too* organised,' Jude replied, joining her parents around the stove.

In a kitchen, Jude's parents really came into their own, having run the family bakery for near-on thirty years before they sold the building to developers and retired early off the money.

Jude drew her grandfather's recipe book from its spot on the shelf, turning to his handwritten instructions for a three-layer celebration cake. She'd never baked it before, but how hard could it be?

'You read it,' her dad said, and all three bent their heads over the familiar words written down so long ago, back when Jude's grandfather was handing the business over to his son. Until then, the recipes had all lived in his memory.

'A fruit cake is almost impossible to get wrong,' read Jude. 'As long as there's plenty fruit and booze and it's stirred with love, you've got a recipe for a smashing celebration. For good luck, make sure everyone on the premises mixes the cake in turn, *especially* if the cake is intended for a wedding.'

It was all coming back to her now. Her mum and dad, who always shared the task of making the wedding cakes, would call to Jude and her gran in the flat above the bakery to come down and 'stir for luck'.

Her dad set to work zesting oranges while her mum prepared the dry ingredients, and the bride-to-be tumbled the port-soaked currants into a bowl.

Crawley and Son cakes must have been cut at thousands of weddings over the three decades her parents ran her grandad's bakery. There was no way all of those weddings had ended in good fortune; a third of them were probably divorced by now. Even though she told herself it was just a superstition, Jude nonetheless wished Elliot was there to help stir the mixture.

Minty's well-meaning wedding planning was beginning to make her feel nervous. Nothing was likely to go wrong, not if Minty had anything to do with it. Only, the wedding had grown from a small, informal ceremony for their loved ones into a far grander affair than either of them had envisaged. If Minty would only stop now, before things got too elaborate, she'd feel calmer and more in control. Still, the wedding cake was all her responsibility, and it was going to be sweet and simple and full of love.

Her mum stopped the whir of the Magimix just as the butter and sugar formed a creamy mass and her dad stirred in the eggs and flour.

Jude had run her own small baking business from this very kitchen to supplement her university studies in book history and conserving. Books and baking were her first loves and she got the best of both worlds in her new Clove Lore life.

Jude lifted the wooden spoon, another relic brought from the Borders.

'I'll stir for Elliot too,' she said.

'Good idea,' her mum agreed.

Each took turns folding in the boozy fruit and the mixture's sweet vapours rose in the warm kitchen.

'Better stir for my dad too,' said Mr Crawley, putting his arm around his daughter.

Jude knew there'd be tears in his eyes so she didn't look up. Her dad was the weepiest man she knew. That was where she got her softness from.

So she stirred and everyone thought of her grandfather as yet another of his wedding cakes took shape.

Chapter Eight

That afternoon, once the sand had been brushed from their feet, Joy surveyed the Borrow-A-Bookshop, where the shelves still stood entirely empty and expectant.

Radia was full of fish 'n' chips, just like she'd wanted, and glued to the phone screen, cackling along with *Bing* bunny, even though she'd protested at first that she was much too old for baby programmes. The respite meant it was time for Joy to get to work.

First, she opened the shop's porthole windows in their deep sills to tackle the fresh-paint smell and the increasingly close afternoon heat. Then she'd opened up her laptop to double-check the contract she'd signed and sure enough, after 'create new stock-record system' were the words, easy to miss, apparently, 'and shelve all titles'.

Joy held her hands together and breathed, trying to remember the calming techniques that Hackney Marshes doctor had taught her way back when Radia was a baby and she couldn't control her anxieties, no matter how many times she checked the front door was bolted and chained or how intently she stared at her sleeping newborn as though it was her job, through sheer will-power alone, to breathe for them both.

'Baby blues,' the doctor had called it, telling her she'd soon feel better if she got out for daily walks. But that was the one thing she couldn't do, terrified Sean was out there, watching them, determined to force himself back into their lives, or worse.

In for five, she inhaled, *and out for seven, six, five, four...* She spread her hands across the shop counter until the room stopped spinning.

'How long have they been happening for, these dizzy spells?' the doctor had asked, and she hadn't wanted to say ever since Sean took it upon himself to move into her flat a year before. That was when the tight feeling in her chest had started at least, and the dizzy breathlessness soon followed.

She'd sat there crying soundlessly while the doctor printed off a leaflet on postnatal depression, telling her a nurse would visit her at home sometime in the next two weeks. She'd left the surgery knowing full well she wouldn't answer the door to any nurse that came prying.

The sound of Radia's cartoons reached her through the memories. The breathing exercises always worked and the dizziness always passed.

Holding her arms in a hug, she picked her way through the boxes and across the shop floor into the café. She poured a long glass of water and downed the whole thing, repeating the inner mantra that accompanied her wherever in the world they happened to be: *Sean isn't here. He doesn't even know where we are. He doesn't want us now anyway. It's over.*

–

By three o'clock she had everything back under control. Anybody peering in through the glass of the shop's locked front door would see a woman, perfectly composed, standing over the new till point and laptop, scanning books from the crates, adding titles one at a time to the stock-management system, her hands working busily and her waist twisting. Everything efficient and methodical. *Lift, scan, enter, stack, repeat.*

She'd have this done in a couple of days, she reckoned. Then she'd get the new website up and running, conceal the SSID for the Wi-Fi, install the phone, security cameras and the passcode entry system. Nothing to it. She was used to working on a mix of hardware and software installations, web design and coding solutions in her job. It was what she was known for. She was a good all-rounder, multi-skilled, a safe pair of hands. She could do it all and had the CV and references to prove it. The components of this shop job were nothing she hadn't done before, except for the small matter of shelving books. That was new.

Dewey Decimal Classification, which would have been her obvious preference, didn't have a look-in at the bookshop, she soon discovered. For a start, the stock was a mixture of old and new books, some of them positively antiquated and very expensive-looking. She'd have to enter those manually on the new stock-control database. They didn't have RRPs, ISBNs or barcodes.

Then, a few moments ago, after seeking clarification from Jowan, the owner, Joy had been told that the books were to be shelved alphabetically under the shop's own – rather random to Joy's mind – categorisation system. He told her he'd written the prices of the second-hand stock in pencil inside their jackets so at least she didn't have to worry about that.

When it was finished, her stock system would be fully searchable by title or even just by topic. The changing holidaymakers working here would be able to find particular books if customers asked for them, as well as being able to easily lay their hands on related titles… but it all still had to make sense for shoppers browsing the shelves. She set about tweaking the library coding she'd written on the plane over to England.

Joy liked it when systems were intuitive and user-friendly. This was just another programming puzzle for her to crack, and crack it she would. This was where her talents really shone through.

She reached for another book to scan, lifting *The Handmaid's Tale*. 'I mean, this one could comfortably sit in non-fiction,' she sniffed a wry laugh, even though her mouth was set in a line with its usual seriousness.

She didn't like feeling cynical. It didn't suit her at all. Was she cautious? Sure. Watchful and restless? Definitely. Since Sean, these traits had shoved their way into her personality, muscling aside her brighter, happier parts. Her abundance of carefree youthfulness had made way for them too. She was fully aware of this fact, but still, she didn't like the cynicism. She tried to tell herself that Radia Pearl was her proof against it; evidence the world still had unspoiled goodness in it. So, she set the book in the fiction pile where it belonged and carried on.

By four, Radia was asking for a snack and there wasn't much in the café kitchen other than surprisingly large quantities of fresh milk, strawberry jam, clotted cream, salted butter, a big sack of plain flour and, on the counter by the shiny new coffee machine – rather pointedly positioned, she thought – a book of baking recipes. Was someone honestly expecting her to rustle up a Devonshire cream tea from scratch?

Sure, she knew all about eating the things, but she was no baker. Her stomach chose this moment to remind her of the big, crumbly, oven-fresh scones she used to pick up at that bakery on the Old Brompton Road when she worked at Tech Stars End User Support. That was her first job out of uni, back in the days before Sean, or before she struck out on her own. She'd buy a bagful of the scones every morning and take them to work, while Gaz, Abi or Steve would bring the coffees, and before they'd completed a stroke of work they'd eat breakfast in the office kitchens and talk about their evenings: clubbing, gaming, going on dates.

She smiled now at the memory, and the taste of the fluffy warm scones came back to her too. Delicious days.

Joy now assembled a plate of jammy rice cakes for Radia with a building sense of mum-guilt. She really needed to get to the shops to buy some fruit.

She told Radia to drink her milk, leaving her slumping lazily on one of the patchwork beanbags tucked under the spiral staircase, and turned to survey her progress.

There were now books piled as tall as Radia all over the floor around the till area. Joy felt the prickling heat of the summer afternoon rising up her back. The shop was a mess, sure, but she'd bring it under control if she worked late into the night and all of tomorrow, hopefully by nightfall it would be cooler for doing some of the grunt work.

Air conditioning clearly hadn't been high on the Borrow-A-Bookshop's list of renovation priorities. Joy had to prop the shop door open as well as the windows. The sounds of the village spilled in too. Seagull cries, water running down onto stones – Joy hadn't yet discovered the beach waterfall so had no idea what the rushing noise was – and children playing in the cool shallows down on the shore.

Just as she was throwing off her blazer and plunging her arms into one of the last unopened crates to retrieve a bundle of Jackie Collins hardbacks, someone politely cleared their throat from the doorway behind her and she sent *Hollywood Wives*, *The Bitch* and *The Stud* tumbling to the floor.

'Oops, sorry,' came a voice.

'It's Montague! The crabbing man!' Radia cried, gleefully, already crossing the shop to drag him towards the beanbag nook under the stairs. 'Why don't you come in and read with me?'

'Magnús and Alex left you all the boxes, huh?' he said, glancing around and looking impressed at the huge mess.

By now, Joy had recovered the spilled books and a little of her composure. 'It's my job to shelve them, apparently,' she told him blankly.

'I didn't put two and two together down on the sea wall. That you were the new Borrowers, I mean.'

'Borrowers? Like my story?' Radia gasped delightedly, holding up her book. 'The last people who stayed here left it for me, just for *being* here.'

'Woah, that's pretty cool,' said Monty. 'Magnús and Alex were pretty cool people, though.'

'But they left?' Radia probed.

'Everyone who stays at the bookshop leaves, once their holiday's up.'

'*Hmm.*' Radia didn't seem impressed by this.

'Can I help you with something?' Joy interrupted.

'Oh, uh, yeah, actually…' Monty ran a hand over the back of his neck and kept it clamped there. 'I need a book about speeches, but uh, it looks like you're not as settled in as I thought the new Borrowers would be.'

Radia was already deeply interested. 'Speeches?' she echoed.

'Yeah, best-man speeches. Did you happen to see any while you were unpacking?' he asked Joy.

Joy's memory worked fast. This kind of thing she could recall easily. Her teachers had found it uncommon until it came to her maths, science and IT classes, then they had lauded her talents.

'There was one on Churchill's oratory,' Joy replied. 'Don't think that's the kind of thing you're after. *We will wed them on the beaches…*' she began with a lopsided smile. Realising she was almost enjoying herself, she let her face fall again. 'Sorry,' she added, squeezing her short nails into her balled-up palms.

Radia looked at her like she'd sworn or something and Joy knew exactly what her daughter was thinking. Swearing would be more in character than this, whatever this was – cracking weird jokes, and in front of a stranger too.

'Can't you just get one online?' Joy asked him desperately.

'Online?' Monty echoed. 'God, no. What would Jowan say? Or Minty for that matter? If they saw me getting a book delivered? Nope, it's the bookshop or nothing round here.'

'Or you'll get told off?' Radia sympathised.

'Definitely.' Monty bared his teeth, looking terrified for Radia's benefit before turning back to Joy. 'Can you get one in for me?'

'I'm not a bookseller,' she said.

They all stood in the awkward silence that followed until Joy was forced to relent.

'But I suppose I do need to test the new ordering system. Can you leave it with me? I'll try tomorrow when it's set up, all being well.'

Monty thanked her and was turning to go when Radia tried to detain him – he was the best entertainment she'd had all day, since the crabbing and the fish 'n' chips. 'What's a best man?' She was standing below him now, far too close and looking straight up at his face with interested eyes.

'It's a special helper at a wedding,' he told her.

'And *you* are one?'

'I am. For my friend, Elliot. He's getting married.'

Radia nodded in approval as though satisfied this information checked out. She'd heard all about the wedding at the ice-cream parlour this morning. 'Mummy was *almost* married,' she pitched in delightedly. '*I'm* not going to get married,' she added thoughtfully, meaning neither adult had to respond to the broken engagement bombshell. Radia was still talking anyway. 'Does he like crabbing?'

'Wh— who?' Monty stumbled. 'Elliot? *Umm*, not sure. He's a vet so he loves animals.'

'Ah!' Radia said, drawing a deep breath before launching into a long story about how she'd quite like to be a vet when she grows up but you need to go to school for that. Joy, sensing trouble, nipped it in the bud with a warning look that made Monty start.

'I really should get going, sorry,' he told her, his hands spread in apology.

Joy showed Monty to the door with a hurry-along motion that he couldn't mistake.

'I'll get that book on order for you,' she told him over Radia's protests. 'They're supposed to come from the supplier within three days so why don't you come back in four?'

Monty tripped on a pile of books, sending them spilling.

'I'll have the place straight by then,' Joy added.

Monty stopped in the doorway. 'You know, the volunteers would be happy to help with this stuff? And I can help too, if you like? And Jowan, he'll pop over. I know Minty's filled his hands with her wedding-planning stuff, but he'll come if you ask. And you haven't met Jude or Izaak and Leonid yet.'

He'd barely finished speaking before Joy shook her head. 'I'm fine.'

'But they love to help.'

'I work alone.'

Monty was having none of it. 'And Mrs Crocombe would be only too glad to nip in and lend a hand, I'm sure.'

'No,' Joy blurted, before recovering herself. 'No, thank you.'

'Ah,' Monty's shoulders dropped a little. 'You've met her already?'

Radia pressed closer. 'The ice-cream lady? She's lovely! *She* talks about things.'

'I'd rather keep to ourselves,' Joy said, through an uncomfortable smile.

'She likes you, Mum,' Radia scolded. 'She even put you in her friend book.'

Joy faltered. 'Her… her what?'

'Ah!' Monty dropped his eyes to the floor and rocked on his heels, smiling.

Joy's heart plummeted. 'Oh god, what?'

'It's uh... She's harmless, honestly, only... Mrs C. has this thing about... about...' He raised his brows. 'Matchmaking.'

'Matchmaking?' Radia's eyes gleamed. 'What's that?'

'Never you mind,' Joy tried hard not to snap. 'Rads, can you get Monty a...' She'd be the first to admit she was panicking as she reached for a distraction. 'A glass of milk. Please. Rads?'

The little girl had been grinning up at Monty, all ears. 'What? Right now?'

'Right now,' repeated Joy, feeling utterly ridiculous. A glass of milk? What had gotten into her? Anybody else she could cope with, but something about this Monty guy made her forget how to act normally.

Radia grabbed Charley fox from the beanbag, stuffed him under her arm and trudged towards the café door. 'Don't say anything interesting, will you?'

'I hardly ever do,' Monty promised her.

Joy leaned closer with a furtive hiss. 'Talk, quick.'

'About Mrs C.? You don't need to worry about her. She's just old and lonely. Her husband passed away years ago and she's got nothing better to do than flog ice creams and try to set up the local residents on dates. There's the primary school, you see?'

Joy only folded her arms, not liking the sound of any of this.

'Her daughter's the head teacher there and it's going to close if the roll drops any lower.'

'And she's trying to boost the population?' Joy's eyes narrowed tightly.

'Exactly. Only between us, I think she's a right old romantic. She just wants to see folks happy.'

'So why does she put them in a book?'

'Ah, well there may be some financial incentive too.'

'Betting?' Now Joy was indignant.

'Yeah, not that it ever comes to much. Nobody had any money on Minty and Jowan getting together last Christmas. And then Izaak surprised everyone by marrying his Russian fella. And it all happened so quick with Tom and Lou, nobody had time to even *think* about matchmaking, though I did make ten quid on Elliot and Jude, so…' Monty shrugged.

'You're involved?'

Monty gulped. 'Not anymore. Listen, don't worry. I'm in her book too, if that makes you feel any better? Probably one of the only locals left who isn't paired up already, except for some of the older folks…'

Joy raised her brows and stared, waiting for Monty to catch on to the ramifications of what he was saying. Monty was a little older than Joy, going by the silvery strands amongst his thick brown curls and the softest weathered lines around his temples, but they were both alone in Clove Lore, and both in the betting book. Monty, however, didn't seem to grasp what this might mean for them.

'You'll like her once you get to know her, honestly.'

Joy looked up at him, unmoved.

'So, listen.' Monty held his palms together, forcing a change of topic. 'What do you say? A book-shelving party? Tomorrow at five? You can have a kind of open house for helpers?'

'Uh… no, I don't think…'

'It's a community bookshop. We help everyone who comes to stay. What do you say? It'll be nice, and you can meet all the volunteers in one go, get it over with.'

Joy glanced around the shop once more. She couldn't deny it was a mess. Maybe if they got things straight quickly she could take a few days off at the end of the fortnight, let Radia have the proper summer holiday she deserved? She didn't often get jobs finished early. Then again, she'd never had the offer of help.

Monty was observing her closely and already smiling.

'OK,' Joy said, with a sigh. 'But only for a few hours. Just to get these books off the floor.'

'No problem,' Monty said it as though all those locals descending on Joy's territory was set to be the simplest thing in the world. 'I'll text everyone.'

'Except the ice-cream lady.'

'Can't guarantee she won't get wind of it and show up.'

Joy gritted her teeth, but Radia was back from the kitchen with a brimming glass of milk.

'Oh, right, my milk, of course. Thank you very much.' Monty rescued the glass from her before shrugging at Joy who didn't know what to say or do. He downed the whole thing in a few long gulps.

'Woah!' Radia was extremely impressed and ran off to the kitchen to see if she could do the same thing, while Joy was left standing on the shop doormat, blinking wordlessly at the sight of Montague Bickleigh with his head thrown back, his throat working, brown curls tumbling, and the slow smile stretching across his lips as he lowered the glass, sweeping his mouth with the back of his hand.

Joy took the glass. 'Uh… right. Well done,' she said, in an inane way that she'd fret about for the rest of the night.

Then Monty was gone, leaving Joy wondering at the strange effects the sight of him pounding that glass of milk had had on her insides. Whatever her traitorous nervous system was up to, she wasn't going to be moved. This was just a glitch in her system. Like that time she was doing an intranet upgrade across those German university campuses and everyone's printers simultaneously disappeared off the network. It had been unexpected and inconvenient but, dammit, she'd put her mind to it and sorted it out all by herself, hadn't she? This was the same thing. A reboot was all that was needed and the next time she saw him she'd be back to processing as normal. Still, she had to admit, the quicker this posting was over and their bags were packed, the better for all of them.

'*And Mu-um?*' Radia called from the café, making Joy shake herself awake. 'There's a big lot of milk on the floor.'

'OK, coming!'

Joy shut and bolted the shop door and turned for the café, but not before pressing the cool glass to her forehead and blowing out a sharp breath.

'Two weeks,' she told herself, 'and we'll be safely out of Clove Lore.'

Chapter Nine

The next morning, Radia had insisted her mum open up the shop door and let her and Charley fox play outside on the steps. She must have run around the courtyard palm tree a hundred times, making up games and singing. She had always been good at entertaining herself.

All day long, holidaymakers had been wandering into the square and asking whether or not the bookshop was still closed. Radia had deflected most of them before they made it to the steps and interrupted her mum's work. Joy didn't know it but she'd told them all to come back tomorrow when the books would be on the shelves and the shop would absolutely *definitely* be open for business.

Joy had been enjoying working on her own, getting every item of stock logged on her system and the whole thing running smoothly, after a few tweaks to the coding. She'd even ordered a book of best-man speeches and wedding etiquette direct from the supplier in the Midlands.

All she had to do was get through the shelving party in an hour, trying not to get too alarmed at the word 'party' (it wasn't, it was just work) and keep a lid on the self-conscious, rattled feeling within her that Monty had set off the day before. For now there was the quiet of the afternoon, and she had Radia to supervise, so she stepped out onto the little square to join her daughter and Charley fox in their tea party, where Radia was pouring water from a silver pot taken from the café.

Sitting in the sun, eating invisible strawberry tarts (Charley's favourite), Joy lifted her eyes to the sky where the gulls circled and swooped and she inhaled the peace of the seaside afternoon while it was set to last.

–

Everywhere around Clove Lore were the signs of renewal after the winter floods. The blackbirds sang in the shade of the camellia grove up on the estate; pink scabious and blue lobelia grew once more in the crevices of every dry-stone wall; children gripped their grown-ups' hands as they gingerly made their way Down-along in wetsuits and armbands, everyone overloaded with bodyboards, beach tents and picnics.

The happy, busy sounds lifted into the warm sea-salted air, confirming what everyone already knew: summer was here and Clove Lore was thriving again.

On this particular Saturday afternoon, pleasure boats criss-crossed the harbour mouth, where a smart cruiser was coming in to dock alongside the Siren's Tail. Sleek and long, its prow was blazoned in deep-blue lettering, letting the locals know this was the *Lucky Boy*.

Once its mooring rope was tied and its engine cut, a figure emerged from the glossy white of the cabin, drawing quite a crowd of intrigued onlookers.

'Aye aye, Clove Lore!' the jolly man called out, clambering up the stone steps and onto the sea wall, more sprightly than most of the younger men who worked in the harbour, even though the gold button of his navy blazer, glinting in the sun, was under quite a bit of strain over his rounded tummy.

Pulling off designer shades, his cheerful, crinkled, icy blue eyes caught the light. Even with the tan lines around his lids, he'd be described as handsome by anyone watching his arrival.

Some of the old-timers who smoked pipes and sipped pints on the pub's harbour-side benches greeted him, even though he was a stranger to them all. As soon as he was out of earshot they turned to each other to discuss him.

One pronounced him, 'No spring chicken.'

'Bit flash, in 'ee?' said another.

'One of them millionaires from Salcombe, I'll wager,' spoke a third.

'S'long as 'ee's got money to spend, we'll allow it,' the first added wickedly, and they laughed in the wake of the self-satisfied captain, who was occupied in surveying the harbour, his chest expanding proudly as though he'd just bought the entire place.

Raking a tanned hand through sleek lengths of white hair, he bit a cigar between teeth as white as his crisp shirt collar.

'It's a fine day for adventuring!' he announced loudly to nobody in particular, striding along, his shiny shoes clacking on the sea wall. 'An ice cream's in order, that's for sure.'

Rubbing his hands together delightedly, he turned heads all the way along past the lime kiln and onto the slope, where he took in everything with an interested eye. 'Oh yes,' he told the air, laughingly, 'I'm in the mood for something sweet!'

—

'There!' Mrs Crocombe was telling the deep-freeze as she sealed the door upon her latest batch of wedding ice cream. It had taken the best part of the afternoon to make it and Bovis had only interrupted her five times to ask how to open the till so he could correct someone's wrong change.

She'd tried to be patient. He was, after all, only learning, but by the time the gooseberry syrup – to be syringed into each sphere of ice cream upon serving at the wedding – was cooling and capped in jars, Bovis was calling for her once more.

When she emerged from her shiny new kitchen at the back of the shop, Bovis was frowning more than usual. This time it was aimed at the gentleman in the white captain's hat and epaulettes, whose grin seemed to be taking up most of the shop. Or at least that was Mrs C.'s first impression as she emerged through the rainbow ribbon curtain.

'Problem?' she asked Bovis, who kept his eyes fixed on the stranger.

'Fella here wants to know if there's real rum in the rum 'n' raisin.'

''Course it is, best Devonshire rum.'

''Course it is,' Bovis repeated, his words aimed straight at the man who he'd clearly taken a dislike to. 'What a daft question. *Is it real rum?* indeed.'

'You didn't seem to know a moment ago,' the customer reminded Bovis, with a jovial laugh, never once taking his eyes off Mrs Crocombe. 'You'll forgive me asking, Miss, only I can't take alcohol when in charge of my yacht.'

Mrs Crocombe, who was used to odd characters breezing in and out of the harbour, didn't bat an eyelid and offered him her dark chocolate and mint crème as an alternative, sensing he was the sophisticated type.

She could usually tell what folks were going to order. When she first opened her shop thirty years ago it hadn't taken her long to figure out that many customers, probably subconsciously afraid of dripping, matched their ice cream to their outfits. This fellow though, looked cultured and adventurous. There was no way he was going to drip.

'Perfect!' he told her. 'You read my mind.'

Bingo! Mrs Crocombe smiled as she rolled a silky scoop.

Bovis watched on, his eyes narrowed like a Victorian maiden aunt chaperoning at a country dance.

'So many beautiful things to taste,' the man continued. 'I could be tempted to extend my visit until I've tried every flavour,' he told her as he took the cone from her hand and pulled a twenty from a thick roll of notes drawn from his trouser pocket.

'You're not docking overnight?' she asked, sorting his change with efficient hands.

'Hadn't planned to. In fact, I was going to take in some more of the coastline, but I think I'd like to see more of Clove Lore. It does seem...' His gaze fell coyly to the cone below his lips before flashing brightly back to her stunned face. 'Enchanting.'

His eyes sparkled in the lights above the counter and reflected in the chrome surfaces and mirrors all around the shop. For a millisecond there was nothing but dazzling blue irises and perfect white teeth.

Bovis tutted and shifted his stance, still glaring, perplexed, at the man who was taking no notice of him whatsoever.

Mrs Crocombe fidgeted with the bow of her apron ties at her tummy and when that wasn't enough to settle the strange sensation the man's smile had sent through her, she smoothed the white cotton over her hips and bravely smiled back.

'That all you come in for?' Bovis asked the man, who hadn't as yet lifted his change from the countertop.

'I've heard there are some pretty walks along the beach here?' the man asked Mrs Crocombe. 'And a famous waterfall?'

'There are,' she told him. 'And now the beach is all sand and shingle since the flood, it's even prettier, if that was possible.'

She'd done her best to recover from the strange feeling that had dragged her back to her awkward teenage years, when she'd wished herself a dark and mysterious Natalie Wood – even though her mother had worked at the Clove Lore estate dairy and all that milk and cheddar had already given her the pale, soft, sweet look she still had today.

She'd made her older brothers take her to see *Rebel Without a Cause* four times the winter it came out and she'd dreamed of being kissed by a wild, doe-eyed boy.

That spring and still under the influence of James Dean and Hollywood, she'd met a big, sandy-haired, cheerful boy fresh from his National Service and they'd married as soon as she was old enough. Ernie Crocombe had remained as rosy-cheeked and devoted – and as far away from dangerous, tragic, dashing James Dean as could be – his whole life.

The man was asking her something. She had to pack away all thoughts of her late husband in order to hear him properly. 'Say again?'

'There was a flood here?'

'Oh, yes, at Christmas. You must have heard about it? Swept through the village, washed away all the beach pebbles.'

'Ah, I was in the Azores over winter, must have missed that. Perhaps you'd tell me more about it? On a stroll, later this evening?'

'Oh,' was all Mrs Crocombe could manage.

'Aren't you 'elping at the bookshop tonight?' Bovis put in.

'Well...' Mrs Crocombe glanced between the two men. Bovis, red-faced and stolid; the other, sun-bleached and dashing, like the time the fish finger people tried to sex up Captain Birdseye on their ads and got loads of complaints.

Mrs Crocombe, however, wasn't complaining. She wasn't one hundred percent sure what was happening but a little flame of intrigue had ignited within her, something she usually only felt when she added a name to her betting book and set about matchmaking amongst the locals.

'I'd like that,' she said, a little shakily, her cheeks blushing.

The man stood straighter, snapping his heels together and offering a hand over the countertop. 'In that case, let me introduce myself. I'm Captain James da Costa of the *Lucky Boy*.' His soft eyes crinkled as he smiled once more.

She slipped her hand into his, while Bovis lifted himself on tiptoe so he could scan disapprovingly down the Captain's body to his shoes and back to his shining eyes.

'Letitia Crocombe, of Crocombe's Ices,' she introduced herself.

James da Costa laughed heartily, making Bovis roll his eyes. 'Splendid, splendid! Until tonight, Letitia.' And he was gone, leaving Mrs Crocombe smiling, dazed, in his wake.

'I don't like the look of 'im,' Bovis told her.

'Oh, Mr Bovis! Since when did you like anyone?' She ran a cloth along the counter and disappeared behind the curtain once more where she immediately pulled out the book from her apron pocket and scratched a name in pencil, *Captain James da Costa of The Lucky Boy*, and beside it she left a blank space, allowing her pencil point to hover for a moment before snapping the book shut, telling herself to give over, and fanning her flushing face.

Chapter Ten

Monty was the first to arrive, at five on the dot. Joy met him at the top of the shop steps, knowing she was supposed to smile and be grateful for the help but feeling nothing but panic at the sight of him. Well, maybe not feeling *nothing* else.

She definitely noticed how his chestnut-brown curls, probably freshly washed, burnished in the afternoon sunlight. He was wearing a blue Henley, rolled at the sleeves, that looked cool and soft and suggested hard muscle underneath. *Not* a convenient thing to be thinking.

Worst of all he was cradling something wrapped in paper. *Please not flowers, please not flowers.*

'Montague!' Radia called out, skipping up to him in the square. 'Come to my tea party.'

'Hallo,' he greeted them both, handing Joy the parcel. 'Tea would be amazing, thanks, Radia.'

'Oh!' said Joy, realising it wasn't flowers, but a big fish. 'What's this?'

'Thought we'd better feed the helpers.'

'Is that one for me?' Radia asked, pointing to a second, smaller package.

'If you like,' he told her, passing her the leafy bundle.

'Lettuce?' Far from being disappointed, she thought his gift hilarious.

'Chinese leaf, celery and dill, and there's a fresh baguette in there too,' Monty smiled, and Radia laughed again. 'Shall we cook it up?'

'How?' Radia squinted up at him. 'Our kitchen's all wrapped in plastic.'

Monty glanced at Joy whose shoulders dropped.

'It's true,' she told him. 'I didn't get a chance to strip the protective wrapping off everything.'

'How have you been eating?' Monty asked.

'We've managed.'

'Yeah, cereal and toast,' Radia dobbed her in.

'Hey, my toast's the best in the whole world, remember? Your words, not mine.' Joy smiled for her daughter, who conceded that much was true, actually.

'I think we can do better than a bit of toast tonight,' Monty put in gently. 'Listen, there's a brick barbeque in the yard round the back of the shop, built it myself in the spring with Alex and Magnús. There's a bag of charcoal too. Let's fire it up.'

Telling him every fish fact she knew, Radia followed Monty round the back and through a little blue gate into a yard surrounded on all sides by the white walls of squat old cottages and stone outbuildings.

A patch of newly rooted turf, already getting over-grown in the summer sun, reached all the way to a completely bare half-moon flower bed by the barbeque.

'You need to get some flowers in there,' Monty told Radia, only just realising Joy had followed them round to keep an eye on him. 'And in the window boxes.'

'I don't have any,' Radia said with a shrug. Charley fox dragged on the grass at her ankles.

Joy wanted to say there was no point planting things they wouldn't see growing but, not wanting to upset

Radia, she didn't. Instead she kept her distance, arms folded, watching Monty start up the barbeque.

'What's that?' Radia asked as he sparked his lighter.

'Oh, it's a, it's...' He turned to Joy as if asking her permission.

'It's a cigarette lighter,' Joy told her.

'You smoke cigarettes!' Radia blurted, dismayed.

'Well, sometimes,' Monty told her. 'But I'm definitely going to stop.'

'Today?'

'*Umm*, well...'

'Come on, Rads. Let Monty sort the food.' Joy tried to pry her away, and Monty smiled back, apologetically.

''Ow do,' called a friendly voice from the courtyard, and Radia instantly abandoned Monty in favour of finding out who it was that sounded exactly like a pirate.

Before Joy and Radia could round the corner, a small, curly coated dog padded towards them.

'That's Aldous,' Monty told them as he tipped the coals out onto the grill.

Radia dropped to her knees to cuddle him.

'Here you all are,' came the voice once more, accompanied by the sandy hair and weathered face of Jowan, the bookshop's owner, his pearl-drop earing bouncing off his jaw as he smiled. 'You don't have any cheddar on you? Dog's got a nose full of somethin' good,' he asked Radia, making her giggle.

Radia told him about Monty's big fish, and Monty waved from his spot over the coals.

'I'm glad to meet you, at last,' he said, offering Joy a hand and apologising for not visiting sooner. 'I've been distracted helping Minty with her wedding plans up at the Big House.'

Joy told him she'd already met his wife and she'd looked extremely busy, to which Jowan only nodded diplomatic-ally, and the three stood around the little beige dog who was now flat on his back having his belly scratched.

'Does he *really* like cheese?' Radia asked, and Jowan told her how, long ago, that was all he'd eaten. 'Well, that and scones and chicken soup! His favourites. But Elliot's got him on a diet these days, and he's all the better for it.'

Radia wanted to know if Aldous ate his soup with a spoon and Jowan chuckled, crouching down beside the girl, telling her all about how Elliot had saved Aldous's life with an operation on his tummy.

Eventually, the smoke got too strong for them so they left Monty to get the flames going and headed around the corner and back inside the shop. Jowan led the way, but made them stop abruptly just inside the doorway while he took in the piles of books.

'Long time since I've seen the place lookin' like this,' he told Joy.

Radia, now carrying Aldous in an awkward kind of doggy stranglehold that he didn't seem to mind, pricked up her ears, thinking Jowan looked like he was about to say more. A wistful glaze had passed over his eyes, but he only swallowed hard and ran a hand down his beard.

Joy knew it wasn't very generous of her, but she was glad he hadn't regaled them with a story about his shop. They were here to shelve the books, not to get all emotional about things.

'You've got a tattoo!' Radia told Jowan, gaping at the faded blue anchor that stretched from his thumb across the back of his hand.

'I do.'

'Because you're a pirate?'

'I am,' he told her, crouching again. 'Only, don't let on to anyone. They'll be pesterin' me for my treasure map again.'

'I found a book about pirates,' Radia said, setting Aldous down and taking Jowan's tattooed hand, pulling him through the piles of paperbacks towards the under-stairs nook where she'd arranged the children's books messily in piles, according to the colours of their spines.

Joy heard him remarking how that was such a clever idea and they should be shelved just like that. 'Jus' like a rainbow.'

Within moments, Radia had Aldous on her lap on one of the beanbags, with Jowan reclining on the other one holding Charley fox on his knee, the four of them enjoying the pictures in a 1960s *Pirate Tales for Children*.

Joy watched them from a distance. She couldn't help thinking of her own father reading to her when she was Radia's age and just getting to grips with phonics. Her favourites had been her Ladybird books, with the spotty inside covers. Her younger sister Patti (short for Patience) loved them too.

The urge to pick up her phone and leave her sister a voice message – the closest they got to direct communic-ation these days – gnawed at her.

She pulled the phone from her pocket and scrolled to Patti's last message, received over a month ago now when Joy and Radia were back in their London flat for a few days between jobs and only a few miles from Patti's place in Richmond, where she lived with her two flatmates.

She clicked on the message and listened again.

'Joy, it's me. I hope you're both doing OK. I have no idea what time zone you're in but I hope you're getting this. There's something I wanted to talk with you about. Nothing major, and Mum and Dad are totally fine, so don't go worrying. They're on their way back from Portugal, actually. Loved it, apparently. And they miss you both, of course. Not that they told me to say that. I'm not interfering or anything. I just think they do miss you. *Um*, uh, right, sorry, that's not what I called to say. Listen, give Rads a big squeeze from her favourite aunt, and I'll talk to you soon, OK? Call me. Or text. Or anything. I'll be here. OK, love you lots, kiss kiss.'

Joy had sent her a voice message straight back, letting Patti know they were both fine and that she was busy as always – and that was it, she didn't want to let on that they were so close to home, knowing Patti would be round like a shot.

It had hurt not to tell her, but in those rare moments when they returned to the flat, squeezing through the door piled up with takeaway menus and important letters, there was always laundry to do, dentist and doctor appointments to catch up on, contracts to look over and the next sets of flights to book. By the time that was all sorted out it was time to leave again, or at least that's how Joy justified it to herself.

And if Patti knew they were back at the flat, there was a slim chance she'd let Mum and Dad know too, and Joy just couldn't deal with that. Maybe they'd want to meet up after all this time apart. Then again, maybe they wouldn't. She didn't know which scenario was worse, and she really didn't want to find out.

It was easier to text her parents now and again, never disclosing where they were exactly, sending the occasional picture of Radia. Her mum would text back about how much Radia was growing, and that was pretty much it.

Economical, to the point, very little in the way of trust or truth-telling.

Patti understood all this, of course. After the big falling-out, she – the youngest of the family – had been the only one to try making amends. Just as Radia was turning five months old, Joy's little sister had got in touch and told her she couldn't lose her again, but she also didn't want to be a go-between.

Joy understood how it only caused upset if Patti talked about her sister and niece at home, and so, as far as Joy could tell, she didn't mention them anymore. But still, now so much time had passed, and with Radia over-shooting school age, she could feel it: the building expectation that they'd go home for good. *That* would be the thing Patti wanted to talk with her about.

Patti must somehow know that Joy was thinking about the school place open to Radia. It would be just like her to offer to help with school runs and pick-ups, anything to encourage her to go back home. But that all felt like far too much unsafe intrusion into The Joy and Radia Bubble. Still, Joy missed her sister terribly.

Retreating to the low café doorway, she recorded a furtive message.

'Hey Patti, it's me. How's the event organising going? I hope you're looking after yourself properly, not working all hours. And I hope Mum and Dad are OK. We're fine. Rads is doing fine.' Joy glanced across the shop. Jowan was swishing an imaginary cutlass in the air and they were both making pirate cries. 'Actually, Rads is probably happier than she's been in a while.'

'So this is where the party is?' interrupted a cheerful voice from all the way across the shop. Joy's nerves jumped at the sudden appearance of the two men in the doorway.

Seeing she was on her phone, the one that had spoken had his hands spread out in apology already.

'I'd better go, love you too,' she told the voice message before quickly hitting send.

There wasn't time to tell her sister she was doing a tech installation in a bookshop. That'd tickle Patti. She loved to read. She was a bigger nerd than Joy, except Patti was born with all the creativity and spontaneity, while Joy got all the practicality and shyness. Though that hadn't stopped them being best friends as kids. The thought heightened the sorry ache within her. She stuffed the phone away into her black pinafore dress pocket and walked towards the newcomers.

'We didn't mean to sneak up on you,' one of the men said; a slight, tall man with a gentle Polish accent.

'Ah, Izaak, come in!' Jowan called from the nook under the stairs.

He didn't, however, come inside, waiting instead for Joy to recover herself and offer him her hand.

'I'm sorry, I was calling someone… I'm Joy.'

'The IT expert,' said the other man. 'Pleased to meet you. I am Leonid.' This man's accent was stronger, Russian for sure.

As the three shook hands, Joy noticed the matching gold bands on their ring fingers. These two matched in other ways too. In their energy, she thought, and the way they waited patiently for her to sweep them inside. Neither moved until she'd said 'welcome' – it had come out awkwardly, hammering home the obvious fact that she wasn't used to playing hostess.

'We brought some cake, made with honey from our new beehives,' Leonid told everyone, making Radia abandon her new pirate friend and storm the gap-toothed Russian man.

'You have *bees*?' she demanded, eyes ablaze.

'I have a garden full of bees and beehives and camellias. Will you visit one day with your mamma?'

Radia told Leonid she'd definitely be doing that, while eyeing the tin in Izaak's hands so hungrily he immediately lifted off the lid for her, revealing a big brown sponge cake shaped like a crown, pre-cut, all grooved and glistening.

'You've heard of Polish honey cake?' Izaak asked, as Radia reached into the tin, lifting a slice.

Her mouth was too full of cake to answer, so Joy had to tell him how Radia wouldn't remember it but she'd tried it as a toddler and adored it.

'That was when we were setting up computers and phone systems in a trendy new hotel in Poznań. It was interesting actually because the room keys were iPhones and they were pre-loaded with all the apps you needed for your stay and I did this clever little bit of check-in-desk coding that meant guests didn't have to queue for anything and... Oh!'

Joy realised that in her nervous state she'd been banging on about her job and looking conceited while she did it, probably.

Sean, after a few months of feigning interest, had begun telling her she bragged too much about her work and that it was selfish to assume other people were interested.

'Sorry,' she said now.

Izaak didn't look like he'd minded, or maybe he was just being polite?

'My mother is in Kraśnik,' he told her, as though glad of the opportunity to mention her. Joy wasn't sure where in Poland Kraśnik was, so she said, 'Is she? That's nice.'

Again, the words came out stilted. These people were going to think she was odd, or rude, or both. She definitely knew the *expected* thing to say would be, 'You must miss her.' But she'd heard strangers say this about her own parents and it only made things awkward, and then, sensing there was more to it than just Joy having to work away from her family, people expected *a story*.

Thankfully, Radia helped draw his attention away by demanding both men tell her all about the bees. Just as they were explaining that they worked for Minty as her ticket-booth operator and general handyman (Izaak) and head gardener (Leonid), Monty stepped inside asking if he could wash his hands and announcing that the fish would be ready in about twenty minutes so everyone had better get on with the book shelving if they were going to get it finished before dark.

This threw everyone into a flurry of activity. Jowan offered to shelve the poetry, while Radia insisted Izaak help her in the Children's section. Leonid chatted away with them from Gardening and The House Beautiful, which ran on to include Arts and Crafts.

Joy gravitated towards General Fiction, where Monty joined her. Its shelves took up much of the shop and spread from the display table by the door, running along the wall towards the low entrance into the café. It was shadier there, away from the little porthole windows by the till.

'How are we doing this, then?' Monty asked.

'Well… alphabetically,' she tried.

'I suppose that should have been obvious.' He was smiling, like a well-adjusted person would, not pained or awkward like her. Joy wished she had some of his calmness around strangers.

'Thank you for bringing the fish,' she blurted, not knowing what else to say.

Monty didn't seem to mind. 'So, Radia was telling me out there that she once ate poisonous Japanese blowfish, in Tokyo.' He lifted two handfuls of books and peered at their spines. 'I'm afraid my Atlantic cod can't compete with that.'

'That's right, *fugu*! That kid remembers everything she ever ate. It wasn't so much delicious as it was… an interesting experience.'

'You were there to work?'

'Yep, installing…' She stopped herself. 'A really boring, specific bit of tech at the stock exchange.'

'Woah, really? That's not boring at all.'

'It's not?' Joy didn't believe him.

'And they let Radia go to work with you at the stock exchange?'

'Oh, no, she was in a crèche during the day.'

'No wonder she knows so much about international food.'

And crèches, thought Joy, guiltily. She knows loads about foreign crèches and childminders and room service. Yet, Monty was looking at her like he was somehow impressed, like she wasn't the world's least attentive mother.

'You must be about the smartest person I've ever met,' Monty was saying. Joy batted the words away like they were angry wasps.

'God, no!'

She wouldn't have been able to pinpoint the moment when compliments had become impossible to receive, painful to hear. It was one of the many things Patti pointed out that had changed about her, around about the time of the big family bust-up when Joy was realising with dawning horror that she was pregnant, and everyone around her was suddenly finding fault and picking at her.

'Where'd you learn it all?' Monty asked.

'Oh, you know, uni, and then a bunch of training afterwards.'

All of that was true, but she neglected to mention how it had always come easily to her. How, if a piece of hardware or software had been well designed she could often intuitively find her way around it, and if it wasn't all that instinctual then the ideas for modifications just presented themselves to her.

She'd learned coding in her bedroom as a teenager from books and online tutorials, and it had all felt absolutely like herself, like the thing she *should* be doing. She'd discovered her talents young and it had made her so happy. She was part of a worldwide network of people just like her, in it for the love of innovation and trying to see further than before. Nowadays, though, it was just work and a way of keeping Radia safe. She'd turned herself into a Jack of all Tech so she could live an untethered existence. All of that early passion was gone.

'Can you keep handing me the A's?' she asked him. 'We should sort them on the shelves, save our backs.'

'Right you are,' Monty said, squinting at the spines, and they worked away steadily, muttering under their breath loud enough for the other to hear.

'Aaron, Abbott, Abrahams.'

'There's a Douglas Adams here, stick him on the next shelf along. We'll get to him in a sec.'

'Pass me that Achebe, thanks.'

Making decent progress, they were soon at the Al's when Jude arrived wearing a white summer sundress and a glowy tan that just screamed 'bride-to-be'.

'Sorry I'm late,' she said from the doormat. 'Minty was talking at me and the caterer about the canapés.'

'Talking *at* you?' Izaak echoed, making Leonid and Jude smile slyly until they remembered Jowan was in the poetry section, although he was too familiar with Minty's organisational zeal to be offended. He was also loyal and wouldn't join in with making fun of her, especially if she wasn't there to defend herself.

Jude came closer and introduced herself to Joy, waved with a cheery 'hiya' to Radia, and then drew from her tote bag a couple of bottles of chilled rosé. 'Shall we?' she asked Joy. 'It is a party, after all.'

Leonid was quickly on his way to scour the café for suitable cups and Jude called after him that it was only a screw top so not to bother with the bottle opener.

Joy was only a little taken aback by how everyone simply made themselves at home in the bookshop, rummaging in the kitchen, striding in and out like it was their own. She supposed it did belong to them, to the community, and not her. She was only the temp, after all.

'After the day I've had, I could do with a drink,' Jude confided in a low voice near Joy's side, which sparked a little thrill of closeness within her that she wasn't used to. How long had it been since she'd been offered a glass of wine at a party by a woman her own age? She couldn't remember.

'Wedding fever?' Joy asked.

'Aye,' Jude agreed in a whisper. 'Only it's Minty who's got the fever. I'm a bit left out in the cold. Still,' Jude sighed, speaking at a normal volume once more. 'There's no one better to organise a do than Minty and I guess it *is* a Clove Lore wedding. It sort of belongs to the community, not me and Elliot. If you see what I mean?'

Joy didn't, and she thought that something so private belonging to a bunch of meddling villagers sounded awful, but she didn't want to say so. Instead she told her, 'Weddings are a surprising amount of work.' Then, thinking Jude might start wondering if she knew that because she was married herself, she added, 'My sister's an event planner. I've seen her throw away whole days on sourcing exactly the right colour chair covers.'

Jude whispered again. 'Ah, you'll have heard about Bridezillas then? Minty's gone a bit Planner-zilla. Shouldn't complain, I know, Minty knows what she's doing,' she added quickly, as Leonid barrelled towards them holding six mugs, signalling to everyone their short burst of activity was already over.

'Al fresco?' Monty called, abandoning his handful of books. 'I'll grab plates and forks. Meet you by the barbeque.'

—

The fresh fish was delicious wrapped up in the Chinese leaf that had wilted and crisped in a sweet, buttery way. There was only enough for a few little parcels each, eaten with torn hunks of baguette and washed down with wine. Monty didn't take one bite for himself, only standing watching everyone else enjoying their food and seeming to be thinking very hard.

His cheeks were a little pink, Joy thought, as she observed him over her plate while Jude told her about her plans for decorating the wedding cake she'd made with her parents. Was he blushing? No, it wasn't that. Not shyness. It was a look she recognised from long ago when she'd worked in a vibrant team and they'd completed projects together. The look of satisfaction over a job done well. The glow of enthusiasm. It suited him.

The afternoon sun and the camaraderie of the simple meal eaten standing around the barbeque fuelled everyone up for the hard work to come, and they passed back inside the shop focused on their shared task.

Joy felt her phone buzz inside her pocket and she stole a moment, hiding in the bathroom at the top of the stairs, to listen to the message. Patti's voice bubbled with wicked excitement?

'So you're having *a party*? With a guy? A guy with an accent? I'm guessing you're someplace eastern European by the sounds of him? *Go you*, Joy! Call me back. Tell me all about him. Anything to liven up this wedding expo. Have you ever *been* to Slough? It's not the first place you think of when you hear the words *destination wedding*. Right, I'm going in to the keynote now. At least it's on working with LGBTQ+ friendly celebrants. That's *got* to be better than the *new ways with napkin folding* demo I just came out of. Call me. We still need to talk. Love you lots.'

Joy couldn't help smiling, even if Patti had jumped to crazy conclusions. It was nice to hear her sister being excited for her, though she'd have to set her straight on the whole hot guy party thing.

Before she could do anything else, Radia was taking her hand and dragging her back down to General Fiction and manoeuvring her into position beside Monty. Radia made sure to squeeze in between the two of them, telling them she was going to help out.

Monty stooped for a pile of books and Radia, who'd got wind of Monty having his own boat, took this opportunity to demand details.

'Does it have a name? All boats have names, don't they? Like *Wallis* at... what was it called, Mum?'

'Staten Island?' Joy asked. 'You mean *Ollis*?'

'That's it. We had macadamia nuts in a jar on the ferry.'

'And... we saw the Statue of Liberty?' Joy reminded her, smiling.

'That as well,' Radia laughed, showing the little gap in her bottom row of teeth.

'They call pop *soda* there, in America,' she informed Monty, who pulled an impressed face.

'I can't compete with famous boats, macadamia nuts and soda,' he said. His voice was kind and laughing. 'My father's little boat doesn't have any of those things. He's called *Peter's Bounty*.'

'Is that your daddy's name? Peter?' Radia was asking, but it coincided with Joy wondering aloud about the boat being a 'he'.

'Aren't boats usually female?' she asked.

Radia laughed. 'Boats aren't girls or boys. Don't be silly,' and having been corrected, both Joy and Monty let their eyes meet with a smile.

It hadn't escaped Joy's notice, however, that Radia had just inquired about Monty's 'daddy' and she got a little lost in her thoughts, wondering why the word hadn't also been shortened to 'dad' in Radia's mind, the way that 'mummy' had.

A twinge in her chest told her that Radia exalted the idea of daddies, even though she hardly ever mentioned Sean. Not that he was kept a secret or anything, only that he never really came up. Why would he? Their little girl had never even spoken with him. Still, there was clearly a deep appeal around the idea of a daddy in Radia's mind. Joy was at a complete loss what to do about that. Telling her the absolute truth about Sean would crush her, or make her pity her mum, or maybe even blame her for the mess she'd got them all in, the way she blamed herself.

'No,' Monty was telling Radia. 'That'll be Saint Peter. He's the patron saint of anything fishy. Net makers, ship-builders, fishermen, that kind of thing. I suppose we call the boat "he" because of him.'

'And you're a fisherman?' said Radia.

'I am,' he said, handing her some books to pass to Joy. 'I was,' he corrected himself.

Jude appeared at Monty's back. 'I've some Charles Dickens and a du Maurier here.'

'We're still on the Alexanders and Allens,' Joy told her.

'Give them here.' Monty took them and added them to the jumble of books around his feet before seeming to remember he had something to ask her.

'Jude, you don't happen to have Elliot's dad's phone number do you?'

'*Umm*, nope,' Jude replied, hesitating at first, then speaking in a low voice which, of course, Radia immediately tuned into. 'They're not on speaking terms.'

'I thought as much,' said Monty. 'Am I *really* not to invite any of his family to the stag do?'

'Really.' Jude was emphatic.

'They're seriously estranged?' Monty replied. 'Seems a shame.'

'Estranged,' Radia echoed, like she was saving the word to her memory banks.

'It happens more than you think,' Joy added, still busily shelving books. 'Sorry, didn't mean to listen in.'

'You'll soon know there's no such thing as secrets here,' said Jude. 'No point trying to keep anything hushed up in Clove Lore.'

Joy tried to smile even though the thought alarmed her.

'Any Andersons?' she deflected, with a wobble in her voice.

Chapter Eleven

Whilst the shelvers worked, out on the slope, the late summer sun was casting long shadows across the cobbles. The air cooled as the sea breeze came in.

'Perfect evening for a walk, Letitia,' laughed James da Costa, while Mrs Crocombe turned the key in the lock of the Ice Cream Cottage.

Bovis – at last out of his T-shirt and back in mossy green corduroys and a checked shirt, like he was on his way to scout the Big House's estate perimeter looking for signs of poachers, and not in fact heading home alone to heat a can of soup – watched on, his face set in an unimpressed scowl.

'Good evening to you,' James threw to him, more as a dismissal than a greeting.

Bovis skulked off up the slope, but not before telling his new boss to ring him if she needed anything. 'Day or night,' he added, giving the Captain one last warning look.

James only crooked his elbow for Mrs Crocombe. 'Will you do me the honour of showing me this beach waterfall I've heard so much about?'

A little unsure of herself, she slipped her hand through his arm and off they went, down the slope. She was surprised to find the familiar sights of the village she'd known all her life stood out tonight as vividly beautiful.

Passion flowers, red roses and dancing fuchsia blooms blazed riotously bright and cheerful this evening. Had they been so pretty the day before? She really hadn't noticed.

Letitia glanced back only once at the windows that looked down onto the slope from her rooms above her shop, fighting the feeling that behind them her Ernest was watching her walking out of doors with a strange man.

She had to concentrate on her step to stop her suddenly-leaden legs stumbling.

James, however, shared none of her awkwardness. He grinned down at her like he was escorting a beauty queen and touched his hand to where her fingers gripped his white jacket.

'Tell me about your day,' he crooned, and that was all it took for all thoughts of her dear, soft husband to drift away on the sweet evening breeze. 'What was your best seller, hmm?'

'Peaches and cream,' she told him shyly, all the while wondering how on earth anything about her life could be of interest to him.

'Ah!' His eyes sparkled. 'Like the song!'

Mrs Crocombe stopped outside Jowan's cottage where the slope levelled out and turned for the lifeboat launch. 'Johnny Burnette? You know that song?'

'Of course I do. It was one of the first records I ever bought. I knew you were a little rock and roller.'

Before she knew what was happening, James swept an arm around her in a swaying hold, and he sang fearlessly on the sea wall, about her walking straight out of his dreams at sweet sixteen with lips like strawberry wine, not caring he was getting the lyrics wrong.

Letitia let herself be danced but drew the line when he tried to twirl her, laughing instead and smacking him lightly on the lapel. 'Oh, give over. It's a long time since I was sixteen.'

'But maybe you were a little rebel?'

The Captain roared a delighted laugh to see her smiling and indulgently shaking her head at him.

As they walked down onto the sand he sang the rest of the tune.

The beach, washed clean like some strange new place by the flood waters, seemed prettier than it had ever been, though Mrs Crocombe didn't say that out loud now. Instead she held James's arm that little bit tighter and strolled bravely on letting him sing as the sun thought lazily about setting.

Chapter Twelve

After a while, Radia had enough of moving books about and went off to read to Aldous in her bedroom. The shelving party had fallen quiet and Joy was fighting the compulsive need she had to fill the silence. Maybe it was something to do with Monty working away diligently by her side, silent and absorbed.

'What do you think of the refit, Jude?' she called out, pleased she'd struck upon something innocuous and easy.

'Much better, isn't it?' Jude replied from her spot by the till, where she was sorting a display of mega bestsellers. 'It's got the same feel it had when me and Elliot came on holiday here, only it's fresher.'

Joy was drawn in. 'You worked in the bookshop? As in, you were holiday renters?'

'Yep,' Jude told her. 'We didn't know each other when we arrived.'

'And they were in love by the time they were supposed to leave,' Izaak put in.

'You made twenty quid out of that one, didn't you Izaak?' Jude said with a wink.

'You were involved in the... *the book*?' Joy said, checking Radia wasn't peering round her door listening to the grown-ups.

'Oh, we were *all* in Mrs C.'s betting book,' Jude told her.

'A lot's changed since then,' Jowan said, steering the conversation back to safer territory, his eyes fixed on his poetry shelves.

He seemed to be faster than anyone else at getting stock filed away. At this rate he'd be on Yeats and the few Zs in no time. Joy supposed he'd had more practice than the rest of the helpers.

'I think Radia's room's much nicer as a bedroom,' Jude was saying, positioning some hardbacks on racks behind the till area so their covers faced outwards.

Jowan wasn't finished yet. 'It was our little private breakfast room when I ran the place alone with my… late wife.' He said this like a man experimenting with a new way of thinking, now that he was married for a second time.

'Luckily, there was the insurance money for fixing the place back up,' Jude said. 'So much of Clove Lore was resurrected with it.'

'But the last little touches, they cost more,' Jowan added.

'Like my beehives,' Leonid called from somewhere hidden in the stacks at the deepest point of the shop.

'*And* the Siren's suite refurbs,' Monty added. 'And the new paint job on the *Bounty*; terrible scratched it was.'

'Those little extras were all paid for by the residents' emergency payments,' Jowan informed Joy, and Jude hummed her agreement from behind the counter.

'Emergency payments?' Joy echoed. 'Didn't you say that's what's paying for my contract?' Joy directed this over her shoulder at Jude, the person she'd corresponded with during the application process.

'That's the one,' Jowan answered for her. 'You wouldn't believe the number of envelopes that arrived after the flood, full of money and cheques. T'was the telly that did it, all them news reports.'

'Minty went viral,' Leonid called out, still unseen amongst the stacks, a smile in his voice, and this was met with a sharp laughing 'Hah!' from Izaak, now in the café and loudly tearing the plastic coverings off the units and machinery.

'She did,' Monty told Joy. 'But it was Moira being airlifted by that helicopter that really brought the money in.'

'Moira?' came a little voice from the bedroom. Radia's. She'd been listening this whole time.

Monty filled her and Joy in. 'She's one of the donkeys from the sanctuary. She got stuck in the mud and had to be rescued by the coastguard.'

'And she weren't the only one,' said Jowan pensively. 'So many lives would have been lost without the airlifts.'

'God!' was all Joy could manage. 'That's horrible.'

'It was,' Jude agreed. 'But afterwards people were so generous. We had to set up a fundraising page when the international donations started coming in.'

Jowan shelved the last of the poetry books and straightened his back with a stretch. 'Minty administered the 'ole thing. Every resident and business owner is being gifted their share. Ten thousand each.'

'Pounds?' Radia exclaimed as Charley fox peeped his head around the doorframe.

'Yep, s'a lot, isn't it?' Jowan told the fox. 'And there's no rules on what to do with it, neither. It's a gift. I replanted my cottage garden, got the gate and railings replaced, an' now the place is ready to sell.'

'He lives up at the Big House now he's a married man,' Leonid added in explanation, emerging from the shelves. 'And technically, Lord of the Manor.'

'Hah!' Jowan chuckled.

'Well, it's nice that people helped out,' said Joy.

'People *are* nice, on the whole,' Jude told the room, standing back to admire her book display. 'Minty's just sorting the last few residents' emergency payments now and then the whole thing will be over.'

Joy felt Jude's words in her gut. *People are nice, on the whole.*

Are people nice? She wasn't convinced. In her experience there just wasn't enough gentleness and understanding in the world, and yet there was Izaak emerging from the kitchen with a tray of coffees and what looked like a milkshake for Radia – how had he conjured that up? – and she had a shop full of volunteers crowding around him and lifting mugs, chatting and smiling. Added to that, the bookshelves were well on their way to being filled and she couldn't remember the last time she'd felt so included in anything.

This was certainly nothing like her other recent jobs. The contrast struck her now and she was left wondering at how lonely her life had become over the last few years, how she could go weeks with nobody to speak to but Radia, how a little of the Clove Lore niceness could have helped them in tricky times lately.

After coffee and big slices of honey cake, the shelvers grew quieter, focusing on finishing their particular areas.

Jowan had shown everyone how to press the spines with their flattened forearm so the books stood flush with the very edge of the shelf. Jude had completed Biography and moved on to the cookbooks. The children's area really

97

did look like a burst of rainbow colour under the stairs. Izaak and Leonid had disappeared into Sciences and The Natural World.

Radia, insisting she wasn't sleepy even though it was way past her bedtime, was given the job of stacking the picture postcards of Clove Lore, fresh from the printer in Truro, in the revolving stand by the counter, a task she was taking very seriously. Monty and Joy found themselves in the furthest corner of General Fiction, over by the café door.

The summer twilight cast itself in the softest way across Monty's dark eyelashes and sun-kissed cheekbones. Joy tried not to look at him a third time after she'd made a double take when he was sorting out the Roberts from the Rogers and Roys.

'Happy?' Monty had startled her, throwing out the question as though it were the easiest thing in the world to answer.

'Am I happy?' she repeated. 'Well, sure. It's been a good night, and look at the shop. It's almost tidy.'

They cast their eyes around. Joy grew very aware that they were alone here in the shadows with the Roses and Russells.

'Have you worked in a bookshop before?' Monty asked.

Joy searched her memory. She'd done retail and recreation plenty of times before. There'd been tech installations on a chain of boba tea shops across the Netherlands, those indie cinema upgrades in the north of England, a series of interactive big screens in sports bars across Birmingham, but no bookshops. 'This is a first for me. It's...' She thought hard. 'Cosier than we're used to. It's nice, actually.'

Monty sniffed a laugh.

'What?'

'You say that like it's a bad thing. Clove Lore *is* cosy and nice.'

'We're used to somewhere more corporate or… you know?'

Monty didn't know.

She tried to explain. 'Like, have you ever been in a nightclub during the daytime? Or a row of brand-new warehouses before the stock arrives? Or in a skyscraper hotel before the plaster's on the walls?'

'Can't say I have.'

'Well, it's all a bit…' Joy didn't want to say it. 'It's all a bit sad, really.'

'But you get home to Radia every night?'

'True, and sometimes she comes with me, when it's safe, you know? Empty offices, that kind of thing.'

'I'm starting to get a picture of your life,' said Monty and he saw something in Joy's shifting expression that made him add, 'Fast-paced. Exciting? Busy.'

'Yeah, I guess.' She stopped shelving and stretched out her back. 'It's varied, that's for sure. But tonight's the first time I've had volunteers helping. If I'm not working by myself there's only usually the engineers there, or the architects, sometimes a poor intern. And it's *definitely* the first time we've had a barbeque. Thank you for that. Again.'

Monty had stopped working now too. He was looking at her in the most unassuming, friendly way, but still Joy wondered if the evening light was playing on her skin the way it was on his.

'It was my pleasure. In fact, it was more fun than anything I've done in a long time.' Monty looked in danger of drifting away into his thoughts. 'Yeah. It really felt like *cooking*. Flames and fish and herbs…' He stopped himself, seemed to grow reticent when a second ago he'd been so passionate. 'Anyway, ah… you… like books?'

Joy couldn't help laughing. He was as bad at small talk as her.

'I'm an eBook kind of woman. You can't travel long haul with a library in your suitcase.' She pulled her phone from her pocket. 'Mine's in here.'

'What kind of thing?' he asked, reaching for a stack of Scotts, leaving Joy to sort the Smiths.

'True crime, psychological thrillers…' she said.

'Oh, really?'

'And audiobooks too, and podcasts. They help me sleep. The grizzlier the better.'

'It's always the quiet ones.' Monty was grinning now.

There was no way she could tell him how, weirdly, they comforted her. She couldn't explain it, even to herself, how they satisfied a morbid curiosity she'd developed lately. They let her safely pick over her fears about what could so easily have been, if she hadn't escaped. She didn't want to give it any more thought than that.

'What about you?' she asked hurriedly.

'Oh, I'm not a great reader. I was always too busy on the boat, and these days it's more searching for new recipes. You never know when you'll find a new salt rub or a sauce that'll bring a bit of salmon or skate to life, you know? Does that sound peculiar? It does, doesn't it?'

'Not at all.' She could picture him turning pages, taking notes, then experimenting alone in the kitchen, tasting things with a teaspoon, scrapping it, starting over. His food tasted like years of experimenting and experience went into it, and devotion too. But she didn't say any of that, no matter how much she wanted to, or however much he looked like he needed to hear it.

His eyes were growing heavy-lidded.

'You're tired,' she said.

'I get up early to do the Siren breakfasts.'

'Shouldn't you get home?'

Monty turned his head in the direction where the harbour lay and his little room down at the Siren's Tail. 'Nah, besides we want to get these finished up first.' He gestured to the last of the books.

When she looked back to the shelf before her it was harder to concentrate than before, their little corner of the shop quieter, and the names on the spines blurrier somehow.

Monty's arms, tanned and strong, worked and flexed as he lifted the last of the stock – the T's through to the Z's – onto the shelves so they could be sorted and rearranged at eye level.

Reaching for an Elizabeth Taylor that needed moving to a higher shelf, her arm brushed his. Not even his arm, in fact, but the soft fabric of his shirt where the curve of his bicep emerged, and still the barely-there brush of cotton sent a warm bloom of heat through her.

She immediately stepped away.

'I'll just get Radia in bed,' she told him, hoping she sounded cooler than she felt.

Once the little girl was tucked in and kissed on the head, Joy hid out in the bedroom and took a second to put Patti right, texting her this time, not daring to leave a voice message in case something in her tone gave away the fact she was hiding in the dark, hugging Radia to sleep, trying to steer clear of whatever that magic, buzzing, electric charge coming from Monty Bickleigh's body was.

> There's no Hot European Guy party, Pats. Don't go getting excited. I'm fitting out a bookshop in Devon and there are volunteers helping with the shelving. It is nice though. Friendly. If a bit eccentric. Have fun at the wedding con. How about you spend your night looking out for a hot girl wedding celebrant or napkin folder instead of jumping to conclusions about my dating life? ;) Take care, J. x

'Your Auntie Patti sent you her love,' she whispered next to Radia's ear as she hit send and decided to hide out a little longer, curled up beside her daughter on the bed.

'I miss her,' Radia said sleepily. 'When is she coming to visit?'

'She's busy,' Joy told her, 'but soon, I'm sure.'

Radia missed the idea of her aunt more than the reality, thought Joy. She could only have the thinnest sense of what she was like, it had been so long since they'd been in the same room together. This sent Joy's heart plummeting again.

—

The whole party had stood for some time admiring their work. Jude had cried and had to be comforted by Jowan who, misty-eyed himself, had read everyone an excerpt from a John Donne poem in a very old book that had survived the floods. When he was finished, everyone applauded before being hushed by Joy desperately gesturing towards the dozing Radia's bedroom door.

Jowan placed the Donne right at the top of the poetry shelves, saying he'd priced it higher than anyone would ever be willing to pay for it because he never wanted it to leave the shop, but he wasn't opposed to customers reading it.

'Like a library?' Radia piped up sleepily from her bed, and everyone groaned and winced. Joy slapped a hand to her forehead.

Jowan admitted in a whisper he'd never been one to chase sales. Bookshops, he said, 'are a place where folks should be able to browse and pass the time of day, even if they don't have the money to buy.'

Joy wasn't sure that was a great business model, but she kept it to herself.

Jude insisted on a group picture for the website and a bleary-eyed Radia scrambled from her bed in her pyjamas to be in it. That girl never missed anything important.

'You can add pictures to the website, right?' Jude asked, setting the camera timer on her phone.

'Sure,' Joy replied, knowing she couldn't post this one. 'I'll start work on the website in the morning. But let me take one with just you locals,' she insisted. 'Without me and Rads in.'

'Don't be daft,' Jowan told her, gathering the very sleepy Aldous up inside his jacket for the shot. 'You're locals too.'

Had Radia not been whispering very earnestly in Monty's ear as he crouched beside her, the little girl would have been thrilled to hear herself described as a local.

They all smiled for a photo which Joy knew she could never share online, just in case she was recognised and tracked down.

After they'd all left and she was tucking Radia back under the covers, she asked what she'd been talking with Monty about.

'His boat,' Radia told her dreamily. 'He's going to take us fishing. Not crab catching but *proper* fishing in the sea.'

Joy only kissed her and let her hold on to the delusion. There could be no more cosy chats with Monty Bickleigh, that was for sure. No more group photos and spilling of life stories. It was getting harder, the holding it all back and protecting their bubble, but she'd have to resist the niceness of feeling included.

Now that the shelves were stacked, she could shut the door and keep themselves to themselves until it was time to leave.

The feeling of Monty's kind eyes upon her, and the way he praised her like she was someone capable of receiving praise, like she wasn't a broken, awkward, terrified thing, all of that would have to remain a memory. A souvenir of the night she was happy in a beautiful, cosy bookshop that smelled dreamily of smoke and charcoal, paper, honey cakes and wine. She couldn't have any more of it, no matter how nice it had felt. So she clambered into Radia's bed beside her and reached for *The Borrowers*.

'Let's read for a bit, yeah?'

That night Radia Pearl fell asleep smiling.

Chapter Thirteen

To prove she really was committing to giving Radia a lovely holiday, Joy had dressed early that morning in her yoga pants and the faded 'Electronic Entertainment Expo 2015' T-shirt that Sean had hated and, out of an odd sense of defiance, she now wore whenever she got the chance.

'What's happened to your normal clothes?' Radia asked, rubbing her eyes in bed.

'I'm not working this morning. We can do anything you want. What do you say? We could go to the beach? The donkey sanctuary? I have it on good authority there's a fudge stall up at the visitors centre?'

Radia hadn't fancied any of those, preferring to stay put in the shop. She had, however, insisted her mum open the door as soon as they'd eaten their toast so she could peer out into the little sunny square, which she did every few minutes until Joy started getting suspicious.

'OK, what are you up to?'

'Nothing, just looking.'

Joy joined her at the door and looked out at the empty square too. A sleepy gull on a rooftop opened one eye to watch them.

'And Mum? It was fun having a party, wasn't it?' Radia said, thoughtfully.

Joy had to admit it was.

'It's fun when there are people in the shop, isn't it?'

'I suppose it is. What are you getting at, Rads?'

The innocence of her wide eyes and little mouth drawn into an angelic 'O' was spoiled somewhat by the smear of jam up her cheek and Joy's slowly dawning realisation that the square was no longer empty.

The gull lifted onto yellow legs at the approaching footsteps. Radia was trying hard not to grin in recognition at the man and woman she'd met yesterday and told to come back today.

'Morning! Open, are we?' the woman – all Cleopatra fringe, big dangly earrings and arty dungarees – wanted to know.

Her husband – thinning hair and thick take-me-seriously specs – was taking a lot of interest in the window display.

Radia was already preparing her mum. 'Last night, Monty's friends said the shop was a charity, didn't they? They need to sell books, don't they, Mummy? To stay open forever?'

Joy's eyes snapped to Radia's, who very much knew what she was doing by reverting to 'mummy' at this crucial point in her plan.

'Nice to see you again,' the woman said, looking in the door at Radia, then back to Joy, a little perplexed. 'Is it *not* your opening day?'

'The till's working, isn't it, Mummy? And the books are on the shelves. I think the bookshop *is* open.'

Joy watched her daughter in amazement, before forcing a smile. 'Of course. Of course, we're open. Please come in.'

'Wait, wait, wait!' Radia spread her palms wide. 'Not yet. You have to cut something. Like when they opened the big white place? When they made the tiny sandwich things? Remember?'

Joy had to laugh. 'You mean the Microsoft place in Denmark?'

Only Radia would remember the canapés at a corporate opening. The CEOs had cut a huge red velveteen ribbon over the revolving doors, corks had popped, and within an hour she and Radia had been in a cab on their way to the airport and onto Joy's next posting.

'I've this?' the woman, who hadn't even made it up the steps, offered, pulling a long red strand off a ball of yarn in her bag.

Radia was beyond thrilled as the woman, Enola, and her husband, Geoffrey – Radia had taken pains to ask their names before the ceremony began – held the wool tight across the doorway and Joy offered Radia the scissors so she had her hands free to snap the picture on her phone. Again, Radia had insisted.

'You have to say, I declare the Borrow-A-Bookshop officially re-open,' Joy whispered in her daughter's ear, and as Radia repeated the words and took quite a few goes at snipping through the red strand, everyone cheered and the gull flew huffily off.

'Now we're going to sell these people books,' Radia told her mum as the pair of them stood by the till and watched Enola and Geoffrey pore over the neatly shelved titles.

'So this is what you wanted to do today?' Joy whispered back.

'Yes, definitely this,' Radia said, grinning. 'I want to be a bookshop helper.'

And that was how the Borrow-A-Bookshop was finally brought back to life after its long rest. The murky flood waters, the rescue helicopters, the tears and all the months of hard work, red tape, paperwork and plasterwork, were all forgotten entirely as these first browsers scrutinised the colourful spines and shuffled their way slowly along the stacks, their heads tipped to the side, all concentration, hunting out that special book they simply couldn't leave without.

Even Joy was a little swept up in the novelty of it all as other shoppers dropped in over the next half hour. She told Radia she wished they had some champagne to serve. Radia decided they'd offer everyone strawberry squash instead.

They'd asked if it was OK to take another picture of Geoffrey as he paid for his book – the very first sale through the new till – and he'd generously smiled and held up his mid-century copy of *Dubliners* with its gaudy dust jacket. Just as he was about to pay, Enola staggered up to the counter and dropped down a great pile of art and craft books on top of his James Joyce, saying they'd take those too.

When Radia misread the numbers on the till as seven hundred and twenty pounds they'd been charmed and made jovial remarks while Joy charged their Visa with the grand total of seventy pounds and twenty pence.

'A bargain,' Enola said as they left, wishing them luck with their new shop.

Neither Joy nor Radia spoiled things by telling them it actually wasn't their shop – they were only borrowing it. Instead they turned back to keep an eye on the other customers from their spot behind the counter and toasted one another with a clink of their strawberry-squash-filled mugs.

By the time the morning rush was waning and customers were looking disappointedly at the door to the café with its sign – written by Radia – that said 'Not open YET', it was becoming obvious, at least to Radia, what they needed to do next.

'Now we have to open the café.'

'You're kidding, Rads! We're not here to actually run the place. Plus, I've got the website to work on and all the security stuff to install.'

Radia didn't say anything, only looking conspiratorially at Charley fox by the till, communicating telepathically their plan to have the best booksellingand-café-opening-holiday anyone's ever had, ever.

–

Joy shouldn't have been surprised that afternoon when, as soon as she'd turned the 'Closed' sign on the door, Radia dragged her across the shop and into the café, demanding her mum bake her something.

'Baking?' Joy raised an eyebrow.

Radia knew she was no baker. The closest Radia got to eating homemade cake was the Mr Kipling Angel Slices they regularly scoffed in airport lounges or during bedtime stories, in whichever Airbnb they were crashing in that night.

'There's a recipe book,' Radia told her, producing the pamphlet that had been left in the kitchen for them. 'That lady told me these recipes are her grandad's.'

'What lady?'

'The one that's getting married. I liked her.'

Joy knew when she wasn't going to get out of something, so she opened the little booklet at the page for 'traditional plain scones' and then found a couple of aprons.

Izaak had stripped away all the plastic from the kitchen last night and now it gleamed white and bright, all new-smelling and clean.

A tiny part of Joy thought of her own little kitchen back in London, a brown and beige relic of the early nineties. Nothing back home was new at all, but it had been hers all the same. She thought of the simple joy of tipping red-wine bolognese into her slow cooker or the smell of pizzas baked on that sizzle stone her mum and dad had given her as a flat-warming gift. She'd loved it there. Even when she was just cooking for herself, learning how to live alone.

In the wobbly post-natal days when she couldn't stop herself crying and the blinds had been drawn all day and she'd shoved a ball of Blu Tack into the peephole on the flat door in case Sean came spying, she'd still found a little sanctuary stirring the porridge over the hob while Radia slept in her Moses basket on the Formica kitchen island. She'd loved it because it was hers. And curiously, the knowledge that it was *still* hers – and Radia's too – brought her a little wave of comfort now.

The café oven bleeped to signal it was now a perfect one hundred and eighty degrees, snapping her out of her thoughts. She'd been wondering why her mind was so strongly directed towards home since she'd arrived in Clove Lore. The same memories hadn't come for her in any of the other places they'd stayed.

'Flour, Mummy?' Radia said, still keeping up the cuteness in case Joy changed her mind and made them order takeout instead of making food of their own.

'Right, yes, of course. Four hundred grams of plain flour it says, so we'll quarter that, since it's just us.'

Radia, however, kept a hand on the bag as her mum poured it into the bowl over the new electronic scales. 'Let's just make a big lot, OK Mummy?'

And so, by eight o'clock Radia and Joy were both fast asleep on Joy's bed upstairs, full of scones, jam, clotted cream and tea, with Radia's copy of *The Borrowers* – already a quarter read – folded open across Joy's gently rising and falling stomach.

Unseen by the sleepers, the sun dipped towards the horizon sending the sky in the west all shades of pink and apricot as Clove Lore slipped into another perfectly peaceful summer slumber.

Chapter Fourteen

The message woke her. So few people had her number, it could be one of only three people: Patti, her mum or Gaz.

> Hey Joy Joy, how's u? More important, where r u? I have a contract in Durham that'll be tricky for me to get to on time now
> Want it? It's for October 3rd
> Swap you anything you have starting on the 4th (anywhere)
> I'm in Brixton installing in a warehouse until Sunday, then Bahrain for 2 wks. Paths crossing?

Joy had met Gaz when they joined Tech Stars at the same time, right after her graduation, and they'd stayed friends when he went freelance and she was going on maternity leave. He'd called her 'Joy Joy' from day one and it hadn't seemed annoying coming from him. He was one of those rare people who exuded sunshine and he was, Joy acknowledged with gratitude, not only a really good contact to have, but her only friend.

Very rarely, they'd meet up on a layover in Amsterdam or Singapore and they'd all go to Snow City to muck about on the slopes together or to the Van Gogh museum. Radia adored him, of course. He always had duty-free Toblerone for her in his bag and, according to her, he was the 'funnest' of all the grown-ups she knew, which admittedly wasn't many.

She texted back.

> Sorry, fully booked. We're at the seaside at the moment. South-west. I'll message you if anything changes and if I can send any more work your way.

Fully booked wasn't quite true. Joy had been nursing a secret. There was the Lisbon weekend job coming up – that would take them into September – and then they'd be back at the flat in London by the fourth. She hadn't booked anything else after that, not until January.

She'd told herself she deserved a break after travelling pretty much non-stop since Radia was nine months old, and goodness knows Radia deserved to stay in one place for a short while.

Only a tiny part of Joy had the courage to admit to herself that she was considering moving home for good – or at least to let Radia have a decent try at primary school.

The whole thing was still barely formed in Joy's mind. She'd worked so hard at pushing the idea away every time it arose, but it was becoming impossible to ignore now.

Maybe Radia wouldn't like school, anyway? After years of travelling, the daily routines of learning might not suit her. It doesn't suit every kid. If that was the case, she could easily arrange some new contracts and take them out on the road again. Then again, maybe she'd absolutely love it. Or maybe there was a future in doing both things; working *and* staying put for school? Joy could always find IT work in London or be a freelancer working from home now that remote connection support was standard. She wouldn't miss hardware installations, or on-site software upgrades, she had to admit. Or hotels.

But then there was the spectre of Sean lurking, not to mention the fact that moving home would put them a few underground stops away from her parents' place. Her stomach turned queasy at it all.

Another message notification appeared on the screen. Joy didn't have to open it to see it was from Patti. This really was unusual. A string of messages over the course of a few days. What did it all mean? Were they suddenly getting back on track, the way they used to be, back when they talked every day? The message said, 'Love it!'

Squinting in confusion, Joy opened their old message thread to see someone had sent Patti the photograph of all the shelvers at the party. Someone had been mucking about with her phone. Someone small and wily who was stirring on the bed next to her.

'Morning, Rads. Did you send Auntie Patti this picture?'

Joy turned the phone to show her the screen where Jowan was smiling in front of the shop counter, his chest swelled in pride and his arm around Jude, who wasn't looking at the camera but scratching at Aldous's head peeking out of Jowan's jacket. Izaak and Leonid were at the back hugging, their heads tipped together, and – shoved to the front and looking like a deer in the headlights – stood Joy with Radia protectively pulled against her side. On the edge of the shot was Monty, caught looking right at Joy, a serious wrinkle of what looked like worry over his brow.

'Did she like it?' Radia asked sleepily.

Joy only sighed and ran her hand over Radia's hair, as dark and sleek as her own.

'She says she did. Listen, Rads, I really have to do the website and security cams today so we'll need to stay in. How about we go food shopping up at the visitor centre first and then I make us some breakfast?'

Radia liked that idea. 'How many scones do we have left?' she asked.

'*Umm*, twelve, I think. Why?'

'We'll need those for the customers, in the café,' she told her, scratching absently at her ear.

'Rads, you think we can run a café while I'm working?'

'And the bookshop.'

'*Pfft!* That's just not possible, Radia. I'm only one mummy.'

'We need a helper?'

'Yes, we'd need a helper. Come on, let's get dressed. You must be starving.'

Radia didn't forget her mum's words on their walk up the slope to the visitor centre, or while they browsed the fudge concession, peeked briefly inside Astral Breeks, the surf-shack clothes shop, dawdled outside the candle-making and silk-printing studio with the pottery wheel in the window, or all the way up to the little convenience store where the locals bought their bread and newspapers, and Clove Lore's holidaymakers winced at the prices of literally everything else. Radia was on the lookout for a helper.

'They said they were *volun-teer*-ing,' Radia pronounced her new word carefully as the electronic counter on the sliding doors beep-beeped them into the convenience store. 'All the shelf-party people? They said they'd come back to help us. Any time.'

'*Hmm?*' Joy was cautious not to encourage this line of thinking, but Radia was right. Jowan had said as much as he zipped Aldous inside his coat for the walk home the other night. *Just give me a shout*, he'd said. But Jowan was nowhere to be seen now, and hopefully he'd keep away too, and all the rest of them.

While Joy distractedly loaded eggs into the wheelie basket, Radia spotted a helper. He was buying cigarettes at the counter and there was someone with him, a woman.

'Montague!' Radia shouted, tugging her mum's arm. 'Look! He'll help us.'

Joy grabbed Radia's hand, holding her by her side. A shrinking instinct told her not to approach him. He was dressed in yellow fisherman's gaiters held up by shoulder straps with a black T-shirt underneath, and he had his arm around a woman who was saying something in his ear. The couple laughed, and then he brought his mouth down to hers.

'Monty?' Radia called again from Joy's hiding place behind the egg boxes and baked beans, meaning she had no choice but to drop Radia's hand and emerge as casually as she could, all the while wanting to slip away entirely so she could pick apart why she'd felt the ground shake beneath her when she'd seen them kiss – and so she could kick herself for believing Monty was single. He'd lied.

Why on earth *would* he be single? He was handsome in a rugged, seasidey sort of way, and his eyes were so dark and soft. Of course he had a girlfriend. Or a wife? Her hand wanted to travel to her chest where something was constricting painfully.

Radia was already on her way over to start firing questions at him, so Joy had no choice but to join her and try not to act too oddly in case he could somehow tell what she was thinking.

The man was grinning down at Radia and making introductions by the time Joy joined them, and although she didn't know it, the most curious thing was about to happen: Joy was about to learn that she seriously liked Monty Bickleigh.

'Oh, I'm not Monty,' he was telling the little girl, and all the while speaking with Monty's full lips and smiling with Monty's sparkling, good-humoured eyes. 'I'm his twin, Tom. Folk are always getting us confused.'

'Twin brother!' Radia said with wonder in her voice. 'You're *two* of you?'

'S'right,' Tom said, kindly, even though he must have had this sort of thing all his life. 'And this is Lou.'

The woman was saying 'hi' and lowering her chin, looking right at Joy, silently prompting her name, but all Joy could do was gape at them in a strange fog of relief and amazement.

'My name's Radia,' came the voice from by her side. 'And this is my mum. Your *twin* cooked us a big fish and we put all the books on the shelves.'

'Ah, so that makes you Joy,' said Tom. Lou seemed to be hiding a knowing smile. 'Monty mentioned you at the pub last night. Mentioned you quite a bit, actually.'

Was she hearing this right? And did Lou really nudge Tom's arm in a very conspicuous way? Was he... was he *teasing* her, about Monty? She felt a burn across her cheeks that told her she wasn't imagining any of it.

Radia, however, was oblivious. 'We were looking for a helper, but we've got nobody. Do *you* like working in the bookshop?' she asked bluntly.

Tom, who was gathering his cigarettes and a lighter from the counter, had to tell her he'd been fishing since dawn and was heading home now. Then Lou put in that she was off to work at the local newspaper offices or she'd definitely have helped.

'We'll manage,' Joy told her daughter.

Radia's heart seemed to swell at the words. She made a high-pitched squealing sound and swung her mum's hand back and forth. 'Are we doing it, then? Even if it's just you and me? Are we going to sell our scones and make drinks and sell books today?'

'It was nice to meet you,' Joy told Tom and his girl-friend, trying to bring this all to an end.

'*Are* we?' Radia wasn't going to drop it now.

'Yes, we are,' Joy told her with a heavy sigh, mainly to keep her quiet and so the couple could get out of the shop without making any more comments or smirking about Monty, who had apparently been talking about her when she wasn't there.

As Lou and Monty's twin left, holding hands and whispering, the small, almost forgotten, part of her that was still an excitable seventeen-year-old wanted to call after them to ask what exactly he'd said about her. The rest of her, which was a circumspect twenty-nine-year-old and afraid of everything, told her to keep quiet.

Joy looked down at Radia, who was jumping and twirling around the wheelie basket.

'OK, Rads,' she said. 'We'll need to get some café stuff then.'

'What stuff does a café need?' she replied.

Joy scanned the shelves with another big sigh. She had absolutely no idea.

Chapter Fifteen

Joy wasn't so set in her ways that she couldn't admit this job was proving to be the most enjoyable contract she'd taken in a long time. Even if it was going to mean getting up early to get her work done so she could spend the rest of the day dealing with the book-buying public, who were, on the whole, quite a bit weirder than the corporate clients she was used to dealing with.

One man had come in alone that morning after their convenience store visit and spent a long time browsing the thrillers, before asking Joy if she had a book in which someone was murdered by an undetectable nerve agent and, he stressed, 'got away with it'.

Joy had gathered Radia behind her, told the man she wasn't sure she had anything like that and attempted to sell him *The Lost Apothecary*, where a lady chemist helps a bunch of women bump off the men who have wronged them. He said that didn't interest him *at all* and left.

That was just moments before the coach-load of women in their seventies had arrived – a 'wild swimming' society all the way from Morecambe, they told her. They'd stormed in like a blizzard, talking over each other and laughing like drains, all the while touching every book in the shop – or at least that's how it felt to Joy, who experienced near-physical pain at the state of the shelves after they'd left.

Between them, they bought only five postcards and two copies of the same Richard Osman novel, which they all discussed loudly as they left the shop and headed down to the beach, while two of them protested, 'No spoilers, please!'

Radia had helped tidy the shop once more and was proving really very good at giving recommendations to browsers – simply pulling a book at random from the shelves and saying, 'This one's good, get this one.'

Joy told her repeatedly to stop, but on the fifth try Radia's tactic actually worked and a young person in elaborate rainbow make-up had bought a copy of *Spells for Modern Witches* on her personal recommendation.

Still, Joy didn't think she could cope with a busy café too. There was a reason the place was supposed to be let to two grown-up holidaymakers at a time. It was too much work for one person alone.

She had been about to tell the first group inquiring about food that she was sorry, the café wasn't fully up and running, and suggest they'd maybe like to come back tomorrow, but Radia had skipped ahead of them into the little white room with the red-and-white gingham tablecloths, saying, 'It's through here.'

Even though Joy's hands were visibly shaking when she served it all up, she had managed to get the espresso machine to produce two frothy coffees that looked reasonably good and she'd made silver pots of tea for the four others.

'See? It's easy,' Radia had whispered from behind the café till, watching them eating the scones which they'd quickly warmed through in the oven and served with a freshly opened jar of strawberry jam, plonked right on the table beside a big blob of the clotted cream turned out of the catering-size tub and onto a saucer.

'We'll have to work on finessing the presentation,' Joy told her. 'If we're going to really make the café thing work.'

Joy had been amazed when they'd left a tip, a whole five pounds, which she surrendered to Radia at four o'clock once all the doors were locked and the sign turned to 'Closed'.

'Your wages,' Joy told Radia. 'Where do you want to spend it?'

There'd been no time for her to answer, however, as a figure appeared at the door, tapping gently on the glass to get their attention.

'Monty! You came back!' Radia sang as her mum let him inside.

'I did promise you a sail on *Peter's Bounty*,' he announced, while Joy mentally compared him to his brother, who she could see – now that Monty was standing pretty close – was probably a bit more tanned and windblown, while there was an appealing liveliness in Monty's brown eyes and around his full lips that she felt sure distinguished the twins further.

'I have to work the evening service at the Siren tonight but Finan's agreed to do the clean down so I can leave at eight, and I thought, if it's not too late for Radia's bedtime, why not tonight? A sunset sail kind of thing?'

Radia stared up at her mum. 'Yes, Mummy, why not tonight?'

Joy hadn't even tried to protest, knowing it would be futile.

As Monty backed away out the door, smiling and bringing his hands together in an awkward kind of way, he'd told them to dress for the sea chill. Then he'd stumbled as he waved to them across the cobbled square while Joy and Radia watched him go from the shop steps.

Joy had to remind herself how much it had shaken her to see Tom kissing Lou, mistakenly thinking she was watching Monty. Not a nice feeling.

It had been enough to scare her and to remind her not to get involved with the Clove Lore community any more than she had to. But with the summer sun wrapping itself in Monty's brown curls and with his shirtsleeves rolled up the way they were, Joy couldn't deny the reckless appeal of an evening spent with him at twilight on the sea.

Chapter Sixteen

That afternoon's shift in the Siren's stuffy kitchens had passed excruciatingly slowly, to the extent that Monty had set an alarm on his phone to mark the passing of each half hour, just to prove that time hadn't stopped entirely.

As the last dishes went out – two well-done steaks and a veggie lasagne – Monty stripped off his apron and made for the bar.

'That's me done,' he told Bella, who was working the beer taps.

'Finan? That's Monty leaving for the night,' the land-lady called across the room to where her husband was setting the plates down in front of diners.

The Siren's rooms were all booked out to holiday-makers, most of whom had already eaten and were now strolling along the beach or sitting on the benches outside enjoying summer cocktails and IPAs. Holiday season was showing no signs of slowing down yet.

The locals were in tonight too. Jowan and Minty were in their usual spot by the bar with Aldous sleeping at their feet. Minty was glued to an iPad, watching celebrity weddings and grumbling loudly about floating candle lanterns being 'the scourge of the countryside', while Jowan listened placidly.

At a booth in the far corner, Mrs Crocombe was laughing along with the captain of the *Lucky Boy*, who refilled her champagne glass with the dreamy look of a besotted man.

She wasn't so distracted by James da Costa not to have noticed Bovis watching them through narrowed eyes from across the room, his orange juice untouched, and she definitely wasn't so preoccupied by her dinner companion to miss the fact that young Monty was knocking off early and Finan was telling him to take a bottle of Cava from the fridge if he liked.

She was soon on her feet and making her way over to the bar, where Bella was trying to signal to Monty to get out quickly.

'Too late,' Bella whispered to her chef as she sailed past him to fetch a picnic basket from the storeroom.

Mrs Crocombe squeezed between the drinkers at the bar to inquire of Monty, 'Going out, are we?'

'Only an evening's fishing,' he replied.

'With bubbly?'

'Um, well…'

'You're not going with Tom and Lou. I saw them leaving for the cinema at four-ish.'

Monty gave an amused, exasperated laugh. 'It's Miss Foley and her daughter from the bookshop. I promised I'd take the little girl fishing. I was being welcoming.'

'*Ah-hah.*' Her voice chimed like a bell. She called through the open door to Bella. 'Pop a big tub of my clotted cream with strawberry in a cool bag for them too, and add it to my bill, won't you?'

Monty protested. 'Mrs C., you don't have to…'

'For the little one. She likes my ice cream.'

'Of course, thanks. That's nice of you.'

'Hope you catch something,' she said, making her way back to the sea captain, who was waiting for the gossip with his arms outstretched in a theatrical way.

'Letitia, you were gone too long,' he boomed, before bursting into hearty laughter that rumbled around the bar, making everyone look over. The pair were soon cloistered again and whispering intently about Monty.

He could predict with full confidence his name was now in Mrs C.'s matchmaking book alongside Joy Foley's and, even though he was sure Joy would be horrified if she ever found out, he didn't mind so much.

Monty had just enough time to shower and change out of his chef's whites and into dark trousers and a favourite oversized jumper in deep indigo. He pulled on boots and styled his hair – which for Monty meant running serum through his damp curls for shine. Out of habit, he rubbed sunscreen across the back of his neck – something his father had taught the boys they must always do at sea – and he was ready.

He stowed the picnic inside the *Peter's Bounty*, having made up a few Tupperwares of snacks from the pub fridges. Bella had topped it up with fresh peaches, the last of the morning's croissants, the chilled Cava, two tall glasses and, of course, the ice cream.

Monty trained his eyes on the slope where he could just make out the straight and elegant shape of Joy advancing Down-along and beside her a skipping, twirling blur of lilac.

He couldn't help sniffing a happy laugh of recognition and the feeling of excitement spread through him.

Tonight had to be special. He had to make sure Joy enjoyed it. She didn't strike him as the kind of person who had much time off, or indeed someone that, while on their travels, went on impromptu sailing trips with local guys. He had seen the way she would try to shrink herself in company. He also hadn't missed the way it had taken her a long time to relax at the shelving party, or the horror she'd shown at the idea of being set up in Mrs C.'s matchmaking madness.

Tonight he was going to keep her safe, make her happy, show her how beautiful his village looked from the water, and then he'd deliver them both safely home. If there was a way to lessen Joy's alarm and help her relax around him, he'd find it. He wasn't going to do anything whatsoever about the way he felt himself blush when she was near him, other than trying his best to stop it happening. Tonight he was just a skipper and Joy and Radia a private charter. At least, that's what he told himself as they approached along the harbour wall, Radia running ahead of her mum in her pyjamas with Charley fox under her arm, practically sending out sparks of excitement.

Monty's heart cracked a little at the sight of the five-year-old in her pink glitter jelly shoes and Joy telling her to *please slow down*, trying hard not to actually shout and draw attention to herself. He could feel the panic coming off Joy, so he stepped in.

'*Woah*, Radia Pearl, careful on these stones, you might trip,' he called out, and he could swear Joy's shoulders dropped in relief as Radia slammed on the brakes and walked up to him by the side of the *Bounty*.

He was already helping her into her life jacket by the time Joy reached him.

'Ready?' he asked the little girl.

Radia held up her drink bottle and told him she was, 'Really ready.'

Monty lowered Radia into the boat by her arms like he was dropping a bundle of wriggling, giggling net into the hull.

Joy told him he didn't need to lower *her* in like that, she'd use the steps, and when Monty laughed he could hear the nerves in his own chest.

'She's cute with her milk and PJs,' Monty remarked, while Joy clambered into the boat, determined to do it without assistance.

'Sometimes I forget she's only little,' Joy replied, watching Radia bouncing around and trying to look at everything at once, screeching so much she scared the seagulls. 'But at night-time, she's somehow tiny again. A baby.'

Monty caught her wistfulness but didn't know how to respond. After all, he wasn't a parent. Didn't have so much as a kitten to care for. He told himself he couldn't understand how Joy must feel about that little girl.

'Are we going to catch a big fish?' Radia asked. 'Like the one you brought us at the party?'

'Maybe. If we're lucky,' said Monty, and once he'd made sure his guests were sitting on the fixed plastic seats inside his cabin, he started the engine.

Joy drew Radia to her and put a blanket over them both. Radia sipped milk between excited exclamations about the other boats and the birds on the water.

'And Mum? Are *we* going to swim?' she asked, watching a bird, which Monty told them was a shearwater, diving beneath the waves and disappearing.

'It's too cold for swimming,' Joy told her.

'I've been in cold water before. In St Petersburg.'

'You mean the Gulf of Finland?' Joy said, taken aback once more at Radia's elephant's memory. 'God,

I'd forgotten about that. We swam at eleven o'clock at night. It was the summer, so the Russian white nights. The sun didn't set at all and our sleep patterns were all over the place. Rads, that was two summers ago. *How* do you remember that?'

'I remember everything,' said Radia proudly.

Not everything, thought Joy, with some relief.

Monty navigated the harbour mouth and out onto open water where the waves made the boat bob and dip, and he cut a course through the evening swells more carefully than he'd ever done before, his awareness that he had two special guests with him burning in his brain, telling him to go gently.

The fishing hadn't quite gone to plan. Once the engines were cut and Monty had set up the fixed reel over the side, Radia had watched for a bite for over an hour and none came.

After a long while spent bobbing gently with the evening tide and sipping her milk until it was all gone, Radia cuddled into her blanket on the padded bench inside the cabin and, clutching Charley fox, fell asleep.

Joy and Monty stood over the sleeping girl and observed one another in the sea-silence. They were only a few hundred yards from shore but there were no sounds other than the slap of waves on wood and the creak and clank of the net machinery.

'We should head back?' Monty whispered.

'*Umm...*' Joy thought this over, looking around at their pretty backdrop.

He took this as a good sign, adding, 'I mean, it'd be a shame when we haven't caught a fish?'

'That's true,' she said. 'How would I explain to Rads that we just gave up?'

'Don't want to disappoint her,' he said, brightening. 'And I do happen to have quite a nice bit of supper here.'

He made his way to the stern where the rod was still dangling into the surf and pulled open the picnic box. Joy followed him to peer inside.

'Bubbly?' Her brows crumpled.

'Yeah, is that OK? It was a present from Finan and Bella, my bosses.'

She glanced back to where Radia was sleeping, saying nothing.

'You had a glass of wine last night,' Monty pitched in. 'So I just assumed?'

'I barely drink,' she told him. 'It's one of the many things you can't really do when you're parenting on your own. What if you have an emergency? What if you had to drive somewhere unexpectedly?' *What if tonight's the night Sean finally shows up at the door,* she didn't say. 'Besides, I usually work when Radia's playing or sleeping. Every spare second is work time. Last night I… I made an exception, I guess?'

'That must be tough.'

'It's our life.' The matter-of-factness broke down into weariness before her expression softened with the temptation. 'Maybe just a tiny bit?'

Soon they were sharing the *Bounty*'s back bench and were deep into their first glass of Cava and the picnic of cool-box bites.

'*Mmm*, what's this?' Joy asked, her mouth watering at the first taste of the tiny savoury triangles topped with toasted sesame seeds from one of the little tubs.

'That's my scampi toast. Here, try the lemongrass and spicy orange dip with it.'

Joy did as he said.

'So nice! You can really taste the lemongrass.' Her eyes widened and she reached for another bite. 'You are a seriously good cook. You know, it took me a while to work out you were a chef and not a fisherman?'

'*Hah*, I guess I'm both, though my brother does the bulk of the fishing now I'm at the Siren's Tail all the time.'

'Where you get to make yummy stuff like this,' she said, sensing he wasn't all that happy about his situation.

'I guess,' Monty lifted a hand to the back of his neck. 'I shouldn't complain. I mean, I could live without cooking twenty fried breakfasts at eight o'clock on a Saturday morning, or turning out another batch of steak and ale pies or yet another Sunday roast.'

'The menu doesn't do it for you?'

'Not really. Bella and Finan know that pub-grub favourites sell, but I think I'm developing an aversion to the smell of bacon, honestly.'

Joy gasped in exaggerated shock. 'Bacon is life,' she told him seriously.

Those first few sips of the drink fizzing in her hand had turned her a little giddy, and that in turn re-awakened her guardedness. She turned her face away towards the bay. After a quiet moment she said, 'Clove Lore really is beautiful.'

Monty's gaze followed hers to the long sweep of harbour, with the ancient stonework of the Siren's Tail perching half upon the sea wall and half upon the craggy rocks jutting out into the Atlantic.

From out here, the white cottages with their frothy red and pink window boxes and balcony planters looked indistinct and soft, like an Impressionist painting.

As they stared, the Victorian lamps – that had once been the talk of the coast when they were installed at the end of the nineteenth century – flickered into luminescence one at a time from the top of the slope all the way down to the bottom, some of them obscured by the twist in the cobbled path.

Somewhere at the midpoint on that lovely slope was the bookshop. Joy wished it had a flag flying from its wonky conical roof so she could make out where it stood.

As if reading her mind, Monty said, 'Can you see that line of palm trees in the backyards there, leading up to the tall spruces? That's your bookshop in there.'

Joy turned to him with astonished eyes.

'Everything OK?' asked Monty.

Joy searched her brain for words and landed on something safe.

'Your speeches book arrived this morning. I brought it with me.'

'Ah, great, thank you.'

Joy looked down at her glass. This was so stilted it hurt. 'We, *uh*, bumped into your brother at the visitor centre store,' she added.

'Yeah, he mentioned it. He said Radia told him smoking is bad for him.'

Joy laughed, glad he was smiling.

'Aw, no, she did? She's kind of judgy about smoking, ever since we saw one of those posters on the Underground, you know the ones with the lungs all bunged up with tar?'

'That'll leave a lasting impression on a kid.'

'Yeah, now she sees it as her duty to let everyone know they're in danger.'

'I mean, she's not wrong.'

'It can be embarrassing though, she's not shy about it.'

Monty laughed heartily. 'I really wasn't kidding when I told her I was stopping smoking, you know? It's a bit of a hangover from when there were loads of boats working off the harbour. We'd bring in the catch, check the nets, sluice down the hull, all while smoking to keep the hunger away before breakfast. At least, that's why Dad did it. It's just habit now, for me. Tom, on the other hand? I can't see him giving up.'

'We all have our little habits, I suppose,' Joy told him.

'Do *you*? I wonder what yours might be.'

She blinked at him, running through her mind, looking for something cheerful to say, something that made her sound happy-go-lucky and fun.

Hiding away? That was definitely a bad habit. *Being afraid of strangers? Jumping at every door knock and phone call? Never asking for help? Taking too many jobs so she didn't have time to think too hard about stuff like this?* All habits she'd formed because of Sean – and nothing she could bring up here on what was feeling increasingly like it was supposed to be a date.

'Coffee,' she told him conspiratorially. 'I can't function without my espresso. That's a very bad habit.'

'Well, I absolve you of that,' said Monty, raising a hand like a priest and making her smile again.

Their eyes were drawn back to the coast by the flicker of lights coming on up at the Big House at the summit of the village, all turrets and sombre stone standing staunchly on rolling green lawns.

'You really ought to visit the Big House before you go,' he said. 'The gardens are open to visitors; Izaak will let you through the gate for free. Leonid's camellia grove is something else, and there's the ruins of the old chapel in the middle of it. It's kind of special.'

'We will. I reckon I'll have the security stuff done in the next couple of days. I'm just waiting for a cable to arrive and then it's website testing and… we'll be done.'

'But you're booked in until the first, right?'

'How do you know… ah, never mind.'

'Like Jude said, there's nothing secret in Clove Lore.'

For a moment, Joy thought about how everyone in the village would know she was sailing with Monty tonight, and yet the gossips felt half the world away out here on the water. And what did it matter, really? They could talk all they liked; she was leaving soon enough.

'When I'm done we can hang around and see the sights, for Rads.'

'A holiday,' Monty said.

'Yep, Radia deserves one.'

'So… she doesn't go to school?' he asked innocently.

'No,' Joy told him, her voice pitching a little in warning.

'Isn't she five?' Monty pressed, not sure why the topic was a sore one.

Joy only drank from her glass and kept her eyes fixed on the shore, falling quiet enough to make Monty panic.

'Ah! Was I being nosy? Sorry. I've spent too much time with Mrs Crocombe. It's obviously none of my business. I didn't mean anything—'

'It's fine,' interrupted Joy. 'Honestly.'

Again, she fell silent, drawing in a deep breath as she turned her eyes to the skies above Clove Lore. There were stars visible and a planet, Jupiter, in the east. She thought about mentioning it, but as a fisherman he'd know all about the night skies, so she just looked on in quiet wonder.

Monty tracked her eyes' progress across the heavens, lighting himself upon the North Star.

'Polaris,' he said. 'He's seriously showing off tonight, right? The sailors' star. I'm guessing you're a seasoned sailor? Radia too. *She* couldn't be more relaxed.' This was said with kind laughter and a glance over at the spot where she slumbered. 'When I've had guests on the boat before there's always one throwing up.'

Joy wondered why she wanted to ask him if he'd brought other women out here for a twilight picnic like this. She mentally batted the thought away.

Monty must have seen the change in her because he immediately got up and made his way to the cabin, fetching a blanket.

When he got back, he motioned to Joy to lift her glass and he draped the blanket over her legs.

'She's still asleep?' Joy asked.

'Sound.'

She tried to carry on the conversation, pulling the blanket closer as Monty took his spot by her side once more.

'You're right, we have sailed a lot. Although I've spent a lot of time in dock too.'

'Having your barnacles sanded?' Monty's eyes flitted to Joy's, alarmed. 'Sorry, that was weird.'

She smiled again, feeling the need to nudge his arm with her elbow to reassure him. She really did have a knack for making people feel ill at ease.

'There was this one time I fitted out a cruise ship with MacBooks and custom charging stations, off the coast of Croatia. It was a tech lending-library sort of thing. That was one of my first jobs when I decided to go freelance and get out of London. Radia came along with me as part of the deal and since it was a family firm and I had insurance for her being with me, they didn't mind her tagging along.'

'How old was she then?'

'We had her first birthday on board,' she said, before falling silent, thinking of the trainee chef bringing a cheesecake with one candle and the way the service staff had sung. No wonder Radia thought of the bookshop gathering the other night as a 'party', poor kid. She hadn't been to many proper parties in her life. The thought dragged her inside herself again.

'You're seriously getting the sea chills,' Monty observed, already on the move, covering the food and packing it away. 'Let's get you home.'

Joy wanted to protest but it was his boat and he'd have an early start in the morning, no doubt, so she'd have to let him take her back to the harbour.

As he started the engine, she joined him in the cabin, the blanket now pulled around her shoulders like a shawl. Radia was still curled up and dreaming by her side.

'Thank you,' she whispered to Monty. 'For tonight.'

'Even though we didn't catch a thing? Well, maybe a cold,' he said, keeping one hand on the wheel, the other reaching out and adjusting her blanket, pulling closed the little gap at her throat.

For the first time in a long time, Joy found herself feeling helpless, but she noted, unafraid. All she could do was look at Monty's earnest face and that soft smile.

Her entire body was telling her he'd be warm and solid to lean against if only he'd wrap his arms around her, but the cautious instinct that had ruled her life for so long now forbade her. She'd need him to do it, to pull her close.

Why couldn't he read her mind now? When she really needed him to. When he smelled of coconut sunscreen and the sea. Now the twilight was playing its tricks again, making his skin glow. She felt for a moment as she gazed at him like she was looped in the loops of his soft curls, now darkest brown under the darkening sky.

Monty wasn't looking out through the sea-sprayed screen now. He was looking directly at her, and the boat seemed to be slowing.

Under his gaze, her consciousness opened in a way she hadn't felt before and suddenly she could imagine what he might be seeing right now: a straight-lipped, rabbit-in-the-headlights thing standing stiffly by his side, giving off the worst standoffish vibes.

There was no way he could be seeing her the way she saw him, all shiny and new, bright eyes and clear summer skin. And yet he was looking so intently at her. His eyes had fallen to her mouth.

Was he thinking of kissing her? The very idea of it made her spine freeze up so she couldn't move. Ridiculous, she thought, and so typical of her, getting trapped in her head, made up of warring instincts of wanting and shame and alarm…

'Joy?' he interrupted her spiralling.

She gulped and let her eyes lock with his. 'Yes?'

'I liked spending time with you.'

'Oh,' was the best she could do. 'Thank you.'

'You're thanking me?'

'Yes, I guess. For not thinking I'm… I'm completely…' She didn't finish her sentence. She saw his eyes flit from her eyes to her mouth and back again. His expression was quizzical, his head tipped, like he was trying to figure her out.

'I don't think you're anything like that,' he said, low and level, obviously reading her mind again. 'Joy, I'm sure you're only *good* things. I think you're… I think you're *all* the good things.'

An abashed laugh burst from him as he seemed to think about what he'd said, giving his head a shake. He looked away to check their course.

They stayed like that; Joy bewildered and wide-eyed, replaying what had just happened, wondering what it meant, and Monty concentrating on navigating round the buoys at the harbour mouth, smiling at his own awkwardness, but not looking sorry at all.

Somebody had to tell the truth and, Monty knew instinctively, it would need to be him.

–

Nobody but Joy had ever carried Radia, not since the surgeon had handed her over the screen and put her on Joy's chest. Yet, here they were, climbing Up-along with Montague Bickleigh carrying her sleeping child in his arms.

There was so little air in her lungs she couldn't tell him the things she wanted to: to please slow down, to not trip, that he was holding the most important thing in the world against his chest, the *only* important thing.

Instead, she gulped at the air and rabbited on, saying anything but.

'Have you ever thought about the last time you were picked up?'

Monty kept his eyes fixed on the slippery cobblestones and shook his head. 'How do you mean?'

'Well, there was a time when you were picked up multiple times a day, and then one day you were just too big and that was the last time you were ever picked up?'

Monty stopped and turned to look at her. 'I hadn't thought about that, but *now* I am. Man, that's sad.'

'But nobody can remember when it was, if they're lucky, that last time, so it's not so sad really, is it? But *I'm* going to remember.' She had her eyes on Radia's closed eyelids and her cheek all squashed up against Monty's jumper. 'I'm going to look out for it and I'm going to make sure I know it's happened. That last time.'

'Joy?' Monty looked stricken.

'What?' Her eyes lifted to his.

'You're crying.'

'I'm not!' With a gasp of realisation, she scrubbed her wrist down her cheek. 'Well,' she tried to pass it off. 'Mums cry all the time.'

'Do they?'

'Yes, it's the love, it's too big. It comes out your face in big bursts.' She was smiling now, her eyes still misted. 'I'm not being morose. I'm just being ready. I don't want to miss anything. None of the firsts and none of the lasts either.'

'Why do I want to rush to my mum and have her sit me on her knee like a baby?' said Monty, falling further into his feelings.

'I think that's why people think men lifting women is romantic.' Joy was growing thoughtful now. 'It's like, your dad stops lifting you, then there's this younger bloke who takes over.'

'Like brides being carried over the threshold by their new husband?'

'Exactly! It's so she feels safe and looked after.'

'I hadn't really thought about it before. Hah! Your brain works in amazing ways.' His feet moved again, pulling himself up the slope, only now he went even slower. 'I won't stumble, I promise,' he said in a low voice, and Radia nestled her head on his jumper and smiled in a way that said she was close to waking.

'I've been told that before,' Joy said, feeling a little calmer now they'd slowed their pace and Monty was placing his boots so carefully. 'The brain thing. Personally, I think it's a bit of a shambles inside here.'

Monty only smiled at her in a way she couldn't read but made her heart sink. Joy scolded herself. *Negative self-talk!* People don't like it. It makes them uncomfortable, she'd learned over the years. Luckily, she had something in her bag to save her. 'Here, I've got your book!'

'Ah, great. Can you shove it in my back pocket?' Monty bobbed his head in the direction of his butt and stopped on the slope once more.

'Oh, uh, sure.' She tried to use the very tips of her fingertips to lift up his loose jumper, followed by the hem of his soft T-shirt, revealing his back pocket. She slipped the book inside.

As soon as it was done, Monty strode on and Joy had to pretend she was having perfectly normal friend-type reactions to having glimpsed the slightest bit of his back.

What was wrong with her? Nobody made her feel self-conscious the way Monty did, and it wasn't anything he did or said. It was all happening in that amazing brain of hers.

Catching up to him, she threw out another question in case he could feel her awkwardness. 'Do you think your mate Elliot will carry Jude?'

'I mean, Jude's about half his height so I reckon he will.'

'I guess by the time there's any lifting going on, you'll be off the hook for best man duties.'

Monty sniffed a laugh. 'Suppose I will. I only hope he forgives me for the stag night. A few drinks at the Siren isn't enough really, is it? I've not had much time to sort anything else. And I don't know if you've noticed, but we're not exactly set up for stag and hen dos round here.'

Radia shifted in his arms and her eyelashes flickered open then closed again.

Monty whispered now, keeping his eyes fixed on the cobbles as he walked. 'What do you organise for a guy you don't know all that well? I mean, we talk most days when we meet at the Siren or around the village, and me and Tom have Elliot and Jude over at the cottage for barbeques, but it's hard when there's no dad or brothers to ask what he's into, you know?'

'Ah, yes, he's estranged from his family? Well, you can't interfere, that's just how things are for him.'

'You reckon?'

'Yes. Don't get involved.'

Monty pulled his neck back, just a little, but it was enough to make her scrabble for an apology.

'I didn't mean to snap. Sorry. I just… know it's best you keep out of things.'

Radia shifted once more and wrapped her arms around Monty's neck, pulling herself into a sitting position but keeping her head down and eyes closed.

'I will. Don't worry. But that's all the more reason to get the stag right. Thing is, as far as I know he likes three things: Jude, working out, and animals.'

'Evening all!' came a voice from the slope above them, yanking them out of their conversation.

'Mrs Crocombe. Had a nice evening?' Monty asked the woman who was standing by the bushy fuchsias outside the Ice Cream Cottage. The yacht captain was still with her.

'Lovely, dear, thank you. I see you're having a little night-time stroll,' she told them, managing to make it sound accusatory and somehow salacious, as though Joy and Monty were kids out past their curfew.

'We haven't met,' Monty told the man, adjusting Radia in his arms in a way that told him he'd shake hands if he could. 'I'm Monty.'

'Splendid!' James da Costa enthused, his cheeks turning rosy with mirth.

'And this is Joy Foley,' Monty said.

Joy smiled, all the while wanting to get away from Mrs C., who was examining her for signs of, what? Post-date rapture? Intentions of singlehandedly repopulating her precious primary school?

'Well, I'd better get Radia to bed,' she said. 'Her fishing trip's tired her out.'

For a second, Joy thought she saw Mrs Crocombe winking at Radia but when she whipped her head around to check, her daughter was smiling sweetly in Monty's arms, her eyes tight shut. Perhaps a little too tightly shut.

'Right you are, don't let us stop you! Nighty night,' called Mrs C., delving for her keys but showing no signs of moving just yet.

As they moved on up the hill, Monty and Joy only smiled warily down at their feet until they'd turned the sharp left into the shadowy passageway between cottages that led to the square where the bookshop glowed in the light of the strings of white bulbs.

'Do you reckon she was inviting him in for a nightcap?' Monty asked wickedly.

'Cone or tub?' Joy laughed. Now it was her turn to find keys. 'Tomorrow this'll be a passcode lock, you know?'

'Ah, how very Airbnb,' said Monty. 'Shall I carry this little one to her bed?'

Joy paused before pushing the door open. 'Uh... OK. Just let me kiss her goodnight first.'

Monty followed Joy up the steps and onto the shop doormat, twisting his body so Joy could press a kiss to her daughter's forehead.

The bookshop was warm and stuffy, the air still and papery. Joy set about opening the porthole windows and flipping lamps on, while her instinct to follow Monty and oversee him putting Radia down contended bitterly with the voice in her head telling her to at least *try* to curtail the panic. They were fine, the door was open, and he'd be back out here any second. Yet she still strained her ears and her neck peering at the doorframe.

–

Monty lowered Radia onto her bed, too afraid of waking her to attempt taking off her jelly shoes. Radia, however, pulled him close and whispered sleepily right into his nose like it was a microphone, 'I know what you should do for Elliot's party.'

'You're awake?'

'No, I'm not,' she insisted, closing her eyes to prove him wrong.

'Ah, sorry, my mistake. So what's this idea then?' Monty whispered back, turning his head so her whisper met his ear.

—

Monty emerged from Radia's room. 'Another amazing brain, that one,' he told Joy. 'But you already know that.'

'Yep,' she said, leaning her back against the counter, holding herself in a hug and telling herself the lie that what just happened hadn't felt so very bad. She could trust this man, if only the worry now hardwired in her brain would let her.

Monty read the signs – she wanted him out of her shop – so he squeezed past her and stepped right out onto the doorstep.

'Thanks for coming tonight,' he told her, turning back and placing a hand on the doorframe. 'Sorry we didn't catch a fish.'

In the sky behind him, Joy caught another glimpse of Jupiter, now competing with silvery streams of moonlight streaking the deep sapphire.

Taking hold of the door as though to close it, she moved closer to Monty, so they stood only an arm's length apart over the threshold.

Neither spoke, they only watched one another.

Monty seemed to be thinking hard. He hung his head a little, keeping his eyes fixed on her, a questioning furrow between his brows.

'We'll catch something next time,' she told him, before wondering why she'd said it. *What next time was this?* He hadn't asked her about a next time.

Monty must have seen her recoiling but he only smiled and kept his eyes trained on her, making Joy's mind race.

He certainly didn't look like he was thinking her presumptuous, and not like he was thinking she was odd either. He was looking at her like she'd seen the guys on her degree programme look at her at the end of uni nights out; carefree, young, desirous, but trying to hold back, trying to be respectful.

For a moment, Joy was back in Halls at the door of her dorm and she wasn't a tired mum, or a travelling technician, or a daughter who couldn't remember the last time she was held. She was a woman who wanted to kiss a beautiful man and there was just enough Cava and moonlight in her system to make her do it, so she stepped across the threshold and brought her face up to meet Monty's, pausing only a breath away from his lips to ask if it was all right.

Monty nodded once, everything soft and slow, before his lips touched hers in an unhurried electric kiss, and there was not a hint of the sea chill between them, only warmth and all the good things Monty saw in her that she could not yet recognise in herself.

—

Early the next morning Joy sprang awake, alone in her bed up at the top of the spiral stairs in the bookshop. Her first thought was to wonder why her sister was texting her this early. Then, *Oh!* Memories of the night before flooded back. Kissing Monty for what must have been half an hour on the doorstep, then giving him her private mobile number because he'd asked for it and she hadn't even considered giving him her other work number.

She should have been alarmed, but all she could do was grin and grab for the phone.

> Dear Joy and Radia, Sorry I don't have time to do proper invites but please come to Elliot's stag at the Siren's Tail on Saturday in the function suite, 6pm. Totally kid-friendly, I promise. Wear old clothes. Monty x

The first thing that struck her was the kiss after his name, which she touched with the side of her thumb. Since she was alone, she didn't have to suppress the urge to throw herself back on her bed with a little squeal of happiness as she gathered the covers around her once more and typed her reply, sending it immediately.

> Love to!

She didn't think how odd it seemed for a mum and her little girl to be invited to a stag party, and the 'wear old clothes' thing had escaped her notice too. All she felt was a curious warm glow and sleep coming for her once more, so she lay back down, smiling woozily, her phone on her pillow.

Chapter Seventeen

'I already told you my name. It's Araminta Clove-Congreve. You *must* have the booking. I'm holding your quote in my hand. Of course, I know the date. Saturday the second, a week on Saturday! Clove Lore Estate. I've engaged your services for three hours. None of your modern rubbish, remember?'

'Mint?' Jowan popped his head into the ballroom where the wedding would take place. Minty had it set out as a makeshift planner's HQ for now, with folding tables and bundles of papers everywhere. 'Elliot's here with his suit and Jude's dress.'

'Hold on one second,' Minty instructed the unfortunate harpist on the line. 'What do you mean, he's here with Jude's dress? He's not supposed to see the bride's dress until their wedding day.'

Elliot popped his head in too. 'It's OK, I've seen it already, remember? In Jude's parents' wedding photos?'

'Well that's not the point, is it? Honestly. We must not *invite* ill fortune willy-nilly.' Her ire was drawn back to the phone conversation. 'What? Yes, I'm still here.'

Jowan gingerly closed the door and smiled apologetically at the young groom.

'I wouldn't have thought Minty was the superstitious type,' Elliot told Jowan, who didn't think it was necessary to remind the younger man of Minty's love of tradition.

'She's jus' got a lot on,' he said instead.

Minty's head appeared suddenly around the door, making Elliot jump.

'What are your thoughts on Jordan almonds?' she asked, her eyebrows raised. 'I've the confectioner to ring next.'

'Uh?' Elliot wasn't sure he had an opinion on them. He wasn't even sure what they were.

'Sugared almonds?' Minty encouraged. 'Do you want classic white or pastels?'

'Um.'

'Just choose one, lad,' Jowan advised under his breath. 'Put her out of her misery.'

'OK, uh, white?'

'Really?' Minty's forehead creased in disbelief. 'For a summer wedding? I'd have thought pastels best, no?'

'OK,' Elliot shrugged, bewildered, and Minty disappeared into the ballroom once more, leaving the men to share weary glances. 'Guess a wedding's not a wedding without a pastel-coloured choking hazard.'

'Best leave her to the decision making, I always find. And she made such a nice job of our own wedding,' Jowan reassured Elliot. 'Mind you, t'was a much smaller task. She weren't tryin' to set up a business then, or hold a glitzy showcase wedding for her brochure pictures.'

'We really just need the basics,' Elliot tried to protest.

'Son, you could sooner stop another flood than stop Minty turning this into the wedding of the decade. I might as well warn you, she wants the photos in all the right magazines.'

Elliot knew only too well what Jowan meant by this, having been pictured in the society pages of *Tatler* and *Town and Country* amongst his parents' smart set when he was younger at events from the Chelsea previews to the last day at Goodwood.

He thanked the universe those days were over and he could be himself here in Clove Lore, with no expectations other than his being happy.

Jowan led him away. 'I was under instruction to hang your suit in our bedroom, so I reckon that'll be the place for the dress too. Did you remember shoes? Minty expressly told me to mention shoes.'

'Got 'em,' Elliot said, indicating the tote bag over his shoulder.

'Belt, tie and handkerchief?'

'Yep.'

'Cufflinks.'

'Just buttons,' Elliot said. 'Is that OK?'

'It's your wedding,' Jowan said, all irony and apology.

From afar, Minty's voice penetrated the ballroom's centuries-old oak door, built to see off raiders with axes and muskets. '*Get the door, Jowan dear!*'

At that, the doorbell chimed, ringing further bells along the corridor in the old butler's pantry.

'She knows people are here before they even ring?' Elliot wondered aloud.

'Eagle-eyed, better than any goshawk.'

Jowan doubled back to the grand lobby to unbolt the doors, finding a rattled-looking woman, visibly shaking and clutching bulging bags of inflated balloons.

'Is Mrs Clove-Congreve here?' she asked.

'Ah! Are you… Jennifer?' said Jowan 'You'd better come in. Minty's on the phone at the minute.'

'I'll just set up here, shall I?' she asked timidly.

'Set up?' said Elliot over Jowan's shoulder, eyeing the bags as Jennifer wrestled them inside.

'She, I mean, Mrs Clove-Congreve, wanted to see a balloon arch and some displays in person before she committed to an order,' said Jennifer with the air of a woman who had a perfectly good online brochure to demonstrate these things but had spent the morning inflating eighty confetti-filled balloons in opaque pastels, shoving them into a minivan and driving all the way from Ilfracombe just because she – like everyone else roped into showcasing their wares for Big House Weddings Inc. – was too in awe of Minty (read: 'terrified') to stand up for themselves. Besides, it would be a big contract if she could land it.

'Done country estate weddings before?' Jowan asked, helping her strip away the bags, and letting a dozen balloons float up to the peeling rococo ceiling where three popped on shards of old lead paint.

'Sorry, didn't know they were helium ones,' said Jowan looking up and thinking he'd better fetch the ladders quick.

'Ah, Jennifer, you made it,' cried Minty, sweeping into the reception hall. 'Perhaps we should see them in the ball-room, *hmm*?' Everyone understood this wasn't a question.

'Aren't balloons a bit…' Elliot began, scratching at his head. Minty's eyes snapped to his face and he remembered why he didn't express opinions when at the Big House.

'A bit what?' Minty wanted to know.

'Well, a bit of an environmental disaster?'

'I've got eco-friendly ones in the workshop?' Jennifer said. 'She didn't ask for eco-friendly ones,' she added with a great deal of bravery.

'I already told you the biodegradable ones you showed me on the Zoom looked like…' she lowered her voice to a whisper, 'prophylactics.'

Elliot stifled an unfortunate burst of glee.

'Not when they're in the shape of a unicorn,' Jennifer protested.

'This isn't a children's birthday party,' Minty snapped, before turning to Elliot to remind him it wasn't a 'hippy commune' either. 'We're having a tasteful confetti balloon arch and four towers in the corners, all in delicate shades of soft cornflower and powder blue.'

Elliot knew when to give up, and indicated to Jowan to lead the way through the back to where he could hang the wedding outfits, leaving a ruffled Jennifer gaping in their wake, afraid to be left with the perfectionist Minty.

Once out of earshot, Elliot confided in Jowan. 'Is there nothing you can do? To keep things… contained?'

Jowan only fixed him with a wise look under an arched brow.

Elliot tried again. 'Jude's expecting a small wedding. She's not the fussy type.'

'Let Mint do all the fussing. All you have to do is enjoy your big day, eh?'

Elliot could only accept his fate as the groom of the year at the wedding of the century.

'Only…' Jowan added cautiously. 'Best prepare Jude for the magician.'

'Magician?'

'Took me the best part of an hour retrievin' that dove from the ballroom rafters yesterday. Be a shame to cancel now.'

'Oh god.'

'They'll follow the minstrels.'

'What's a minstrel when it's at home?'

'You know, *Hey nonny nonny*, strumming their lutes, singing romantic ballads from long ago. Big hats. Mint's roped them into helping serve the cheese twists as well.'

Elliot drew a deep breath. 'I'll warn Jude.'

'That's the spirit!'

The men shook hands on parting at the grand lobby as two subdued-looking lads carried a rolled red carpet from a van into the ballroom and Minty boomed into her mobile about a late delivery of thrones, 'And *not* the gold ones, we want the burnished oak.'

'Do I want to know what that's about?' asked Elliot.

'Shouldn't think so.' Jowan patted him on the shoulder with a stoical smile and sent him on his way.

Looking up, Elliot followed a cloud of drifting balloons of, it transpires, not *quite* the right shades of cornflower and powder blue, now lost to the summer sky. They'd escaped in Jennifer's hurry to get them back in her van.

'If it's any consolation, she's like that with everyone at the moment,' he called out to the poor woman over the lawns, but she didn't seem to hear him as she slammed the van door shut.

He watched as she sped past without so much as a nod, and Elliot, being an affable, take-life-as-it-comes sort of soul, didn't think to consider the escaped balloons, now way up amongst the blue, a warning portent for his wedding day.

–

Hidden away in the camellia grove behind the Big House, a couple were secreted on a picnic blanket amongst the greenery, enjoying the view of the Atlantic breakers.

Mrs Crocombe poured two cups of tea from a Thermos while a smiling James da Costa fixed a pink bloom behind her ear, neither of them minding it was the last flower of the season and more than a little faded.

'Letitia,' he cooed softly, just for the sake of enjoying the sound of her name.

The summer breeze made the petals at Mrs C.'s temple flutter.

'To us?' she proposed, coyly, lifting her cup to his.

'And a prosperous future,' he added with a curling smile, as the balloons floated out of sight far above them.

Chapter Eighteen

Joy felt bad that, in the end, the shop's website was so simple. It hadn't taken long to make, using her own tried-and-tested template which she knew how to adapt and expand with ease.

All the stock that she'd put on her system on their first day in the village was now listed for sale in the Borrow-A-Bookshop's online store and configured so the laptop, connected to the EPOS, would receive a notification as soon as someone bought anything online.

The second-hand stock still needed descriptions adding but that was a job for Jowan or someone who knew the first thing about antiquarian books – and that definitely wasn't her, though she might have given it a good go if he'd asked. Now all she had to do was test it and the site could go live.

Saturday had come around quickly in the midst of all Joy's hard work. It hadn't been easy juggling it with serving people in the shop every day, or baking the scones each evening ready for the steady stream of customers who kept the café ticking over. Joy had just about managed to keep on top of clearing plates and washing up, which was a job in itself.

Then there'd been the task of installing the shop's security systems – discreet cameras linked to a mobile, where Jowan would receive alerts if ever anyone tried the doors or windows after nine at night.

Joy had tackled this part of her job in the early hours, setting an alarm for five in the morning so she had time to complete her work before the first customers arrived.

As always, Radia had slotted into the whole arrangement, only this time, instead of sloping off with a tablet to watch YouTube Kids or being entertained by a childminder or tutor, Radia had helped out all day long, crashing only around two o'clock for a few episodes of *Bluey* and a nap. Whenever they got hungry Joy served up pasta or sandwiches, soup and crackers.

There'd been a particularly exciting instance when a card with no stamp had arrived for them on the doormat amongst the morning junk mail and Radia had ripped open an invitation to Jude's hen do.

'Sunday, seven until late, at Jude's place,' Radia read aloud, before telling her mum they were *definitely* going.

When Joy tried to invent reasons to get out of it, Jude had texted a reassuring message that it would absolutely be suitable for Radia, even though she'd be the only child there; it was just some pizzas and fizz with her family.

There was no point in protesting any further. Radia had danced around her bedroom, pulling the closest thing she had to a party dress from her suitcase and singing, 'Two parties! Two parties in one weekend!'

Joy had to admit Radia's excitement was catching. She'd enjoyed the last couple of days in the shop, even if she hadn't seen Monty again. It hadn't escaped her notice that every time the shop door chimed she'd turn her head, hoping it was him paying a visit, but it never was.

He had, however, texted during extra-long shifts at the pub, apologising that he couldn't get away, saying he would if he could, and asking her if there was anything she and Radia needed. Each was signed with a single kiss. Each one had told her she wasn't forgotten.

By Saturday, as they closed up the shop just before five and made their way down the slope to the Siren's Tail, Joy had dark shadows under her eyes and she'd have happily spent the evening snoozing on Radia's little bed in between episodes of *Gilmore Girls*. Instead, they were going to a stag do, of all things. The promise of seeing Monty was the only thing motivating her. That and Radia's explosive excitement.

After the sailing date/not actually a date and the kissing on the shop doorstep, a stag do was another departure from her closed-off life. She could not have guessed how it was going to turn out as she filed into the Siren's Tail function room, where Elliot sat cross-legged and blind-folded in the middle of the dancefloor and Monty held open the door for his guests, a silencing finger held to his lips, high-fiving Radia as she clamped a hand over her own mouth to hold in the happy squeal.

The last time Joy had seen Monty, they'd been kissing. It was almost impossible to believe. That whole evening had a dreamy, moonlit cast over it now.

As she passed him with a shy smile, a sudden memory of the way he'd moaned low and quiet against her lips sent a shockwave racing up her spine.

It had been real. The whole thing had been real and kind of amazing, and seriously hot, and he was smiling back at her now, not in the least trying to hide it, looking for all the world like he was thinking the same exact thing.

–

Elliot grimaced beneath the blindfold that shut out the afternoon sun still spilling in through the function room's new blinds. Everything in here was new, in fact, and just like the rest of the village, it smelled of fresh emulsion and new carpet.

A woman approached, instructing Elliot to hold his arms out and not make a sound.

Elliot tipped his head. 'I can hear a kid giggling, so this can't be what I think it is.'

'True, it's a kid-friendly surprise,' chimed Monty, rocking on the heels of his boots with glee.

'This is making no sense, mate,' Elliot replied with a nervous laugh.

'OK, *shhh* now, hold very still,' the woman urged before placing the warm, heavy bundle gently onto Elliot's lap. He instinctively wrapped it up in a hug, and Monty pulled away his friend's blindfold.

'You got me a puppy!'

'We got you a whole zoo!' Radia cried, delightedly, coming to sit beside Elliot on the floor with her legs crossed, patting the carpet beside her.

'That's right, don't be shy. Come and form a circle,' said the petting-zoo lady, who was dressed in a safari costume, complete with khaki helmet and with the words Bideford Bay Kids' Party Petting Zoo in a jungly print across her back.

'We got you the *mega* party experience,' added Monty, joining his friend.

'It was my idea,' Radia blurted. 'I always wanted a petting-zoo party and you love animals, so…' She tailed off into a happy shrug, her eyes fixed on the puppy which the zoo lady told everyone was her own dog, only five months old and called Pickle.

At the carpeted edge of the dancefloor, tables were set with a finger-food buffet, also Radia's idea. The paper plates and napkins printed with cartoon monkeys and tigers, which Finan had ordered online especially, were an added surprise.

'Everyone gets a balloon animal and a cupcake when they leave,' Finan announced from the doorway, his eyes fixed on Radia.

'I *love* party bags,' said Radia, making Joy wonder if the Siren's Tail men had planned this more for her than Elliot. Had they been talking about the strange new Borrowers? Had they taken pity on Radia? It wouldn't surprise her if they had. This was the most they'd had to do with any community of people in years, or indeed ever. It wouldn't have taken the locals long to work out that Radia was a seriously lonely kid. Then Joy got to thinking whether her daughter had ever actually had a party bag before. She mentally added another guilty notch on the Bad Mum post of parenting fails.

Elliot, who had been rendered helpless as the beagle pup licked at his ear, had to agree – the mega party *was* an excellent idea. The puppy's waggy tail thwacked against the freshly polished dancefloor. The vet reached a fist out for Monty to bump. 'Thanks, mate.'

'Thought you'd prefer this to the usual kind of thing,' Monty told him. 'Well, Rads did.'

Radia was too busy taking hold of a gecko to reply. The zoo lady reeled off well-rehearsed facts about her little menagerie in the same enthusiastic voice she'd use with a gaggle of pre-schoolers, and Elliot truly looked like he couldn't be happier with his lot in life.

Joy watched the whole thing from behind Radia's back, where she snapped photos on her phone. Monty had asked her if she'd help document the party.

She smiled at the phone screen as she took shots of Elliot passing the wriggling, tumbling Pickle to Monty. Tom, now squeezed in between Monty and Elliot, gently cradled a white baby rabbit. Three men Joy hadn't recognised were now introducing themselves to the group as Jude's dad, Jude's best friend from the Borders, Daniel, and Ekon, Daniel's boyfriend. They were fussing over a fat grey chinchilla called Cilla who, the zoo lady said, was unlikely to wake up for the party, being such a sleepy girl.

Meanwhile, Leonid was teasing Izaak about not wanting to hold Craig, a giant stick insect, and it was all hilarious until the zoo lady brought Leonid a friendly rat called Louis, who she promised wouldn't bite so long as he sat still. Now Izaak laughed and filmed his husband sitting stock still and wide-eyed while Louis scuttled up Leonid's arm and onto his shoulder, sniffing the air.

The whole scene made Joy smile as she snapped image after image, even though the sight had set off a chain of thoughts that discomforted her. Seeing all these men interacting so tenderly contrasted sharply with Sean and the men he called his friends.

She saw them now, crashing through the door of her flat, drunk after a night at the pub. She used to scrabble out of bed, pulling on a jumper over her baby bump, knowing from experience she'd have to bring them beers and crisps while they swore and told lewd jokes around her dinner table, spreading out the bank notes and shuffling cards where earlier she'd been reading her baby books.

There was nothing friendly and tender about those men, and there was nothing she could do to prevent Sean turning up with them whenever he'd felt like it. Some-times they stayed all weekend, sleeping where they fell, using her bathroom, jeering at the football, searching in her fridge. That was when her flat had stopped feeling like her own, around about the time she was realising she really was trapped.

She'd made the mistake of complaining after one of their post-pub nights ended in her cleaning up someone's vomit. It was her flat, she'd insisted. Sean couldn't just let them run riot in it, especially when she was pregnant and needed the place kept clean.

He'd been so shocked to hear her pushing back, he'd sent all his friends away immediately and she'd stood gulping and nervous, full of instant regret as the flat grew quieter.

He'd sat her down for a long lecture about how much he did for her, how ungrateful she was. How these men were important business friends and she'd embarrassed herself, and him, in front of them. It had lasted hours, the haranguing, and when she started to cry with exhaus-tion and bewilderment, he'd told her she had no business crying, not when she'd been the one hurting *his* feelings. Then, to her amazement, *he'd* cried.

Flying into a frantic state, he'd asked her why she didn't love him, and wasn't she happy she was having his baby? It had rapidly descended into a desperate, overwrought scene from there; he'd wept on the floor, wondering why she didn't want him when he gave her literally everything he had to give. He'd stumbled out the door in the early hours, leaving her gaping after him, begging him not to leave, convinced she really must have done something awful to hurt him, believing she was the ungrateful one.

He'd stayed away, not answering her calls, until she was unable to think straight. He'd turned up again three days later, only an hour after sending a text message where she'd told him if he really didn't want her she understood and she was sorry it was over.

There'd been a ring at her doorbell, a huge bunch of red roses, and he'd swept back into her life with smiles and apologies and kisses. She'd been so relieved he was back and in a wonderful mood, like he had been at the start when they first met, she'd convinced herself she was happy he was home again, and the rollercoaster of emotions that was their relationship set off on another confusing, disorientating circuit, until she didn't know what was pleasure and what was pain anymore.

By the end, he'd made sure he was so closely insinuated into every part of her life that she couldn't see how to ever disentangle him.

He'd finally put off her own friends with his grouchy, put-upon behaviour, making them feel like inconsiderate intruders when they called round or rang (he always beat her to the phone and told them she was resting or she was in the bath – she wasn't, of course), and it wasn't worth the aggro of him discovering she'd replied to their emails on the sly, so she didn't try that either.

She still tried to convince herself it wasn't really all that bad. Sean would tell her so as well. She should loosen up, he'd complain, stop being so uptight. He loved her, didn't he? He'd taken her to the big baby superstore and spent a fortune on the best buggy on the market, hadn't he? He took her out if she ever needed anything. She didn't even have to worry about bills, he was dealing with everything for her.

She was lucky, he'd tell her, but she wasn't sure she actually felt lucky. Then for a long time, she hadn't felt anything at all, other than a yearning to disappear entirely. If it hadn't been for Radia maybe she would have done.

'Joy, you have to pet something,' a voice broke through to her. Monty's. He was watching her with a little crease of concern between his brows. 'You're not allergic, are you?'

'*Hmm?* Oh, no, not allergic,' she said, blinking herself out of the vision of her lovely flat occupied by all those men who probably never even knew her name.

'Try Wallace,' Elliot threw in. 'He's great.'

Wallace, it turned out, was an enormous toad, who pulsed and gurgled on her lap. She patted his bumpy back, unsure exactly how you're meant to pet a toad.

Radia, between animals of her own, took her mum's phone and snapped pictures of her, giggling at the mock horror on Joy's face.

'Couldn't I have the puppy?' Joy said, and everyone had laughed, everyone except Monty who only smiled at her from across the chaotic circle, his eyes soft, his chest rising and dipping heavily as though he was holding himself fast to his spot, mastering self-control, trying not to get up and move beside her. Joy knew because she could feel it radiating out of him, an unmistakeable attraction, as strong as the moon pulls the tide, invisible and irresistible.

He'd sighed against her lips, her brain reminded her, and the whole time he'd kept his hands gripped tight around the doorframe of the Borrow-A-Bookshop, letting her wrap herself around him, and his breathing had turned ragged and urgent like the kiss was gnawing into his core like it was hers.

Her brain replayed it now as she watched him across the circle, everyone else's heads lowered and fixed on the animals. Monty looked back, directly at her, his eyes alive.

He'd kissed her without grabbing at her, or darting his tongue about like some sloppy teen intent on claiming her, or making her want to pull back and find air. He'd kissed her like he really, really wanted her to like it. She tried to suppress the shudder the memory provoked.

He was still looking at her. Someone was going to notice. But even Radia was absorbed in the way the puppy was now tumbling around the circle looking for fusses and making the men say *aww* and exclaim at his cuteness.

She tried to tell him, with nothing but an unequivocal stare, how much she'd liked him kissing her.

He'd loved it too, she was sure of that. He hadn't released his grip on that doorframe the whole time. He'd held back. He'd not wanted to constrict her. The whole thing had been on her terms, and it had been her who'd broken away in the end, breathless and blinking, telling him she'd better go check on Rads, and he'd only smiled and slowly turned for home. There'd been zero pressure or expectation, nothing that left her feeling conflicted or coerced. It had been lovely. *He* was lovely.

The puppy tumbled onto Monty's lap just as she was reaching that conclusion, and she watched helplessly as he booped his nose against the dog's.

It was a kind of exquisite torture, being this close to him and having all her common sense failing her, and yet her imagination ran completely out of control for gentle, hot, respectful Montague Bickleigh.

Blushing, she was sure of it, she tried to concentrate on the toad and its bulgy throat. She could feel Monty's amused eyes boring into her as he seemed to reflect all her feelings right back across the room, so strongly she wondered how the rest of the party couldn't feel it too.

The hour passed quickly in a blur of animal facts, the gentlest cuddles, reminders about frequent hand washing, and one particularly exciting bit where nobody could locate Craig the stick insect and, after a lot of searching, he'd been found clinging to the back of Izaak's T-shirt.

They'd all drunk craft Devonshire lager or orange squash from monkey cups and the whole buffet had disappeared right down to the last Pom-Bear crisp – again, Joy suspected the buffet had been planned with Radia in mind – and then Elliot had got a bit weepy when the puppy had to go back in the zoo lady's van with the rest of the creatures.

Outside on the harbour wall, waving the van away, Monty had to hug the emotional groom until he'd recovered himself and announced he'd had the best day ever.

'How many of those has he had?' Jude's dad asked, nodding at Elliot's empty monkey cup in his hand.

'He's had three orange squashes,' stated Daniel.

The men all agreed it hadn't been a bad party after all and they might as well head back inside the bar for dinner and some proper drinks now that Monty's shift was about to begin.

Radia gripped Charley fox and her mum's hand very tightly as it sank in that it was almost bedtime for her. Joy had to pretend she couldn't see the tears on her overwhelmed little girl's cheeks – she'd only have been mortified and insisted she wasn't exhausted from all the excitement.

Monty may have noticed too because he insisted on walking them a little way up the slope. Daniel and Ekon followed close behind them. They weren't staying for the meal but going back to Jude's to help her prepare for her party tomorrow.

'Are you coming to the hen do?' Radia asked Monty, sniffing back sleepy tears and trying hard not to yawn.

'Ah, no,' he told her. 'It's a girl's party.'

Daniel took over. 'We're allowed to go because Jude's my BFF.' Radia turned her face up to his and squinted as she trudged up the slope. '*Best friend forever*,' he added in a dramatic whisper.

'Bee eff eff,' Radia echoed dreamily, thinking how she wanted one of those more than anything.

'You don't have to walk us all the way up,' Joy told Monty once it became clear Radia was absorbed in quizzing Daniel about how Jude came to be his friend and whether he and Ekon were going to get married like Jude and Elliot.

'Wow! Don't *you* like to know all the details!' they heard Daniel fluster while Ekon listened in, amused.

Hanging back a little, Monty told Joy, 'It's OK, I just feel bad the party had to end so early. Work, you know? But, listen, um, tomorrow night. My shift,' he blurted. 'I'll be finished about ten. If you…'

Joy kept her eyes fixed on the back of Radia's bouncing bob, but she was definitely smiling at his words.

'If it's not too late, I mean, would you…' he continued, while she flushed pink.

She should tell him she'd be asleep by ten, most likely. She should tell him she couldn't have a guy coming over to the shop at night, not with Radia there. She also wanted to stop dead and kiss him hard on the lips and make him promise he'd come find her the second he was finished with work. Instead, she shrugged helplessly and shook her head, her lips moving and no words forming. All too soon they reached the turning for the shop.

Ekon called back that he'd see them tomorrow, and Daniel chanted, 'Girls' night! Girls' night! Girls' night!' as he walked on up the cobbles, encouraging Radia to join in.

All Monty could do was surrender the two party bags with jelly snake cupcakes inside and bid Joy goodnight.

'Will I see you tomorrow night?' he asked again. He seemed not to know what to do with his hands, so they both ended up behind his head.

Joy gripped the bags and told him she didn't know, before fixing him with a panicked look which she broke off after a second's indecision. Then she followed after her daughter, down the alleyway and into the bookshop square.

–

All the next day as she worked on the shop tech, keeping the doors locked against customers or any handsome chefs who might come strolling by, Joy was plagued by the image of Monty booping his nose to the puppy dog's. The memory made her smile then frown in frustration in equal measure. To fight it off she'd worked as hard as she could, and she'd kept Radia busy with some BBC Bitesize lessons on iPlayer, all the while totally at a loss for how to handle these wholly inconvenient impulses racing through her body, telling her that Monty Bickleigh was the only thing she wanted right now, while a weaker impulse warned her he was the very last thing she needed.

Chapter Nineteen

The first thing that struck Joy as she was hugged and welcomed into Jude's place was the sight of a wedding cake in clear containers stacked up on the counter, a traditional tiered thing in white fondant icing. Then there was the immediate air of expectation and festivity and a wonderful, warm feeling of family too.

Evidently, Jude had popped the Prosecco long before her guests arrived. Her mum, Mrs Crawley, was also a little flushed when she welcomed them inside. A regal, elderly woman on the sofa was introduced as Jude's grandmother.

'Come and sit with me, little one,' Jude's gran said to Radia as soon as she came in, producing a bag of toffees from her handbag, telling Radia she ought to help her eat them – even though they played havoc with the teeth.

Radia dived into the spot on the sofa between her and Mrs Crocombe.

Jude was rapidly pressing bubbling glasses into her guests' hands and asking Joy how the stag do had been yesterday. She'd been in on the petting-zoo surprise.

'It was lovely,' Joy confessed, hoping it sounded innocuous and light, feeling very much as though she was being observed. 'So, how are the wedding plans?' she asked, trying to deflect Jude and Daniel's evaluating eyes.

Jude pulled a not very bridal face and said she'd just had Minty on the phone for half an hour asking her how she would go about making a wedding website.

'A website for her wedding-planning business?' said Joy.

'Well, she doesn't have one of those yet either, but she meant a website specifically for mine and Eliot's wedding.'

'Ah! Yeah, that's definitely a thing,' Joy told her.

'That's what Minty said too. What on earth do we need a website for?'

'My sister makes them for all her event clients to share with their guests. It's a good place to put all the information – timings, menus, that sort of thing – and you can have a place to share photographs and a chat room for all your guests to get to know one another. Works for weddings and corporate stuff too, makes it more personal.'

'Ugh!' Jude suppressed a shudder. 'Isn't that what the incredibly long drawn out wedding meal is for?'

'So, you don't want a website then?'

'I don't know if I've much choice. Minty gets what Minty wants. She *is* footing the bill, after all.' Jude crumpled a little. 'I know how ungrateful I sound, I really do. I just don't want Minty going to all this trouble when she already has the estate to run and the Village Recovery Committee to oversee. Oh, Mrs C.? That reminds me. Minty wanted your bank details, for the transfer?'

'Righty-ho,' replied Mrs Crocombe, saluting. 'I'll ring her in the morning. Pity she can't come tonight.'

'I think she was afraid it would get wild,' Jude told the room with a laugh that turned nervous when she saw Daniel and her grandmother turning to smirk at each other.

'If it helps, I can talk to Minty about websites. Offer some advice?' Joy said.

'You would? Really?' Jude turned and called to Mrs Crawley who was standing over the hob. 'Mum? Joy's going to calm Minty down about the whole website thing. That's nice, isn't it?'

'I can't guarantee calm,' Joy threw in, 'but I can get her started with it all.'

Jude squeezed Joy's arm in gratitude and carried on handing out glasses while Mrs Crawley asked how her husband had been at the stag yesterday, hoping he hadn't had too much whisky and cried. 'He's a terribly weepy man, bless him,' she added gently.

'Actually, it was Elliot that cried,' Radia told the room. 'Well almost, over Pickle.'

'Who on earth is Pickle?' Mrs Crocombe wanted to know.

Radia filled them all in and repeated as many animal facts as she could remember and Daniel piped up to say he and Ekon were *definitely* getting a puppy now, until his boyfriend reminded him they were both nurses and how were they supposed to manage with their shifts, and that got Radia onto her favourite topic of how she'd never *ever* had a pet.

Sensing trouble, the bride-to-be got the room's attention by asking, 'So, Mrs C. How are things with the Captain?'

Everyone was suddenly quiet and watching Mrs Crocombe, who'd been tucking into Jude's mum's excellent cheese plaits.

'Well, um...' she faltered, scanning the room and looking timid. 'He's good company.'

'Bovis told me he was supposed to have left the harbour days ago, but he's changed his mind and is sticking around?' At this, Jude threw Joy the slightest smile and a wickedly sparkling wink as she innocently lifted a plate. 'Pinwheel pizza, anyone?'

'He's getting to know the area,' replied Mrs Crocombe defensively.

Even though it felt like sweet revenge watching her getting a taste of her own meddling, Joy still felt sorry for Mrs C. Right up until the old matchmaker made use of her as a human shield, that is.

'I see young Monty Bickleigh is still helping you settle in, Joy, dear?' said Mrs Crocombe.

'He is,' Radia cheeped.

Now Daniel was grinning with prurient interest. 'Elliot's best man?' he asked.

'That's him,' Mrs C. confirmed, with some relief that the pressure was off her. 'A lovely boy, but lonesome, I've always thought. He's not been happy since he got off the boats and into the kitchens.'

'He was cute,' Ekon interrupted.

Daniel looked like he might protest before thinking again and finding he had to agree with his boyfriend there. 'But he didn't *look* lonesome.'

'Yeah, he looked pretty chilled to me,' Ekon told Mrs C., and Radia took in this whole exchange, her head whipping back and forth like it was a tennis match.

Joy flashed warning eyes at Jude, nodding almost imperceptibly towards her little girl. It was excruciating to hear Monty discussed in front of her like this and, knowing Radia, she might repeat it right to his face the next time she saw him.

'I think he's… *splendid*!' Radia exclaimed, using a new word she'd picked up from *The Borrowers*, and Joy clamped her lips.

'That's an excellent word for him. He *is* splendid,' said Mrs C., smiling approvingly.

Jude's grandmother chuckled from the sofa, enjoying the drama very much, but evidently taking pity on Joy. 'My husband was splendid. Did I ever tell you the story of how we met, Jude?'

Jude had heard it before, many times, but she'd never say so, and the room was going to hear about it anyway, there was no stopping her.

Daniel turned in his seat to listen and everyone fell silent.

'When I was just a girl my mother told me about *the recognition*,' Jude's grandmother began, her musical Scottish accent turning dramatic. Radia was already hooked.

'Ah, yes, the recognition,' said Jude's mum, bringing her Prosecco with her from the kitchen, where she'd pulled the mozzarella sticks from the oven and tipped them into a dish with a chilli dip. She perched on the arm of the sofa next to her mother-in-law, who continued her tale.

'My mother told me that one day I'd be going about my business and it would simply happen. I'd meet a stranger and I'd recognise them as my own.'

'*Is* that what happened?' Radia asked.

Joy tipped back her glass in a long gulp.

'It was. Of course, I hadn't believed her at the time,' Jude's gran pressed on. 'Nobody listens to their mother when they're young, but she was right. One day I was walking down Marygreen High Street with my friend

Gayle Dodds, on our way to the pictures, and there he was.'

'What was he doing?' Jude asked, even though she knew all this.

Radia shoved a second mini pizza into her mouth, transfixed.

'He was standing on the pavement all by himself, looking right at me. He told me later he couldn't move. He just *knew* he had to say hello.'

'*Did* he say hello?' Radia struggled to ask through her mouthful, making the grown-ups chuckle at her interest, which in turn made her scowl. 'Wha's funny?'

Jude's gran took pity on her, taking her hand. 'Not quite, actually. He said, *Toffee?*'

'Toffee?' Radia echoed, tickled.

'That's right. He offered me a toffee, and it didn't strike me as odd in the slightest. And we went into the pictures together and watched the film and he held my hand even though he'd only said that one word to me.'

'Gran!' Jude laughed.

'It wasn't me, it was *the recognition*. I just knew I'd be holding that man's hand for the rest of his life. It didn't seem strange at the time, more like magic really, and yet it was the most normal thing in the world as well.'

'That's how it was with my Ernie,' said Mrs Crocombe, who seemed to be staring blindly into the past, no longer in the room but back in her memories and laying eyes upon her husband for the very first time. A sorrowful look passed over her face, and only Joy recognised it for what it was. Guilt.

'I couldn't recognise Elliot,' said Jude. 'He was behind a door when we first met.'

'Behind a door?' cheeped Radia, still thoroughly enjoying herself. Adults talking about important things, a lovely granny holding her hand, and no grown-ups paying any attention to how many little pizzas she'd had.

'It's true,' said Jude. 'I was hiding in the bedroom upstairs in the bookshop and he'd just let himself in. He was gate-crashing my holiday! I was terrified.' Jude thought for a second. 'Although, I knew I liked the sound of him, even then. Even through a door.'

Ekon and Daniel had slipped their hands together, squashed up on the couch, and Ekon took the opportunity of telling everyone how he'd liked Daniel *for ages*, but Daniel was ridiculously slow on the uptake and hadn't understood what was happening.

'Until I intervened,' Jude said, 'and told you to actually *talk* to Ekon.'

'Matchmaker,' accused Daniel, smiling over the top of his champagne glass at his friend.

'Nothing wrong with giving love a nudge in the right direction,' insisted Mrs Crocombe.

The Spotify playlist Jude had made for the evening changed to a jarringly happy Harry Styles song and the little moment of hen party sentimentality melted gently away, but Joy was left thinking about it for a long time, even while the mozzarella sticks and even more mini pizzas were passed around. She wondered whether it was really possible to meet someone and just know they were the one.

It certainly hadn't been that way with Sean, even with all his charm and confidence and compliments. He'd swept her off her feet with fancy dinners and presents, made it impossible not to feel flattered and wanted. He'd told her how amazing she was and how he'd never met anyone like her. Three dates in and he was declaring that he loved her. She'd been so overwhelmed by it all, and so young and caught up in thinking that this was what it was supposed to feel like. Then there'd been all the flashy stuff that, she was ashamed to admit it now, had bowled her over. Like the cars he'd pick her up in (always a different one, and fancier than the one before), and he'd always worn the nicest suits and taken care of himself. Everything seemed to come so easily for him.

She hadn't recognised any of these things as red flags, and nothing warned her off – even if her sister had met him once very early on and immediately nicknamed him 'Del Boy', and he'd not liked her one bit, and it had caused a fight that night after they'd been out at a nice bar. Sean had flown into a rage and shouted at Joy for the first time, really scaring her, and then he'd cried and apologised and grovelled, telling her it was Patti's rudeness that had done it. Joy's little sister had set out to turn Joy against him and he had simply wanted to defend himself. Didn't Joy see that her own family had it in for them, wanted to split them up?

He'd somehow made his control look like romance, like it was them against the whole world and he'd take on anyone who, for whatever pathetic reasons they might have, wanted them to separate. It was jealousy probably, he claimed, or possessiveness over Joy, who was a grown woman, couldn't they see that? She could make her own decisions about who she spent time with, he'd railed.

They'd swung from intense romance to a different pitch of intensity so fast she'd not understood it was happening, and by then it was too late.

He'd somehow got himself a key made, then he'd sort of moved in. Or at least he was suddenly coming and going as he pleased, and her life shrank imperceptibly until her mum was leaving messages in tears, telling her daughter it felt like she didn't know her anymore and she *really* didn't like this guy.

Yet, Joy always defended him. He was good to her. He loved her. And all the time she didn't fully see what he was doing to her. He was cutting her off, keeping her all for himself.

No, there'd been no lovely romantic 'recognition' there, unless it was Sean recognising she was going to be easy to control.

Joy quietly slipped into the kitchen and set herself up as the glass-washer and bowl re-filler. The feelings in her chest didn't match the happy wistfulness of the rest of the group. She plunged her hands into the too-hot, soapy water, letting the hot tap run and run, wanting to feel anything but the bitter, cynical feeling that was threatening to overwhelm her.

Weddings and forevers weren't for everyone, her brain told her. No matter how many heart-warming stories of love and marriage the Crawleys and Crocombes of this world told.

Joy kept her hands busy, the scalding water drowning out the feelings of having been taken for a ride by a nasty narcissistic man who had dropped her and Radia like stones and was out there somewhere right now doing and thinking who knew what.

Soon, however, the food was all gone, and the dishes washed up. Everyone had broken into chatty little groups and Jude's mum announced it was time for games.

Joy watched from the kitchen where she wiped down already clean surfaces and Mrs C. planted a white veil over a bemused Jude's head, telling everyone she'd run it up from some old net curtains.

Daniel and Ekon conspiratorially produced a big box from behind the sofa, then, thinking better of it, Daniel said, 'Actually, maybe we should hold off a bit,' looking over at Radia and then back into the box, sending Jude into a panic about what could possibly be in there.

'We're heading off now anyway,' Joy said, sensing the part of the evening that was suitable for kids was most definitely coming to an end.

Jude's grandmother had produced a hipflask encased in a little crocheted sleeve and was offering Mrs C. a swig of her homemade sloe gin, telling her one whiff of it would put hairs on her chest, and Radia, despite complaining that she really wasn't sleepy, was hauled off the sofa and told to find her shoes.

'I'll call a cab,' Joy said into the rising rabble, feeling a little forgotten about already.

'No need, dear,' Mrs Crocombe told her, over the sound of the oven timer bleeping to say there were still some forgotten garlic dough balls on the way.

Ekon was draping Jude in a pink bride-to-be sash while Daniel handed round plastic tiaras with flashy lights.

'Rads, can you find Charley fox,' Joy instructed, looking around the room, just as the doorbell rang and Jude, still in her homemade veil, escaped for a moment to welcome inside two more women, one of whom Mrs C. made clear was her daughter, Edie, a head teacher. The other lady was one of her teaching assistants, Monica Burntisland.

'*Teachers?*' Radia repeated as the room filled even more, another cork was popped, and summer jackets were removed, sending new perfume scents mingling.

'Do you have a car seat?' Radia asked sleepily.

'Ah! No, no I don't.'

Joy told him it didn't matter but she'd sit in the back with Radia if that was OK, and they clambered in and made their way along the main road and down the narrow lane that led to top of the village, neither of the grown-ups talking, and Joy hoping Radia would fall asleep on the drive.

She didn't, of course. She was telling them there was a school here, and those nice ladies were teachers, and *how lucky* are the children who get to go to school here, Mummy?

It lasted the entire way down the slope too – Monty had a parking space and a special key fob to get into the visitor centre car park after hours. He'd pointed out the cottage where his brother now lived alone as they walked by, but Joy and Monty couldn't get another word in all the way down to the bookshop. Radia was complaining about how she *longed* to try a school dinner.

Joy had caught the sympathetic smile he'd thrown her. She rolled her eyes and smiled back.

The street lamps glowed warmly in the summer darkness, and the honeysuckle and stocks in the gardens heading Down-along released their sweetness. Joy wanted to remark on the calm navy-blue strip of sea glimpsed between the cottages, or how cheerful the Siren looked tonight, all its windows aglow, but Radia talked on and on, between gaping-mouthed yawns, about how she'd seen this pencil-case unboxing video by her favourite YouTuber and it was also a calculator *and* a notebook and she'd have liked one of those. She'd have to ask Santa for it, she supposed, since she wasn't getting new school stuff. This was said with a deep sigh.

'Straight to bed, it's way past your bedtime,' Joy announced, as she punched in the new passcode.

Amazingly, Radia only looked back and forth between her mum and Monty – who was hanging back in the little square under the strings of lights – and she tramped straight through to her room at the foot of the stairs without any complaints, flipping on the big lights as she went. Joy watched from just inside the shop door.

'Right, I'll… head back, then,' Monty said, already taking a step away and hiking a thumb to indicate he wasn't expecting anything else.

'Wait.' Joy's mouth had said it before her brain could intervene.

He held himself still in the middle of the square.

'If you give me a minute, I'll do her a cocoa, then we could…' Joy had no idea what they could do. 'We could…' Her eyes fell on the little blue tables and chairs of the courtyard. 'We could have a drink?'

Monty didn't need to hear more. He pulled up a chair and sat with his back to the palm tree in the big pot.

Joy followed her little girl inside, trying not to think too much about anything and especially not about Jude's gran's theory of 'recognition', which was obviously romantic nonsense and not at all a real thing any sensible woman would be daft enough to succumb to.

Chapter Twenty

'Wine?'

'Cocoa please,' Monty joked and it only took Joy a moment to register.

'Hah, sorry, Radia's had the last of it. I've got this though.' She showed him the half bottle of Jude's rosé left over from the shelving party.

'Perfect,' he told her.

'Aren't you tired? Breakfast and dinner shifts *and* a stag weekend in between?'

She poured the wine and pulled up the seat opposite Monty and facing the open bookshop door. From here she could see all the way through to Radia's darkened bedroom.

Monty waved the suggestion away, even if his eyes had a tired softness about them. 'Cheers,' he said, lifting his glass to Joy's.

She had to look away as she drank. Monty's eyes stayed gently fixed upon her and it was all too much after her long evening of being around people, all of whom, she felt sure, had suspected her secret: she really liked this guy.

'So… what is this?' she asked, a sweep of her hand gesturing to the courtyard.

'I think Jowan intended it to be an outside meeting place, an extension of the café maybe, somewhere to read and eat?'

'A meeting place? *Hmm.*' Joy supposed she could allow café customers to sit outside if she kept the shop door propped open. She could even set out a little display of books here to draw in more passers-by.

It struck her that she was thinking more about book-selling than putting the finishing touches to the security and camera systems or to helping Minty with her wedding websites problem.

Monty watched her but didn't pry into her thoughts. He seemed contented enough just to see her looking happy. He drank again and rested his head on his hand, a hazy smile fixed on his lips.

Joy inhaled the cool quiet of the evening. The way the light fell against the whitewashed walls of the cottage backs put her in mind of the little yard outside her own flat, with its white render over London red brick. When she'd moved in there were only bins in the yard out the back. She'd planted herbs in pots, scrubbed the flagstones and hung a hammock. Gaz and her co-workers would come and drink beers there after work, and they'd make pizza and look at the stars through the light pollution. Again, her safe little space back home seemed to be calling to her, reminding her of all the good times she'd had there, times she could have again, if she was brave enough.

Her eyes settled on the palm tree in its big terracotta planter with its cracks visibly repaired with silvery mortar. She supposed it must have been a result of the flood damage.

'I like how you can see the repair,' she told Monty, absently, and he followed her eye line to the pot. 'All the cracks are filled in but they're still there too, not covered up. It reminds me of *kintsugi*. I took Rads to an exhibition about it in Nagasaki. There were all these ancient dishes and cups, all the broken bits filled with gold, fixing them back together.'

'Kin…?' Monty prompted.

'*Kintsugi.*'

Monty soundlessly mouthed the word before saying, 'I like that idea; repairing things so the damage can still be seen? So the cracks are part of its story.'

'Exactly,' said Joy. 'And it makes you think of the person who made it, and how it might have got smashed in the first place.'

'And the hands that put it back together?' said Monty, thoughtfully. 'It was Magnús and Alex's handiwork, actually. The ones that vacated the shop before you?'

'Right. Well now Alex and Magnús are part of its story.'

Joy wanted to talk more. She strongly wanted to tell Monty about the scar across her abdomen from where the surgeon had pulled Radia, or the vaccination mark on her arm from her BCG, the completely failed piercings that had never healed on her earlobes because it wasn't a good idea to trust a teenager with a pink plastic piercing gun in a shopping mall when you're fourteen. It was enough just to think these things herself, and so she smiled, and although she didn't know it, her eyes sparkled under the bulb lights.

A heavy kind of silence settled around the pair now.

'Listen,' Monty said eventually. 'I'm sorry about all the school stuff tonight. I could've warned you that Edie Crocombe and her TA would be at the hen do.'

Joy swept a dismissive hand. 'Radia would have reacted just the same, even if I'd had warning.'

'She'll not let that go now, will she?'

'No, but that's nothing new. She wants a normal life.'

Monty's brow crumpled a little. 'She has a normal life.'

183

'*Hmm*, maybe,' Joy said, reluctant to dig deeper but the wine wanted her to keep talking. 'I can't help feeling guilty about all the things she's missing out on.'

Here it came, the same old stuff she thought every night. Would it help lessen the guilt if she told a sympathetic listener? The way Monty was watching her with quiet interest told her to try.

'She misses her auntie, and the flat, and…' Joy faltered. 'And my parents. She'd love a granny to spoil her.' Shifting in her seat she pushed her hair behind her ears and took a deep breath. 'She could have gone to school last September, you know? I deferred her place. She's missed so much.' Joy stubbornly refused to give in to the tears welling.

'Or, there's another way of looking at it,' Monty tried, ever so tentatively.

'Tell me.'

'Well, when we were loading up at the buffet yesterday, at the zoo party, Radia was telling me about the hot dog carts in Central Park and how one time you let her have two chilli dogs *and* a Big Gulp.'

'I did.' Joy laughed. 'She remembers that?'

'And she told me about a pizza slice you bought her from a hatch in a wall in Venice and you ate it on the Rialto Bridge. She *told* me that. At five years old! And her face was all lit up too. It must have been one tasty slice!'

'Hah, it was.' Joy inhaled through her teeth and her eyes shone at the memory. 'And it was sunset,' she said, exhaling. She could see the scene now: Venice, all golden and sparkling, and the gondolas gliding by.

Monty hadn't finished. 'And she was trying to tell me about eating the biggest nectarine she'd ever held, but she couldn't remember where that was.'

'Barcelona. She was practically a baby then. How does she know all this stuff!' said Joy in wonder.

'You did that.'

'Hmm?' She wasn't following.

'*You* gave her a lifetime of amazing experiences, and she's not even six years old yet. You've given her an education she'd never get normally. How many kids even know what the Rialto is? Huh? She's seen the whole world. Eaten it, swam in it, flew around it. What a gift!'

'Oh.' Joy slumped, a little happier, in the chair. 'I hadn't thought about it like that.' She vowed to try to remember it the next time the guilt was gnawing at her. It was certainly working now. 'You know she'll be telling people about the fish you barbequed for us for years to come, right?'

'So will I,' he said with a laugh. 'I haven't enjoyed cooking for people like I did that night in… *oh*, a long time.' Monty spoke sighingly. 'It felt like *real* cooking, just fire and fresh air and simple ingredients. I'd do it every night if I could.'

'You should then,' said Joy, shrugging like it was obvious.

Monty absorbed the words before letting his gaze settle somewhere on the ground by the shop's steps.

Joy didn't want to interrupt his thoughts so she sat quietly and looked at the stars beyond the glowing lights. It really was lovely to sit here, wine-warmed on a summer night, and Monty so easy to sit with, nothing on edge, nothing difficult.

'I can't believe I'm doing this,' said Joy at last. She inhaled the late-August night air once more, filling her up: the sea and night pollen, wine and whatever that good stuff Monty was wearing that smelled of summer holidays. 'I wanted to do this,' she said.

Monty tipped his head again, letting her go on.

'When we arrived. I took one look at this little square and I distinctly remember thinking, I want to sit there with a glass of cold wine on a night like this.'

'And now you are.'

'And now I am.' Her eyes danced between the gently swaying lights, the deep navy of the sky, and the palm fronds arching over Monty's head. 'This is my third drink tonight.' She said this like it was a confessional.

'And it's my first,' Monty replied.

'I definitely liked this weekend.'

'So did Radia, I reckon.' Monty glanced into the stillness of the shop.

'She loves a party. And people. Not like me.'

'You didn't do so badly.'

'It's exhausting. Peopling.'

'I hear you. Uh, listen… I should probably go, let you have some alone time.'

Joy jumped in her seat. 'That's not what I meant. *You* don't exhaust me. You're… easy to be around, actually.'

'OK, good,' he said, resting back into his chair, smiling, and one hand lazily propping up his head.

Joy, totally unaware she was doing it, mirrored him, her fingertips resting against her cheekbone. His eyes followed their movement as she let her nails graze gently over her skin. His pupils dilated a little more, making his brown eyes browner. *That* she noticed.

'I feel like we've met someplace before, actually,' he said suddenly, his thoughts drawing him inside himself. 'You and me.'

'You do?'

'Yeah, that's how easy it is. I kind of *knew* you, you know?'

Joy did know, and the way he was looking at her now sent an instruction to her legs, making her rise slowly to her feet.

'Like we recognised each other, or something?' she said, half alarmed, half courageous, fully acting on compulsion.

Monty stood too, watching her with caution, not sure what was happening yet, abandoning his glass on the table.

'It was like I'd been waiting for you.' He pushed his chair away with his boot then stepped into the gap between them, stopping only inches from her, mirroring her parted lips. 'What should we do?' he asked, then smiled at the question. 'I mean, what do you *want* to do?'

She slipped her hands around his waist and into the curve of his lower back, pulling his stomach against hers. There was some awkward foot shuffling that made their toes bump and they both had to laugh.

His hands hung in surrender by his sides.

'This is what I want to do,' she told him, her voice barely a whisper, bringing her mouth up to his in a slow kiss that instantly turned his breathing ragged.

When she eventually pulled away again, his heavy-lidded eyes stayed fixed on her lips.

She spoke again. 'Only don't hold back this time.'

The words were enough to make him take her in his arms, drawing her as close as possible. This time he kissed her, withholding nothing, still determined to make sure she liked it.

When she wordlessly led him into the shop, letting the door lock behind them, leaving their empty wine glasses out in the moonlight, Monty followed in her irresistible wake up the curve of black iron stairs and into her bedroom.

Everything, from undressing in the soft light from the summer's night sky beyond the glass, to pulling him down onto the bed and making him sigh and shiver as she kissed down his neck and over his taut chest and stomach, felt easy.

Monty had condoms but told her he wasn't expecting anything at all and she only smiled and reached for the foil packet, sending him almost delirious with wanting.

They talked in whispers, instructing each other softly, making sure it was still all right, saying it felt so good, growing increasingly breathless and trying not to cry out loud as they moved together harder and faster, gasping for air, pushing closer to the edge, until Joy felt her entire nervous system come alive under his weight and she writhed and kissed him hard to stop the sounds escaping. Seeing her, feeling her, come undone around him, was all it took for Monty too, and they collapsed, gasping and laughing and kissing, looking in wonder into each other's eyes like they were waking up from a long time spent in a dreamless slumber, recognising that they were perfect at this, perfect for each other in all the important ways.

Chapter Twenty-one

It was the journey of Monty's hand over her back as he shifted in half-sleep that woke her.

Joy wasn't sure how long she'd been out, but the sun wasn't yet risen in the sky.

She allowed herself the luxury of taking him in; the way his chest rose and fell softly, and how soft the skin was over his stomach. His arm lay between them now, unmoving against the sheets, his fingers at rest. There was something of the summer light in his skin, as though he'd absorbed it all season long and emitted it now.

She had to lean in and kiss the soft spots that drew her gaze, working up over his ribs and onto his chest. The trail led her to the spot on his neck that, she'd learned last night, maddened him. The press of her lips was enough to awaken him fully and he drew her to him, stroking her hair back behind her ear.

'Water?' she asked in a whisper and he nodded. She pulled on a T-shirt and quietly left the room.

Once back in bed, having tiptoed past Radia's room and drawn her door closed on the way to the café kitchen, they both drank.

'All quiet?' Monty asked.

'She's a good sleeper.'

'What do I do in the morning? Should I leave before she wakes up?'

Joy had to think about that. 'She won't think anything of you being here, I mean, as long as you're dressed. But she might tell people.'

'Ah! And we don't want Mrs C. profiting from any gossip about us?'

'Exactly.'

'You can both follow me down to the Siren, if you like, for breakfast?'

'OK.' The idea turned her shy again, but it was still totally impossible not to grin when presented with Monty, all earnest and sleepy in her sheets. Arriving at the pub together from Up-along, everyone would know. How could they not? In a nosy place like this.

Somehow the possibility didn't feel as bad as she might have imagined. That was all Monty's doing. He was so well regarded here, any gossip would be gentle enough. She tried not to think too hard about how it didn't matter anyway. How she'd be leaving the gossips behind in a matter of days.

As if reading her mind yet again, Monty asked, 'So, you're going on to your next job soon?'

'Lisbon.'

The word hung in the air. It meant this couldn't become anything more than it was. It meant Monty shouldn't get his hopes up. Joy wished for the first time in a long time that things were different.

'Then London afterwards,' she added.

'Yeah?' Monty lifted his eyes to hers and she saw the hopefulness there.

'For a little while. All autumn. Through Christmas, maybe.'

Monty didn't say anything, only wetting his lips, listening.

'Maybe we could...' she began. The sentence felt impossible to finish.

The idea of Monty coming to see her at her flat – in the real world – was utterly outlandish. Here in Clove Lore anything seemed permissible, but in her little flat? That was where all the ghosts of her old life were hanging around. And yet, she could picture herself handing him a coffee over her little breakfast bar. She could see him reading with Radia at the dinner table. The idea was dangerously appealing.

'Meet in London?' he said, tentatively.

'Could you do that?' she said. 'Get away for a while?' What was she doing? And yet the words spilled out.

'Yeah, of course! If Finan ever hires a sous chef. In fact...' Monty impulsively grabbed for his phone in his trouser pocket on the floor.

'What are you doing?' She didn't know if she was delighted or horrified.

Monty tapped out the words, reading them back to her. 'Finan, PLEASE hire me some kitchen cover. Just please!'

He smiled as he showed her the phone, hitting send before her eyes. 'There.'

In the silence that followed, Joy slipped closer to him, back into the cosy nook under his arm. They settled against the pillows. Monty pulled the covers around them and Joy told him she could stay like this, lying against his chest, forever. Her words alarmed her but were nonetheless true.

Monty seemed to think for a long time after that, while the dawn brightened the room with its pink glow. The silence took on a new kind of heaviness.

'You, uh, you said you deferred it,' Monty said at last.

Joy shifted in his arms. 'Huh?'

'A place at school, for Radia? You deferred it. That sounds different to you turned it down.'

'She doesn't know it, but she can start school on the fourth.'

'Of September?'

'Yep.'

'Wow.' Monty ran a hand through his hair. She felt the muscles in his chest move and his heart seemed to suddenly beat faster.

'Why haven't you told her?' The question was so tentatively asked, Joy knew he was trying not to spook her.

'In case I can't do it. In case, when the time comes, London just feels like too big a step.'

'But you own a place there?'

'My flat.'

'You can tell me,' he told her softly. 'The thing that's keeping you moving. You can tell me. I won't judge.'

It took a long time to answer.

'Well,' Joy began, and her throat constricted at the things lining up, things she found she really wanted to tell him.

He pulled her closer and pressed a kiss to the top of her head, tucking the covers around them again until she felt like she was in a nest.

'It started with Sean.' Just saying his name in the little safe bubble they'd formed brought up a heavy, stifling weight in her chest.

But it was too late to go back to silence so she talked him through the whole thing. Telling him how, after months of holding her breath in her flat, waiting for the moment he would crash back into her life, though he never came, she had the idea to begin travelling for work, carrying baby Radia with her. European jobs at first, then further afield. How it had taken her ages to get back in command of her fears. How she had only just recently, since coming to Clove Lore, in fact, begun to remember who she'd been before Sean.

Monty took it all in. The way Sean had insisted he drive her whenever she needed to go out, restricting her mobility and making it look like attentiveness. How he'd set impossible standards she couldn't possibly meet, and then he'd make her feel she was to blame when she fell short.

'I know people might think I should have reported him to the police or something.'

Monty didn't say anything, only pulling a face that suggested he hadn't been thinking that at all. Joy was too wrapped up in defending herself to notice.

'But what would I say? That I lived with a guy who purposefully burned dinner every night for weeks so he could blame me for not being home in time, even though he *knew* I finished work at five thirty and got home at six, but he wanted me home for half-five when he served up. Can you report someone for making you walk on eggshells? Nobody handed him all my passwords and online accounts but me. I did that myself. What could the police do with that? How could I tell them I'd let myself get pregnant with this guy? I'd brought it all on myself. That's how it looked. How it *still* looks.'

Monty's jaw was flexing and his grip tightened around her as she spoke, but he didn't say anything, only kissing her head and stroking her arm all the more.

'He visited us once in the hospital,' Joy spoke on. 'Gave Rads her Charley fox, and that was it. He walked out smiling, saying he'd be back that evening, and he never came back, didn't call, nothing. I waited for him to pick us up from hospital, rang his mobile, left messages. It didn't occur to me that this was our chance to get away from him; all I wanted was for him to come and get us. I'd forgotten how to live without him running everything. In the end, the midwives said I couldn't just hang around anymore so I called a cab and a locksmith. When we got home the guy was already waiting on the steps. He changed the locks there and then and I shut me and Radia inside. And we stayed inside.'

Remembering the feeling of waiting, wondering what was going to happen to her next, made her chest tighten and she rubbed at the ache, taking a moment to breathe through her mantra the way the doctor had told her. *Sean isn't here. He doesn't even know where we are. He doesn't want us now anyway. It's over.*

Monty didn't ask if she was all right. He only waited. Finally, she recovered her breath enough to go on.

'We lived so quietly, with the blinds shut all the time, trying to be invisible. I was afraid to step outside in case he was waiting, watching us. I was paranoid.' She gave a wry laugh. 'I was more afraid of him once he disappeared than I ever was while he lived with me.

'Anyway, I knew we couldn't go on like that, but I just couldn't bring myself to sell my little flat. I was adamant about that. That was *my* place, not his. It was all I had. That and loads of good tech contacts. Instead of going back to where I worked, a place called Tech Stars, after my maternity leave was up, I bid for loads of freelance stuff, didn't matter where in the world they were, and I lined them all up in my diary. Got Rad's passport sorted out too. Pretty soon we were out of there. And we've been moving around ever since.'

'And your flat's standing empty? Not rented out?'

'Nope.' How could she hand over keys to strangers, no matter how well she vetted them? Not when Sean could turn up any time and insist it was his place, making them leave, moving himself back in. The idea of him inside her home made her shudder. 'Peace is priceless,' she said.

Monty hesitated before letting the words out. 'Are you living in peace?'

The question, so innocently asked, shook her down her spine. She ran through her mantra once more in her mind. 'We're safe,' she told him afterwards. 'As long as we keep moving.'

'Do you think he really is looking for you?'

Joy didn't know how to tell him there'd been no sign of Sean since that day at the hospital, but the menacing sense that he was out there in the world, possibly wanting contact with his daughter, was too terrifying a prospect to test out by allowing him to find them.

'Are you going to sell the flat? He'd never know where you were then? There'd be no point on the map where he could potentially locate you.'

'I would... I mean, I should, but...' She thought of the little primary school around the corner from her home, and the place waiting for Radia. You don't just give up a spot in an outstanding primary school, or a flat a stone's throw from countless IT start-ups and some of the biggest tech companies in London. If she was going to go home and find work again, that was the place to be. That was the reason she'd chosen her street in the first place.

It was the flat she'd worked for, which she owned outright. Which she'd loved. An increasingly large part of her wanted to turn the key and say the words, 'Rads, we're home and we're here for good.'

'The longer I've been here, the more I've remembered all the things about my old life I used to love. I was part of a team at work. We worked *so* hard, then we'd have LAN parties, stay up all night gaming, and in the morning we'd do these scone and coffee runs. We'd hit the bars some nights, cinemas and restaurants. And I loved being alone in the flat, cooking or sitting out in my little yard, and I loved Radia being in there with me, in a weird way, even after everything Sean was putting me through. I loved it being just the two of us there.'

'Sometimes you give up the good stuff so the people you love most can have what they need,' said Monty. The next words flew straight from his subconscious: 'Like I walked away from the boat so Tom can keep fishing. I still top up the family bank account; I doubt he even knows that. It helps when there's a run of bad catches, and I always, always pay off his tab at the Siren.'

Tipping her head to look up at him, she said, 'And it's working?'

'Kind of,' Monty told her with a shrug. 'In some ways. Tom's happy, that's what matters.'

'But you're not?'

'I am right now.' He sealed his words with a kiss to her temple. 'The boat, prepping the fish, being outdoors, that's still in my make-up. So what if I'm stuck in a kitchen plating up Caesar salads most of the time? I still get so much of what I love. The sea's right there, and the *Bounty*. Besides, I told Mum I'd look after Tom, so I am.'

'OK, but you should get to be happy too.'

'And you shouldn't?' He tipped his head so he could see her face.

'It's not me that matters.' Joy didn't need to say the rest. Radia was what counted. 'Since coming here though, it's been getting clearer to me. I'm not just made up of all the sad stuff that happened, all the things that Sean did to my life. I'm all the good things too, like Radia being born. I did that. And every time she ever said she loves me, and the way she laughs. I don't know why I only just figured this out, but I've realised I'm not just twenty-nine-year-old Joyce. I'm myself at Radia's age too, back when I was much, much happier than her.' The thought pained her and brought a tremble to her voice. 'And I'm still myself when I was fifteen and mad about Paul Kushner in the sixth form, and I'm me when I graduated with honours, and when I smashed the interview and got the job at Tech Stars. I'd forgotten all about those earlier versions of me. Sean made me forget. But she's coming back to me. *I'm* the person who changed the locks that day, even when I was scanning the road and shaking like a leaf, thinking he was about to storm up the path and ask what the hell I was doing. Even when he was destroying me, there was a part of me that could still defy him. I still knew I belonged to myself, even when Sean believed I was his.' The thought brought her strength now. 'I've always belonged to myself.'

'That's right, you're Joyce Foley, no matter what. Your own person, made of all the good things you ever did.'

Joy let herself lean closer into Monty's body, knowing she'd never let anyone make her forget it again.

'You must really want to go home,' Monty said, dragging his lips over her hairline and kissing the soft baby hairs there. Joy felt the effort it took for him to say the words, but in that moment she was decided.

'Radia needs to go home. But you'll come to see us?'

'I will, as soon as I can. I can just see myself in Laandun!' He said it in a terrible Mockney accent, just to make her smile.

Laughing sleepily she told him wryly that yes, that's exactly how they spoke in the capital. He'd fit right in.

As the summer dawn turned from pink to the soft blue of daylight once more, Joy wriggled down onto the pillows and Monty drifted off to sleep with her head on his chest, holding her hand flat against his heart.

As sleep claimed her too she tried very hard to picture Monty Bickleigh – the man with the sea-salt curls and the sun and stars in his skin – walking down her street, past the primary school and the taxi rank by the all-night chemist, encountering the endless traffic and sirens, the pigeons and the dirty rain. The place she had loved so dearly. Her home.

She tried to imagine him walking up the path, standing on her doorstep, picking out her name on the buzzer, coming for her. But before her brain had managed to place beautiful, wholesome Monty – the twin who loved his brother and his family business, the fresh air and the whole Clove Lore community more than anything – at her door, the picture in her mind faded. Monty's fine features greyed and blurred, morphing horribly, and the man she threw open her door to in her half-dream wasn't Monty at all. It was Sean, standing over her with mocking eyes, fists clenched by his sides. And in the fuzzy darkness of the dream flat behind Joy, a little voice cried out excitedly, 'Daddy!'

Chapter Twenty-two

Joy didn't register what it was at first. The sound of the shower had covered it, the ringing.

As she emerged from the steamy bathroom towel-drying her hair, wondering what she should wear for breakfast at the Siren, she heard it more clearly: Monty's lovely voice. Only he was putting on a posher tone for the benefit of someone. A customer in the shop? Not likely at eight-fifteen.

'That's right,' he was saying. 'The Borrow-A-Bookshop, Down-along, Clove Lore.' A pause, and then, 'No door number. All the locals know where we are. Hard to miss us really.'

Joy pulled her robe closed and made her way down the stairs as Monty told whoever was on the phone that it was nice talking to them too, then hung up.

'There you are. I told them you'd ring them back, thought you'd be longer,' he said, coming to meet her where she'd stopped on the bottom step.

He reached his arms around her, tipping his head up to kiss her, and they both smiled at how for once she was taller. Radia's bedroom door was still closed so Joy took her time with her good morning kiss.

'You're late for work,' she told him.

'*Meh*, Finan can fry bacon,' he said dismissively, leaning in for another kiss.

'Was that a customer?' she asked, after pulling reluctantly away. 'Seems a bit early for book hunting.'

'Hmm?' Monty was hazy-eyed and dreamy from the kiss. He kept her close. 'No, it was your mum.' He said it so casually, like it was nothing.

Joy stiffened in his arms. 'My mum? *My* mum?' she repeated.

'Yep. We had a nice chat about her holiday in Portugal. You can catch massive tunas off the Portuguese coast. Mind you, you'd need a licence. It's not—'

'My mum called me?' she interrupted him. 'Here? On the shop phone?'

'Uh, yes?' Monty stepped back, not understanding at all what was happening. 'I didn't want the ringing to wake Radia so I grabbed it. Shouldn't I have?'

'How did she know we were here? How did she get the number? I…' Joy's brain had jolted straight into panic mode.

She turned and ran for her mobile upstairs, Monty watching her go, open-mouthed.

There was a missed call from her mum's mobile ten minutes ago, the first time in six years she'd actually rung it as opposed to texting, and a voicemail sent late last night. She already knew who it'd be from before she hit play.

'Joy? I'm sorry,' the message began. 'I thought I should tell you. When I popped round to Mum and Dad's place last night I checked my messages like I usually do, only my phone had connected to that new Bluetooth speaker thing Dad's got in the kitchen… and they heard the whole thing. You saying you were at the borrowing bookshop in Devon. And I tried but I couldn't get it to switch off, and then Mum grilled me about where in Devon you might be, and I told her I had no clue, but she was already googling the place and… I'm so sorry. She said since you were in the country she was going to try to see you both, and I just… I'm sorry. You know how she gets, she's worried about you and Rads, and, look, I don't want this to spoil things between us, not when we were getting better at talking…' Her voice shook. 'And you never know, she might have had time to chill about it all. Only she did say she was going to ring you, so…'

Joy heard the resignation in her sister's voice. Sure enough her mum had been that missed call.

'Everything OK?' asked Monty from the bedroom doorway. Joy jumped and hung up on her sister's apologising.

'No, not really. You shouldn't have spoken with her. You can't just involve yourself in my family stuff.'

'I, uh, I'm sorry, I had no idea who was calling. I thought it was a customer or a supplier or something, and you were in the shower, and Rads was asleep.'

'Radia.'

'Huh?'

'Her name isn't Rads, it's Radia.'

'OK, sorry.'

'What did you tell her?'

The abruptness jolted him. 'Just that you were staying here for a few more days, then Lisbon, then home again to London.'

'You didn't!' Joy felt her blood still.

'Shouldn't I have?'

'No, you shouldn't! She could have been anybody and you're just telling them our address?'

'But it wasn't anybody, it was your mum. She sounded nice, really happy that you were in the country. What… what have I done wrong?'

'Nobody knows where we are. Nobody. Not ever. Especially not Mum and Dad. We're not like that. Not in each other's business. Not anymore. Radia doesn't even *know* her grandma, not really.'

'Grandma?' a little voice said from behind Monty and his eyes widened as he turned to reveal Radia on the landing, Charley fox dragging beside her. 'Is Grandma here?'

'No,' Joy insisted. 'No, she's not.'

'Did Grandma call? Was that her on the phone? What did she say?'

Joy glared at Monty. 'We keep ourselves to ourselves. I told you that.'

'I said I'm sorry. What can I do to fix it?'

Joy didn't answer. Her mind was racing. Maybe if she ignored the calls, simply didn't reply, that'd be the end of it?

Radia pushed past Monty. 'Can I call her back? Face-Time her? Please!' Radia was pleading, and the panic continued to work its way through Joy's system.

Monty took another step closer towards the stairs. 'I'd better leave you two to sort this out, I reckon. I'll be down at the Siren, OK?'

'You're leaving? You're just going to turn my life upside down and now you're leaving?'

She knew she should stop talking right now, but the fear, shame and squirming embarrassment over not having a functioning relationship with her own parents whipped her up into anger – a much easier emotion to process.

The words spilled out. 'Or are you on your way to sky-write it? Joyce Foley is hiding out in Devon.' She cast the words in the air with her hands. 'Come and get her!'

Monty shook his head, exasperated, no idea what to do other than apologise.

'Let's call her, Mummy,' Radia pestered, pulling at Joy's fingers. 'Give me your phone, we'll do it now.'

'No!' shouted Joy, snatching her phone away. Radia flinched. It took a horrible, frozen split second before the little girl's face crumpled and the tears fell.

'Rads, I'm sorry, I didn't mean—' Joy began, but Radia was already running downstairs, making the metal steps clang.

She fixed her eyes on Monty. 'We were doing fine on our own,' she told him, her voice shaking, tears on the way. She pulled her robe tighter around her. 'This is what happens when you let people in.'

She was talking more to herself than Monty now and dragging her wheelie case out from under the bed. The sounds of Radia crying downstairs rose to meet them.

Monty gasped. 'You're not leaving? Just because your parents know you're here? That's crazy!'

'You don't know the first thing about us!' Her eyes were fierce like a cornered animal's when she turned to face him. It made Monty halt on the spot.

'Well then. Why don't you tell me about your parents so that I do understand?'

Joy's fight-or-flight trigger had fired and she seemed to be set on doing both at the same time. She tugged the zip and started pulling clothes from their hangers, tossing them into the case.

'We don't talk. We don't let them know where we are. We can't trust them. They really hurt me,' she spat.

Monty backed away. 'I'm sorry,' he said again, weakly this time.

Radia's crying grew louder, the kind that Joy knew wasn't going to subside with an apology and the promise of an ice cream. This was why she stayed away from people. The upset that invasions of their privacy caused was too great.

Joy's mind raced as Monty watched her packing. How did she explain to Radia that the grandparents she thought so wonderful had turned their backs on them, just like Sean had? They'd blamed her for what happened. They'd told her she was weak, at least her mum had. Her dad had been his usual silent, busy self and said nothing at all. But he'd been there listening to the phone call and not intervening when her mum gave her the ultimatum. It was Sean or them.

At eight months pregnant and with Sean holding her credit cards and her flat keys, what was she meant to say? Especially when her mum had turned against her, calling her selfish, saying she was trying to keep the baby from them, telling all the family how mean she was being. And they'd all believed her – her aunts and uncles, her cousins too.

By the time she'd gone into labour she hadn't seen or heard from another soul for four weeks, and even Patti had gone quiet, apart from the odd text begging her to chuck the father of her child out on his ear. They'd abandoned her and her baby when she needed them most.

How could she say any of that to Radia? And why should she explain it to Monty? She'd already told him far too much and it had burst their safe little bubble. This was why she hid. She couldn't trust anyone.

'Please just go,' she told him, her back turned, hiding her tears. She listened to the reluctant pause, his huffing sigh, followed by the slow retreat of his boots on the stairs, over the sounds of Radia wailing.

The shop bell rang out as he pulled open the door, and the latch clicked behind him, locking them alone inside again.

Chapter Twenty-three

The Borrow-A-Bookshop didn't open its doors again that day, or the next few days either. Even when holidaymakers crowded the steps and peered in the glass, forcing Joy to tape a sheet of brown wrapping paper over the front door to stop the intrusion. Even when Izaak came down the slope intending to ask if there was anything they needed, he'd found the place shut up. No amount of knocking or calling through the letter box was going to make Joy throw open the doors and sell books or serve up scones.

Instead, she sat unseen at the shop's laptop, working steadily away at the last of her tasks. Even though she'd packed most of her stuff, she wouldn't leave without fulfilling her contract, but that was all she was going to do.

What had she been thinking? Bookselling? Baking? Ridiculous! It had been far too public, too risky. And dating? Downing wine and kissing Monty? Going to parties and showing Radia off like she was public property? Like she was a part of this community?

She'd let herself slip. And yes, it had been fun. Seeing the same locals every day and having a routine that wasn't simply work, eat, home-educate, sleep, repeat. But it had been illusory.

The hard facts were they were only visiting for a fortnight and she had a job to do, with professional standards to maintain, and she'd totally thrown them out the window at the first glimpse of a handsome man who showed an interest in her after a few glasses of cheap vino.

She'd been sure to block Monty's number on her phone and delete his messages in the frantic, tearful hours that had followed their Monday morning fight. It didn't matter now though. After a few solitary days of intensive work, everything was completed, including Minty's wedding websites, and early too. She'd hoped to spoil Radia a bit, and enjoy some holiday time off, but there was no way they could venture out and about in Clove Lore now.

She'd done everything she could think of to help Radia settle again after she'd snapped at her, starting with a big apology.

She'd tried to tell her how her daddy hadn't been a very nice person and she had been cross with Monty because he hadn't understood that, and she'd accidentally shouted at Radia when she was actually only upset with him.

Radia had listened and, very magnanimously, told her mum, 'It's all right.' But she hadn't understood why Grandma wasn't meant to call the shop.

Joy had made them both some tea, thinking hard as the kettle boiled about how the worms were ever going to get back in the big opened can labelled 'family dysfunction'. She'd had to concede that keeping Radia in innocent ignorance just wasn't an option anymore.

'Rads, darling,' she'd began, sitting Radia at a café table safely behind the lacy curtains, unseen by passers-by. 'You know how we don't really see my mummy and daddy?'

Radia rolled her eyes. 'Obviously,' she'd said, like a snarky teenager, and Joy saw through her attitude right away. Radia was confused and hurting, thinking all the adults in her life very stupid indeed and just wanting it all to make sense.

'It's because they didn't like your daddy. They didn't like me having anything to do with him.'

Radia squinted. 'But we *don't* have anything to do with him.'

'Right. That's right. Only, they're still cross about him, and they're cross with me. And I don't really want them getting too involved with us now because…'

Radia waited, her big round eyes utterly uncomprehending. Joy wanted to cry but held her nerve.

'It's complicated. Grown-up stuff can be really complicated.'

'Are Grandma and Grandpa *not nice*?'

Joy hesitated. 'It's not that they're not nice. It's just they walked away when we needed them. When you were born.'

'Grandma phoned the shop,' Radia stated blankly. 'I wanted to say hello. She could come and visit us for a holiday.'

'God no!' It was out before Joy could censor herself. 'I mean, we're busy. I'm working.'

'They live in London?'

'Yes.'

'And we're going to be in London?'

'Yes, for a few days.' Her voice hitched as her throat constricted, but she wasn't going to cry in front of her child. The school place and the prospect of autumn at home in their little flat felt like it was slipping further from their reach. Joy was glad she'd not told Radia about any of it.

'We'll see them then,' Radia told her mum. 'We can go to their house.'

'Is that what you want?' Joy asked, already knowing the answer.

That was how mother and daughter had made up; with the distant promise of a meeting with Joy's parents.

She'd meant it too. Joy would never agree to something she didn't think she could deliver. She wasn't sure about going to her childhood home though. They could meet at the play park off Birdcage Walk. Radia would be fizzing with innocence and excitement and goodness knows how her mum would be. Fussing, maybe? Weepy? Cold towards Joy but sunshine with Radia? She couldn't anticipate how it would go.

Her dad would most likely stand there with a straight smile, not saying anything, holding the coffees, watching Radia play.

And how would they manage the hugging thing? Would her mum be expecting a big reunion scene? The thought of it made her queasy. All the suppressed feelings and resentment would be there, still unspoken, and they'd have to act normal for Radia's sake.

She pictured the silent painfulness of it all and Radia's excitement tinged with awareness that something wasn't quite right between the grown-ups. It would probably leave her with the impression that the adults in her family were generally silly and disappointing.

Maybe Patti could be convinced to join them? That would help. Her little sister would be a good buffer, acting cheerful, asking easy-to-answer questions and keeping their mum under control if she got too crazy.

She'd played the scene in her mind umpteen times, trying to imagine the best-case scenario, and always resorting to the worst possible one, where Radia was rejected again and how that would prompt a real break with all of them, leaving things irreparable forever.

Yet, Joy knew she had to meet her mother halfway. That's what adults did. And her mum had phoned, hadn't she? Her mum had left that voicemail saying she knew they were in England and she hoped they could put aside their differences and meet. Pamela Foley had been holding back but Joy had picked up on the tears and eagerness building in her voice. The fact she'd immediately tried the bookshop landline after leaving the message told her that her mum was desperate for real contact this time.

Joy had felt it too; the pull towards the familiar. It buzzed within her like a sick excitement. But at the same time there was a force just as strong repelling her, reminding her she'd been dropped like a stone by her own parents. How do you recover from that after nearly six years?

Joy drafted and redrafted her text message, and eventually had to settle on something short and efficient.

> Hi, you called the bookshop where I'm doing a tech refit? That was one of the volunteers you spoke to. We're leaving here soon. When we're next in London we'll meet you for a bit in the park, if you want? Radia would like that. J

When she read it back it sounded so cold, so withholding. She imagined how it would feel to get a message like that from Radia at some point in the future if it had all gone horribly wrong. The very idea stung wickedly. But *she'd* never abandon Rads. *She* wasn't going to hurt her daughter and let her down the way Pamela and Mike Foley had.

Still, when she was by herself in the silent shop, Joy couldn't escape the thought that in her desperation to keep Radia safe from all the hopelessly selfish adults in her life, she'd still messed her daughter up in her own unique way.

Was it inevitable? No matter how hard she tried to break the cycle? Was she on the path to having a ruined relationship with her daughter anyway? Were things spoiled already because years ago she'd prioritised Sean, because she'd been naive and young?

The nice things Monty had told her about how she'd given Radia a childhood anyone would envy had no impact now. She couldn't even remember them. Radia was suffering because of Joy's weakness; that was all she knew in this moment. Her daughter had missed out on a normal childhood and she would blame Joy for it, just like everyone else had, as soon as she was old enough to figure it all out.

The searing self-hatred that Sean had seeded within Joy grew and bloomed once more and she let it take hold like bindweed, choking out her sense of proportion, telling her this whole thing was her fault.

By the time she let the text message fly to her mum's mobile she was sobbing and cursing herself.

Now Joy's work was done and the fight with Radia was over, they cuddled on the big bed while the lightest summer drizzle fell over the village. They read and re-read picture books taken from the Children's section, which Joy would end up having to put money in the till for, and she'd kept her little girl close and told her she loved her over and over.

Radia only tutted in response and wiped kisses from her forehead, but she still read along, chattering about the characters, delighting in the illustrations.

They were going to get through this. They were going to get back inside their bubble and be OK, though Joy didn't know how. She knew one thing, though: they were leaving Clove Lore.

Chapter Twenty-four

On what Joy had decided was to be their last day in Clove Lore, Thursday, the last day of August, mother and daughter had woken up on the big bed surrounded by books. Radia had laughed so much the night before at *Oi Frog!*, her happiness had turned into a big torrent of emotion and tears. Joy wanted to put it down to tiredness but worried it was all because of the prospect of another airport and another hotel-concierge-arranged babysitter. She couldn't blame her for being confused and emotional; Joy felt exactly the same and hadn't the excuse of being five years old. She'd booked a cab. They were leaving for the airport hotel this afternoon, and flying off to Lisbon as planned on the second.

They'd hugged it out, read and slept, and now Radia was dozing in her mum's arms while Joy stared at the shimmering light cast over the duvet. It was a watery white that hinted at the changing season. Summer was coming to an end.

She tried hard not to think about September and what would happen when they called in at the flat after the Lisbon trip. All the London shops would have their Back to School stuff on display, from the stationers to the supermarkets. It would be impossible to avoid seeing it at this time of year. It would not be easy to face up to.

Her phone was out of reach by Radia's feet so she had to quell the impulse to message Gaz and tell him she'd take the job in... Durham, was it? Starting on the third, he'd said.

Early September in Durham sounded good. North enough to propel them away from London and to delay having to deal with her parents, at least.

Her mum hadn't rung again but she had texted back a heart emoji and the words, 'We can't wait to see you both!'

How could so much excitement be squeezed into one exclamation point? She had been able to feel her mum's anticipation radiating off the screen and it almost made her cry again. It had whipped up memories of when Joy lived at home.

She hadn't thought of it for years but it all came flooding back in. The pride they had in her before she let them down. She replayed the way her mum had been when she'd got her A-level results with all those A*s, when they knew for sure she'd got into Goldsmiths to study computer science.

Her mum had told everyone in the family, brought in a catering company and boxes of supermarket bubbly and they'd had a summer party in a gazebo in the garden with all the neighbours – who'd probably resented hearing about what a 'clever girl' the Foleys' daughter was for the hundredth time.

Nobody in her family had gone to uni before; they hadn't needed to. Her dad had taken over his father's car dealership and they'd been modestly 'minted', as he liked to call it, since the mid-nineties.

Remembering all of this set her on a path of remembering her mum at Christmastime in the kitchen in her Harrods apron and Dad beside her, fussing over the turkey. Her mum had been fizzing with festive excitement, waiting for the doorbell to ring and all the family descending. Pam Foley knew how to enjoy life. She loved family and big occasions. She loved her home and her girls.

It wasn't all happy memories, however. There was prickly stuff too, and Joy remembered that much more vividly than the cosy times.

There'd been that entire weekend house party at Pam's (faddy fitness-fanatic) brother's place for his fiftieth, when she wouldn't speak to anyone because Joy's uncle and his wife had the gall to suggest Pam shouldn't have brought her own stash of Kettle Chips and KitKats just because she didn't want to eat their special Keto diet.

It had come to a head when Pam shouted over the buffet table that celery sticks with peanut butter did *not* constitute a birthday meal, even when he pointed out crossly he'd done her a special plate of chicken and cheese fajitas because he *just knew* she'd be like this.

The whole thing had ended in rolled eyes and laughter once the wine was going around after the (rather restrictive) Sunday lunch the next day, when he'd admitted his rubbery green bell pepper 'sandwiches' filled with cucumber slices and cream cheese were no substitute for a nice roast with Yorkies.

There were shops in Pam's neighbourhood she couldn't set foot in because she'd taken exception to the way the teenager behind the till had spoken to her and she'd kicked off before discovering it was the owner's kid earning a bit of pocket money. But by then it was too late and she had '*said what she said*' (Pam's favourite saying) and flounced out.

One thing everyone knew about Pamela Foley was that she could hold a grudge. It was not a good quality to have and such a shame when there were some really nice qualities within her too: like her generosity and her confidence, or the way she'd throw her head back when she bellowed a laugh, as well as her fierce protectiveness that had made the bullies' parents on the school yard quail when she'd marched over to confront them about their child picking on her little Joy or Patti.

Joy's brain was hazily showing her highlights of her mum handing out her foil-wrapped breakfast rolls in the Gatwick departures lounge at three a.m. – proudly brought from home because she knew the Starbucks closed overnight – and telling Dad she had his favourite: egg, sausage and bacon. At times like that he would kiss his wife, grinning, calling her, 'my wonderful Pam'.

They'd been a normal suburban family with all the ups and downs, faults and feelings you'd expect to find, and all the love too. Joy could never have imagined as a kid she'd end up estranged from them by the time she hit her mid-twenties, but life was full of unexpected twists, it seemed.

Visions of the way things used to be still circulated in her brain while she came round that morning; her unconscious telling her it really was time to address this mess because the pain wasn't going away.

Joy would have lain there a lot longer, holding Radia and trying not to think about the packed suitcase by the bedroom door, if it hadn't been for the sound. A sharp metallic scratch on wood. Someone trying the keyhole?

Her eyes flicked wide open.

The noise came again, and then some banging, and muttering.

In an instant she rolled out of bed and shoved pillows against Radia to support her, tucking the duvet tightly over her, all done in complete silence.

Joy held her breath so that she could listen all the better for the sounds downstairs.

A shoulder thumped against the shop door. *Bang!* More muttering, angrier now.

This was it. Red alert. The moment she'd known was coming.

Tiptoeing, she snatched up her phone and dialled the emergency services, her thumb hovering over the green call button.

She couldn't see the door from the top of the spiral steps but crouching halfway down she clearly made out the shadow behind the brown paper. Tall, male, agitated.

The muttering had turned into louder grumbling. The shadow fumbled at the lock, trying a key then their shoulder alternately.

Each bump at the doorframe made her heart palpitate wildly, jumping in her chest like it knew these were her last moments.

Out of habit, her brain landed upon her mantra, but it didn't work.

Over and over as she made her way to the door, she heard it whisper, *Sean's here. He knows where we are. He wants us. It's over.*

'Joy?'

The sound of her name made her entire nervous system seize up, had her doubled over, dropping the phone, her hands pressing her knees for support, utterly winded. That voice…

'Joy? Are you in there?'

It wasn't Sean. It was a gravelly, piratey West Country accent. She gasped, standing straight once more, hauling breath into her lungs.

A scratch low against the doorframe told her Aldous was here too. A whine confirmed it. Joy hurried over the last few steps and unlatched the door.

'Good grief, lass. You're ill!' Jowan said, the second he saw her.

'No, no, I'm fine,' she tried to tell him, but it was no use. She couldn't control her breathing.

Jowan led her to an armchair. 'I'll get you a glass of water. Where's the little 'un? Is she sick too?'

All Joy could focus on was the wide-open door. 'Close it,' she told him. 'Close it, quick.'

Jowan did as instructed and Joy clamped her shaking hands over her mouth to keep the sobs in, as tears streamed down her face.

What followed was a long round of mutual apologising. Joy, embarrassed and weeping, couldn't stop saying sorry for hiding away the last few days, since the morning after Jude's hen party; for not letting Jowan know she'd fulfilled her contract and was ready to leave.

Jowan was full of remorse for getting flustered at the door. He hadn't understood the new electronic security system meant the old lock was now redundant.

He hadn't meant to terrify her and couldn't fully understand why she'd reacted like she had, and Joy didn't want to explain.

'I woke up groggy and disorientated, that's all,' she told him, shrugging it away, unconvincingly, and putting her specs back on over red eyes.

As they exchanged apologies, Aldous had determinedly hobbled up the spiral stairs and shoved his way into the bedroom to sniff out the sleeping Radia, who he woke by leaping onto her, his skinny tail whipping loudly against the bed.

They heard the delighted squeal from down in the bookshop and Jowan called his wayward Bedlington downstairs again. Radia followed, wide awake in the way only five-year-olds can be seconds after a long, stuffy sleep.

She greeted Jowan with a big hug which turned him all abashed and delighted.

'Radia Pearl, my favourite little pirate!' He pulled her up onto his knee.

Before, Joy would have felt strange about that kind of closeness but, she was surprised to find, so many of her old reservations were gone. She knew not everyone was a threat. Jowan was nothing but kindness.

Radia was examining the pearl-drop earring at his grizzly jaw, then, finding he wasn't complaining about that, she decided to grill him about the anchor tattoo on the back of his hand for the second time, asking the same questions she had at the shelving party.

'Didn't it hurt, the needles?' she wanted to know.

Jowan began explaining that it wasn't something he'd recommend for fun, and Joy slipped away.

'I'll make us some breakfast,' she said, but they were busy chatting.

–

By the time they were all eating jammy toast and draining their mugs, sitting by the shop's unlit fireplace surrounded by books, Joy had recovered herself enough to remember to ask Jowan if he'd had some special reason to come to the shop that morning.

'Ah, yes, I did. Let's see.' Jowan was on his feet and moving to the door where he'd abandoned a big rectangular parcel wrapped in white paper when he'd discovered Joy scared witless.

'Thought I'd bring this down, get it out the way before all the wedding's eve hoo-hah kicks off tomorrow. Do you want to unwrap it, Radia?' he asked.

Radia delightedly tore at the paper. 'Is it a present?'

'It's a present from me to Borrow-A-Bookshop,' he said, just as the little girl revealed a picture frame, the kind with lots of little spaces for photos.

'I jus' picked it up from the framer. Might look nice behind the counter.'

Radia took the cumbersome thing to her mum and all three tipped their heads over it. Ten framed colour pictures, mostly of beaming bookselling-holidaymakers that Joy didn't know, and in the bottom right corner was the photo from the shelving party.

Joy tried not to look at it, but for a second all she could see was Monty and the easy way he stood with his hands shoved into his pockets. He looked gentle and uncomplicated and happy. The image took her right back to how he'd appeared the first time she saw him on the harbour wall, when he'd helped them with the crabbing rod and she'd had the protection of The Joy and Radia Bubble of isolation. Things had been simpler then, though not necessarily happier.

No matter how she tried to resist, her eyes dragged themselves back to him. Just by looking at it she could feel the softness of that shirt, and the softness of his brown eyes and brown curls. How could so much softness hurt like this?

She was glad when Jowan pointed to the image in the centre of the frame, all washed-out colours and blurred the way only old film could be. It was of a couple in their forties, standing on the steps of the bookshop, grinning at the camera.

'That's my Isolda,' said Jowan.

The woman wore an ankle-length dress in flowy florals, her long hair whipping up in the breeze. Jowan beside her was in a sky-blue suit and brown paisley tie that definitely didn't match. It was plain for anyone to see, even after all this time and in a faded photograph, that the couple had been made for one another.

'She's beautiful,' Joy told him.

He only smiled.

'What are those?' Radia asked, pointing at the blurry objects hanging from Isolda's hands. Jowan peered closer.

''orse shoes, maybe a chimney sweep or two.'

'Huh?' Radia was no more enlightened.

'Wedding gifts. For luck? We were just about to leave for our honeymoon.'

'You got married here?' Joy looked around the shop as if the echoes of a wedding party could still be detected.

'We did. Didn't bother with a vicar or paperwork, mind. Just us saying we'd love each other for good, and all our friends tipsy on homemade wine.'

Jowan sniffed away a wistful laugh and told her that back then they'd been considered the village's 'resident hippies'.

He shrugged and smiled, marvelling at his old life, as though Isolda had been a beautiful dream of twenty years' duration, magical and unreal.

'We stood in that doorway there and made our vows, and after that, well, I'm not sure anyone remembers. T'was quite a party.'

'And what's that?' Radia had already moved on to another picture. A dismal scene. The shop in disarray, the floor hidden under sludge.

'That? Well, that was the best day of my life. *Joint* best day.'

Even Joy was surprised. 'The shop flooding?'

''Bout an hour later, I was engaged to my Mint.'

'Ah, right. Makes sense,' Joy said, and somehow she couldn't lift her eyes from the pictures in their mounts again.

'Who are all those children?' Radia wanted to know, pointing at the image of a small circle of kids, or rather the backs of their heads as they sat on the floor by the fire where they were huddled now. There was a woman in the armchair holding open a picture book and pointing at something on the spread pages.

'That was Annika,' Jowan explained. 'She did a daily story time for the kids during her fortnight here a few years back. Nice thing to do during the holidays.'

'They're all children on their holidays?' Radia said to herself more than to Jowan.

'And some are locals. That tiny one is the eldest Burntisland boy,' Jowan said, pointing, 'and that's the two eldest of Mrs C.'s grandkids, those ones there, in yellow, see?'

'Story time at the bookshop,' whispered Radia as though incanting a magic spell. Then she fell silent, peering all the harder at the little group.

Joy knew what her daughter would be thinking, no, *fantasising*. The look in her eyes showed it all. How much she longed for friends and fun activities like this. Maybe she could sign Radia up for some weekend clubs in whichever cities they'd be in next? She hadn't learned much for certain in Clove Lore but she now knew she could allow Radia a little more freedom to mix with other people and the world wouldn't come to an end because of it.

'And that's Jude and Elliot, of course,' guided Jowan, pointing at another image showing the pair standing behind the counter on a summer's day.

Elliot was stooping to get inside the frame beside Jude, who only reached up to his shoulder. Jude was beaming straight down the lens while Elliot looked directly at her. They were a cute, mismatched couple, but squashed together in the image with absolutely zero space between their bodies, they looked just as joined at the hip and dopily in love as Isolda and Jowan did in their wedding picture.

'And that's Alex an' Magnús,' said Jowan, directing their gaze to another image. 'They brought this place back to life after the flood.'

This couple – him all shaven-headed and bearded, her with a huge grin and cascades of long, almost white, blonde hair – were wearing matching Scandi jumpers and standing in front of a window display of books hanging artfully by their spines on clear threads as if floating behind the glass.

'She looks like a mermaid,' decided Radia. 'But that's not taken here?' she added, quite correctly.

'That's their very own bookshop in Reykjavík,' Jowan told them. 'First bookshop you can borrow in the whole of Iceland. Doin' well, it is.' This provoked a welling of misty tears and a big gulp in Jowan, which surprised Joy. He was proud of them, like they were his own kids.

'They fell in love here an' took the things they'd learned out into the world.' He kept his eyes on the picture. ''Tis a romantic place, the Borrow-A-Bookshop.'

Joy's eyes flicked to Jowan's in alarm.

He knew, of course. They must all know, about her and Monty and the brief fling that had stolen all her common sense. It was clear from his expression there was something he wanted to say.

'Radia?' Joy said hurriedly. 'Can you go get your back-pack filled up? And I'll need the passports out of the drawer in your room, please. Taxi's coming after lunch.'

'But Mum!' Radia complained.

Jowan helped by lowering the picture frame out of view, leaning it against his armchair, signalling the fun was over.

'And you can choose any books you'd like to take with us,' Joy added. 'Start with the pile by the big bed, OK? *Oi Frog!*'s a keeper, right?'

This was enough to get Radia moving, and she disappeared up the stairs calling Aldous, who bounded along in her wake.

'Last morning, then, eh?' said Jowan, picking up Charley fox from the floor where Radia had dropped him.

Joy began clearing their empty breakfast dishes. Jowan sprang up too and followed her through to the café kitchen.

Not wanting him to prod and probe, Joy reached for business talk instead. 'You should have mentioned those pictures before. I could have scanned them and put them on the website.'

'It's not too late, you know?' he said in a discon-certing way that told Joy he wasn't referring to copying the images.

Her voice was pitchy when she said, 'I've a photo scanning app on my phone, I could quickly—'

'He's been very quiet, you know?' Jowan interrupted, his tone all urgent caution.

'Who has?' said Joy, mortified, focusing on rinsing the cups in the sink.

Jowan lifted a tea towel like this was his own kitchen, which, she supposed, it was. 'He's a good fellow, maybe not the boldest, or even the best at knowing his feelings, but he's good where it counts.'

Joy listened, knowing it was all true.

'I can't ask anything else of you, I know that,' Jowan went on gently. 'And I don't know the details of what happened, he's been as quiet as a clam, but… please say goodbye, before you go. I've never seen him so pale. Like seasickness, it is.'

'I'll take that,' she cut in, lifting the towel from his hands, drying the plates and stacking them neatly in the cupboard above the sink.

Jowan watched her as she worked. 'Regret can eat a man from the inside out,' he said softly. 'So can longing.'

She wiped the crumbs from the countertop and rinsed out the sink, the water gurgling down the plughole.

'There, spotless,' she said, and they both looked around the kitchen. 'Ready for the new booksellers.' The words weren't easy to hear once they were out. She knew she was at risk of crying again.

'Jus' say goodbye. Let him know it's all right. Please?'

She couldn't help dropping her head as the tears came.

'Ah, come here, little one.'

Jowan held open his arms to her and she stepped inside so he could rock her like a dad would, shushing her like a child.

'All will be well,' he soothed. 'Jus' don't leave here with regrets, is all. Leave here happy, knowing nothing was missed, no opportunity to do as your heart wants. You deserve that, at least.'

Joy let herself be held, gripping his jumper and feeling small. She didn't deserve a thing, she told herself.

Selfishness and fearfulness had spoiled her for everyone she encountered. The idea of Monty suffering now, and not understanding what was going on because *he* wasn't damaged in the ways she was, caused her chest to burn with shame and sadness.

'I'll tell him we're leaving,' she told Jowan, wiping her hand across her nose but not letting him go.

She'd tell him too that none of this was his fault and that there wasn't a thing to feel seasick about, and then she'd drag her cowardly heart and her little girl out of here, leaving Monty in peace.

Chapter Twenty-five

If she was going to do it, it had to be now. Leaving Radia with Jowan, promising she'd be half an hour at the absolute most, Joy made her way Down-along.

The morning's drizzle had left the cobbles slippery and she had to grip gateposts and fences as she went down the slope. It struck her as she struggled downhill that this was the first time she'd been out all by herself in the fresh air on a damp, sunny day in years. Since before Radia was born, probably.

Time alone when not working wasn't a luxury she could afford guilt-free these days. On her corporate gigs, when Radia was left with a childminder, Joy would work flat-out all day, cutting short lunch breaks and drinking coffee on the go so she could get back to her daughter all the faster. There was never time to take in what passed for 'scenery' in whatever anonymous grey office block or corporate shiny glass box she was working in that day.

But today, in Clove Lore, exhausted from crying and self-recrimination, and knowing this was her last chance, she slowed her pace and allowed herself to look around.

Watery grey clouds still clung to the far horizon but the rain was gone for the day, replaced by a wonderfully heavy blue sky. There was warmth in the sun. The kind that reminds you that summer is clinging on tenaciously until the first of the leaves fall.

Gulls sailed overhead and a few of them swooped down to settle on the cottage chimneypots, fixing their beady eyes on her in case she had a picnic, which she kind of wished she had.

Or at least a coffee to sip, some warmth and comfort would definitely help, but the idea of encountering Mrs Crocombe chattering in front of the espresso machine in her Ice Cream Cottage put her right off that idea.

Each little garden she passed had the look of newly established planting. She supposed the floodwater had ripped out most of the old stuff as it charged down the slope.

One or two straggly palm trees that had survived the deluge leaned out over freshly painted fences, lending the quaint Devonshire scene a touch of the tropics. She stopped for a second in front of a cottage near the bottom of the slope where the path widened out onto the harbour wall and lifeboat launch.

There was a homemade 'For Sale' sign outside it that she hadn't noticed before, and below the rather eye-watering asking price was a mobile number and the name 'Jowan de Marisco Clove-Congreve'.

This must be Jowan's old place. He did say he was selling it now that he'd moved in with Minty at the Big House.

On either side of the stepping-stone path leading to the cottage's white front door were frothy clouds of late-summer bedding in full bloom: a sea of feathery pink achillea like the ones in her mum and dad's garden; low clusters of tiny purple flowers she couldn't name; silvery spikes of thistle-like sea hollies and, bobbing over the beds, great tall spheres of brilliant blue agapanthus like exploding fireworks.

The low buzz of the garden's hoverflies and bees hummed in harmony with the rhythmic shushing sound of the tide going out.

The lacy-curtained cottage windows stared back and Joy shook herself, packing away the daydream threatening to form in her brain of dragging a suitcase behind them for the last ever time and leading Radia up the path of a cosy cottage just like that, letting themselves in. Lucky Jowan, having lived in such a lovely place.

She moved on, but slower now because she wanted to delay seeing Monty and because she wanted to savour it too, the curious feeling of knowing she was making her way towards him. He was down there somewhere in the Siren. It was perversely exciting, knowing that he was nearby and she could look at him once again. Not a prospect that would be open to her ever again, so she took it easy, passing down the curving slope and onto the seawall where the warm breeze lifted her hair. Boats clanked at their moorings in the harbour as the outgoing tide dropped them down onto sandy beds.

Tourists bustled around, carrying drinks from the bar down onto the dry greyish sand at the top of the beach where laid-out towels and windbreaks made a patchwork of rainbow colours. Kids in wetsuits paddled in the shallows and scrambled around the rock pools further along the curving bay.

And there it was, in front of the sleek white lines of the imposing yacht *Lucky Boy*: the trusty *Peter's Bounty*, the Bickleigh brothers' boat, moored to the stone steps of the seawall, a sturdy little tub of a thing. She smiled to see it, but then, unable to ignore why she was coming down here, her face fell once more.

She was almost at the propped-open doors of the Siren when she spotted the figure alone on the beach, sitting hunched on a rock, his back towards her and his head down. Definitely Monty, and not his twin Tom. She'd be able to tell them apart at any distance now. Now that she understood Monty's Montyness. Kind, straightforward, warm Monty – his whole bearing showed it, even now when he seemed so forlorn.

Doubling back along the wall to the short concrete causeway that led to the sand, she kept her eyes on him.

Jowan was right; he looked seasick and terribly pale. She watched him reaching into his shirt pocket and pulling free a cigarette packet, going as far as shaking one loose before looking hard at the thing, heaving a sigh, and crumpling it in his hands.

That's when he saw her.

'Joy!' He sprung to his feet, shoving the crushed packet into his back pocket with some difficulty. 'You're still here?'

'Yeah,' she said, smiling weakly.

He watched her wordlessly, utterly still, his hands by his sides, as though he was afraid of spooking her again.

'I, um, I came to say goodbye.'

'Right.'

'So, uh, thank you.'

His head tipped a little. He obviously hadn't expected gratitude. 'For what?'

'For the shelving party, and the stag do, and for picking me and Rads up from the hen do, and… for everything… generally.'

He swallowed. 'Right. Well, you're welcome.'

An incongruously happy party of kids and grandparents passed noisily by, heading out along the shoreline.

One of the kids kicked water at a sibling and the spray glistened in rainbow colours that were gone again so quickly only Joy noticed.

'I should probably…' Joy hiked a thumb behind her in the direction of Up-along.

Monty shifted his feet, his wide eyes turning pained.

'So…' She backed away, nodding in acceptance, and smiling with her lips hidden entirely. 'Bye then?'

'Wait!' he said, trying to keep his voice soft.

She froze, not knowing what else to do.

'Is, um, is Radia OK? I didn't mean to cause a scene the other morning. She was upset.'

'She's fine.'

'I really am sorry I messed things up.'

Joy's eyes fell to Monty's shadow across the sand.

'I don't mind hurting,' he added, 'but it's not right that she should. Just because I didn't listen well enough and respect your… family situation.'

His shadow clasped its hands together then advanced a step closer.

'No, no,' Joy protested, meeting his eyes now. 'It wasn't you at all. *I'm* sorry. I was the one getting involved with some guy when I was supposed to be working—'

'Right,' Monty interrupted, visibly wounded.

'No, not some guy, I didn't mean just *some guy*. I mean…'

'It doesn't matter,' he waved her words away, then shoved his hands into his pockets with a quick shrug. 'So, you're off then?'

She nodded. This did not feel good. Her eyes briefly lifted to where his curls shifted in the breeze. It was easier if she didn't look directly at him.

'I hope things will be OK with your mum and dad, and that my answering the phone the other day doesn't make things hard for you.' He spoke decidedly, and his feet moved, advancing, she thought, towards her, but then he passed straight by her instead. 'You deserve a happy family life,' he said as he left.

Her brain screamed at her to grab his wrist as he passed by, telling her to stop him by any means necessary, rugby tackle him if she had to, just hold him there until she could make sense of the feelings crowding in on her.

Yet the old familiar fearfulness had already won out and frozen her up like a statue, and she let him walk away.

She was dimly aware that he'd be up on the sea wall already, grains of sand crunching under his boots. Maybe he was looking over at her? More likely he was looking down at the ground as he went. Any second now he'd be shoving through the pub doors, almost out of view for good. She pictured the kitchen doors swinging, him grabbing his chef's jacket, buttoning himself in, disappearing, disappearing, gone.

She'd have stood there, just another rock on the beach, for who knows how long, had it not been for the footsteps behind her, slow at first, cautious, and then faster, and she heard her name called out. She whipped around to see a woman dashing towards her, smiling and waving, getting faster.

'Joy?'

To Joy's overstimulated brain the woman, a slightly younger mirror-image of herself – though her dark hair was shorn short and her clothes were a thousand times cooler – appeared like a mirage.

'Joy, babe? What's wrong?' she called out, as she pounded down onto the sand, her smile fading, turning to deep concern. 'Where's Rads? What's happened?' the woman asked.

All Joy could do was fall into her little sister's arms and grip her tight. 'Patti?' She didn't ask why she was here. She didn't need to. There was an intervention going on, that much was obvious.

Their tears fell, and Patti held on to her big sister as they folded down onto the sand.

'Oh, Patti, I've made a mess of everything,' Joy sniffed. 'Things can't get any worse than this.'

'No, don't say that,' Pattie cajoled, rubbing her sister's back in big comforting circles. 'Mum's not even *got* here yet.'

This took a second to register before Joy fixed Patti with a blinkless stare.

'Mum's not *what*?'

Chapter Twenty-six

'OK, pick one. I've got veggie sushi, cheese ploughman sarnies, or this sort of noodle slaw thingy with edamame beans?'

Patti had dragged Joy up off the sand and they'd flopped down against the locked shutters of the old lifeboat launch above the beach. She was unpacking her canvas tote bag onto the concrete.

'You stopped at a motorway M&S?' asked Joy, still dazed at her sister's appearance.

''Course I did, it was a five-hour drive, and I also hit every Starbucks I passed on the way here. I'm ninety per cent matcha green tea latte now.'

'Got any Percy Pigs?'

'Obviously.' Patti reached into the bottom of the bag and revealed two pink packs, passing one to Joy. 'So, do you want to tell me why you were staring out to sea all alone on a sunny day, no sign of Rads…'

Joy tore the bag open and bit into a pink gummy pig. 'Rads has a sitter for half an hour. I need to get back there in about…' she paused to calculate, 'about twelve seconds. How about *you* tell me what you're doing here? And what's this about Mum coming?'

'Couldn't talk her out of it, once she knew where you were. You know what she's like. Once she gets a bee under her blanket she's unstoppable.' Patti shoved an *uramaki* roll into her mouth with her fingers.

'But we're leaving today,' Joy contemplated. 'Where even is she?'

'Last seen circling Southampton shouting at her satnav,' Patti laughed through the mouthful of sushi.

'Mum's driving? Alone?'

'No.' Patti swallowed her food down, shaking her head. 'Dad's with her, only he's just had the laser-eye thingy, and…'

'He's had eye surgery? When?'

'Last week, just after they got back from Portugal.'

'You didn't tell me?'

'Uh, I didn't think I had to. It wasn't a big thing. And he's fine to drive now, only Mum won't let him. He's been wearing shades everywhere since the op.'

'Not the aviators?'

'Yep. He's gone full *Top Gun*.'

'Jeez!'

'I know!'

'It's bonnet by the way.' Joy delved into the bag and disappeared another Percy Pig.

'What is?'

'Bee in your bonnet?'

Patti shrugged this off. 'Yeah, but what are the chances of that happening, you know? Blanket seems more real-istic.'

Joy rolled her eyes. 'What do Mum and Dad even want? Coming here? It's… it's…'

Patti shrugged. 'They want to see you and Rads, I suppose.'

'But they could see us any time.'

Patti shot her with a stare that said *Really?*

235

'OK, maybe not, but I don't understand the rush? Why now? When they couldn't forgive me before. They've just changed? After all these years?'

Patti shifted round, still cross-legged, so she faced her sister, setting down the sushi container and sending Joy into panic.

'Oh no, what? There's something wrong with Mum. Is she ill?'

'No, god no, she's fine. It's not that. It's…' Patti took a deep breath. 'I've been trying to talk to you about it for ages, but we kept missing each other, and it's not something I could leave in a voice message or show you in a text or anything.'

'You're scaring me, Pats. Just tell me.'

She reached behind her for her backpack, the kind you'd take hiking up a mountain of a weekend, exactly the sort of thing Patti might be doing now if she wasn't wild-goose-chasing her sister to Devon. She unzipped the bag. 'Promise you'll take a few breaths, OK?' She slowly drew out a folded *Evening Standard*, a bit dog-eared, definitely weeks old.

'What's this?' Joy unfolded the newspaper.

'Page two,' urged Patti, her eyes fixed on Joy with caution, clearly afraid of how she'd react to whatever this was. 'It's good news, honestly, only I didn't know how to tell you.'

Joy scanned the columns, not understanding. 'This is all a bit weird isn't it, Pa—' She paused. Her mouth fell open.

There he was in black and white, cuffed and being led into a van by two burly court officers. Joy read the headline aloud. 'Six-year sentence for serial girlfriend swindler, Sean Jackson.'

Joy's eyes flicked to Patti's, who looked back gravely, then back to the story. She read at speed under her breath.

'A man who got off with a twenty-four-month suspended sentence and two hundred hours' community service five years ago for the crimes of coercive control and bank fraud has today been sentenced to six years' jail time after being found guilty of, amongst other crimes, forging a girlfriend's signature multiple times to take out high-interest "pay day" loans she knew nothing about.'

Joy let the paper fold in her lap. 'Five years ago? So when he disappeared after Radia was born, he was probably in court?'

'Yep, I guess, and about to do a serious stretch of litter picking.'

Joy scoffed and shook her head. 'And there was me wondering where the hell he'd disappeared to.'

'You had no idea the police were after him back then?'

'None. None at all. When I was in the maternity ward waiting for him to come and get us and he never showed, I was frantic. My calls were going straight to his voicemail. I got the registrar to ring around all the hospitals thinking he'd had an accident. I even called his mum's place.'

Even when the universe had presented her with the opportunity to get away from him and start a new life with her baby, Joy had been worried for Sean, thinking he'd been hurt or killed. She hadn't just been ringing round looking for confirmation that he definitely wasn't coming back – confirmation that she never got anyway. The sickness that he'd cruelly seeded at her core had still felt loyal to him then, still felt horribly like affection, even when it was mixed in with all the resentment and fear and hate.

She could see herself standing there with her bags, postpartum, staring wide-eyed at her miraculous little Radia Pearl, holding her phone to her ear, torn apart, not knowing what to do. If he had turned up, she'd have gone back to her flat with him and then who knows what their fate would have been? She shuddered at the thought of how her life might have turned out, might have ended, had Sean not been arrested.

Patti was repeating a question next to her. Her voice made its way through the fog of horrible memories to reach her.

'Did he rip off your signature, like he did that woman's?'

Joy shook away the visions and cleared her throat before she spoke. 'I don't think so, but…' she swallowed. 'He had my bank cards.'

'No? That arsehole!'

'And my pin numbers. I gave them to him. Who's the arsehole now?'

'Still him.'

Joy pushed her glasses back onto the bridge of her nose and looked back at the paper. 'He didn't clear us out or anything. Didn't take out any loans.'

'Didn't have time to,' Patti said, knowingly. 'You had a lucky escape. He was nicked before he could do any real damage.' In the silence that followed Patti seemed to reconsider her words. 'Well, you know what I mean.'

Joy smiled thinly and read on.

'Sean Jackson, 45, of no fixed address – variously known by the assumed names of Sean Tilley, Jon Jackson and Sean Sampson – has a history of swindling women out of their savings and running up huge debts in their names through the practice of coercive control.

'Jackson was convicted at Westminster Magistrates Court on Friday on three accounts of fraud by false representation and two accounts of controlling and coercive behaviour as defined in Section 76 of the Serious Crime Act, 2015, as well as absconding to avoid arrest. He is sentenced to seventy-two months in jail. His arrest followed a police report filed by Ms Annabelle Chapman, 32, of Clerkenwell, earlier this year.

'Chapman, who testified via video link, said life with Jackson had become intolerable: "It was like a fairy tale at first, all flowers and champagne. We got engaged on a weekend trip to Paris a few weeks after we met and once the ring was on my finger he suddenly flipped. He wanted me to stop work, expected me to stay home. He took my house keys and my mobile and he had my whole family turned against me. When I stood up to him, he'd turn nasty, calling me ungrateful for all the things he did for me. He'd rant and rave, saying I'd upset him on purpose. It was always somehow my fault. I thought I was going crazy. That's what he's like. He convinces you you're in the wrong, and by then you've no one to turn to for help because he's scared all your loved ones away."'

Joy could feel Patti's eyes upon her, brimming with tears and sympathy.

'That's what he did to you, wasn't it?' she asked.

Joy only nodded. This was the first time a family member was acknowledging how it had all unfolded, how Joy had come to be cut off. She couldn't face looking at her little sister, so she read on.

'Senior District Judge Benjamin praised Ms Chapman's bravery in making the police report that brought Jackson to justice. During the investigation, two other women were revealed to have been subjected to his coercive control and it is believed there will be more who have yet to come forward.

'Detective Sergeant Alain Cho, from the City of London Police Fraud Enforcement Department, said: "Whilst looking into Ms Chapman's allegations of coercive behaviour, we discovered that Sean Jackson had been up to his old fraudulent tricks once again. His modus operandi remained the same: targeting young, single women, isolating them from family and friends, and taking control of their finances, homes and in one instance, obtaining multiple sports cars over a period of weeks from a girlfriend's central London supercar rental business."'

'Hah!' Joy laughed, wry and bitter. 'Well, that explains why he had a different car every week then. He had the supercar woman and me on the go at the same time, and when I was pregnant too.'

Patti grew animated, running through the most vivid expletives in her vocabulary, aiming them all at Sean. Behind the spite in her voice there was a tremor of emotion. Joy spoke over her, wanting to get to the end of the newspaper report.

'D.S. Cho added, "Clearly Jackson's previous sentence wasn't enough to deter him, but this second conviction will reinforce the message that coercive control of domestic partners is a serious crime in itself and won't be tolerated."

'When under examination in court, Jackson answered "no comment" to all questions. The convict, said to be temporarily residing at his mother's home in Croydon at the time of his court appearance, began his sentence on Friday. He was also ordered to pay £18,000 in damages as well as court costs and surcharges.'

Joy folded the paper again and handed it back to Patti. That was not a souvenir of her trip to Clove Lore that she wanted to keep.

'I will have that sandwich actually,' Joy said, and Patti hurriedly tore away the wrapping.

'Here you are.'

They ate for a moment in silence, Joy looking out over the harbour to the blue horizon and Patti sneaking sidelong glances at her sister, clearly not believing she could be this OK after the bombshell.

Finally, Joy spoke. 'It's over then. He's actually ended up in prison.' Her voice hitched and tears threatened but Joy wouldn't let them fall. She took another voracious bite of sandwich and chewed thoughtfully.

Patti attempted to draw her out. 'He's not coming back from this. There'll be more women too, I bet, more days in court. He could go down for decades if they add up multiple sentences.'

'I don't think I can do that,' Joy said hurriedly. 'Testify.'

'Nobody says you have to. Not if you can't bear it. You never have to see him again. You don't even have to think about him. It's over.'

Now Joy felt the heave in her chest as a sob made its way out. Again she refused to give in. *It's over*, she told herself. She turned to smile through eyes shining with tears at Patti, wanting to reassure her she wasn't broken.

'You must have been so afraid,' said Patti. 'And we were all just… useless.'

'You were a kid, Patti.'

'I was twenty-two, well old enough to come storming through your flat door and kick him in the balls! But I didn't do anything.'

'You did. You were the one running intel on Mum, keeping me in the loop.'

'Yeah, telling you how pissed off she was. Hardly helping, was it?'

'I needed to know, and you were great at texting me, checking in.'

'Until I stopped.' Patti's eyes were deep round pools of sorrow now. She looked just like Radia and the sight made Joy's heart swell.

'You were the one who started texting again when Rads was tiny. You reached out. Anyway, you had no idea what was going on with Sean. Nobody did. I pushed you away.'

'He *told* you to push us.'

'Well, yeah, subtly, he did. But I agreed to it all, didn't I?'

'You didn't *want* to though.'

'You don't understand. At the time, I thought I did. He'd say you were all busybodies and you were trying to poison me against him, and some days it really did look like that.'

'I get it now. I didn't understand at the time, not really. I just thought you'd taken up with a shitbag bloke. I didn't think it was like, literally pathological. That he was…' Patti stopped herself.

Joy faced her sister and finished the sentence for her. 'Abusive?'

Patti looked down at her abandoned food. 'Did he hurt you?' she asked in a small voice.

'No. Never.' Joy put a hand to her sister's arm. 'I thought maybe he might, but he never did. He shouted, a lot, right in my face, threatened me sometimes, but…' Her voice trailed off. She didn't want to say, 'but that was all it was'. Because that had been bad enough, she realised. The shouting, the gaslighting, the million micro-aggressions that had left her head spinning, not knowing who she was anymore. It *had* been abuse, even when he'd never hit her.

Joy squeezed Patti's arm. This was more than Joy had ever confessed and it felt like a buried chest of secrets being unlocked within her.

'He really is gone,' Joy said, as much for her own sake as for Patti's. 'And he really doesn't know where we are. And he doesn't want us at all. He's probably got loads of daughters and sons all over south-west London. And all those women? He doesn't want any of us. It really is actually over.'

Patti was on her knees in an instant and putting her arms around her sister. Joy wrapped her up in a hug that swiped the breath from both of them.

Patti spoke into Joy's hair. 'Are we going to be all right, Joy? You and me?'

''Course we are,' Joy said, putting her down again with a tearful sniff, but she was smiling too.

'Joyce and Patience,' said Patti, barely a whisper.

'Team Foley,' replied Joy.

They smiled at each other in silence for a beat in which the sisters' entire worlds became righted again, having been spinning wildly out of their orbits for five whole years.

'Can I see Tiny now, before you guys have to leave?' Patti asked tentatively. 'Where is this childminder anyway?'

'Oh my god, Jowan!' Joy cried. 'He's got a wedding to help with. Minty's going to be mad as hell!'

The pair stumbled up onto their feet, brushing away crumbs and sand.

'Jowan? A wedding? *Minty?*' Patti was incredulous. 'What kind of a name's Minty?'

'A posh one?' Joy suggested.

'You really have got yourself involved in the community here, haven't you?'

They walked together up the slope, Joy holding up the ploughman's sandwich so they could both share the last bites and Patti could cling to her sister's arm with both hands.

'Where are we going?' Patti asked, as they passed Jowan's old cottage.

'Up!' said Joy. 'Didn't you come down the slope to get to the beach?'

'No, I parked behind the pub. I had no idea you were basically clinging to a seventy-degree incline in this place. How do the locals get anything delivered round here? Is it flown in by drones?'

'If you really want to know…' Joy gestured at the tourist signpost up ahead with its multiple pointy arms directing visitors to all the attractions: the waterfall, the beach, the visitor centre, the Siren's Tail.

'Does that say "To the Donkeys?"' Patti snorted a laugh, stopping dead for a moment to gaze in amused judgement.

'Yep,' Joy replied matter-of-factly. 'It's pedestrians only. The donkeys cart stuff up and down the slope, apparently. I haven't seen them though. Basically, it's donkeys, sleds, or *carry it yourself and risk falling down the slope and into the sea* around here.'

Patti hauled on up the hill, still not letting go of her sister.

'It's the way things are in Clove Lore,' Joy shrugged. 'It's got its own… unique charm?'

'It's beautiful, I'll give it that,' conceded Patti. 'Some might say it's romantic. *Hmm?*' She faced Joy in exaggerated inquisition, her eyes shining wickedly.

'Don't be daft.' Joy shook Patti's arm in playful warning. 'There's nothing like that going on here.'

As they passed the Ice Cream Cottage, Captain James da Costa strode out in his black tie, crisp white shirt and white trousers like he was fresh from the wheelhouse of a billion-dollar cruise ship. He turned Down-along, clawing back his sleek white hair at the sight of the sisters and slipping on dark shades. 'Good morning, ladies, beautiful day for it!' he said with a winning smile.

Joy only nodded to him, but Patti was grinning in unconcealed glee.

'Who was *that*?' she whispered once he'd passed by.

'Just one of the many, *many* potential candidates for a red-hot summer romance that this place is crawling with. Sadly, he's sleeping with the old lady who runs the ice-cream shop.'

'Bad luck,' Patti consoled.

'*Such* bad luck.'

'And was he at one of the parties you've attended recently?' Patti's tone made it clear what she was getting at, but Joy only replied primly that she didn't know *what* her sister could mean.

Even through the laughter and teasing, Joy couldn't help thinking of Monty down on the beach that morning. He'd looked so decided, so stern and cold, and here was Patti genuinely believing there must be some dreamy holiday romance going on.

Patti knew well enough not to pry any further and Joy wasn't going to say anymore.

245

'Have you got an ETA on Mum, yet?' Joy asked, by way of changing the subject quickly.

Patti cocked her head as though listening to the air around them. 'She's not in the vicinity yet, but believe me, we'll hear her before we see her.'

'I don't want a big scene, Pats,' Joy cringed, as they turned to the left and off the slope, heading into the shade between the cottages that led into the bookshop's square.

Patti rubbed Joy's arm, diplomatically not saying anything but very much suggesting that a big Pamela Foley-centred scene would be unavoidable.

'Ugh! It's going to be awful, isn't it!' cried Joy, dramatically, but deep down there was something new taking hold of her, something other than the worry, dread and shame she'd felt when dealing with her mum these last few years. There was a tiny, glowing scrap of hope. Her little sister, and that newspaper report, and all the police officers and lawyers and judges who'd listened to Sean's incredibly brave victims and crucially, *believed* them had done it. Everything felt different now because of them.

With Patti on her arm, Joy led the way up the stone steps and in through the open door of the Borrow-A-Bookshop, where the scene before the sisters drew them to an abrupt and silent halt on the doormat.

Chapter Twenty-seven

Radia had been reading, very loud and very slow, perched on the edge of the armchair. 'And that is really the end.' She closed her copy of *The Borrowers* in triumph and looked at the little circle gathered around her on the floor.

Jowan, reclined awkwardly on a beanbag beside her, led the applause.

Two blond boys Joy didn't recognise clapped and grinned, and Aldous, who was for some reason wearing a little T-shirt, barked happily and turned in circles. The rest of the story-time crowd was made up of Charley fox – who was propped up by a pile of books – and a large blue teddy wearing round plastic trainers on its paws, which must have belonged to one of the boys.

Jowan tried to stand when he spotted Joy at the door but was thoroughly stuck in the beanbag. Joy strode inside and helped pull him up, apologising for being away for so long.

'Mum! We're having story time!' Radia announced delightedly. 'And these are my friends!'

'These are Mrs Crocombe's grandsons, the two youngest ones anyway,' Jowan informed her, now he was safely on his feet.

'Oh?' Joy said, looking around the shop.

'My fault, sorry,' Jowan pressed on. 'Once I'd mentioned Annika's story time at the shop there was no putting Radia off the idea, and Mrs C. just happened to call in with the boys. Radia pressed them into stayin' for a story.'

'I finished my book, Mum!'

'Well done, Rads!'

'I give it ten out of ten!' she said grinning.

Joy was about to suggest Radia take the Crocombe boys through to the kitchen to look for some squash and a snack but Patti, who'd hung back on the doorstep, joined her sister now, watching Radia with eyes full of feeling.

'Is that…' Radia started. 'Auntie Patti? It is! It is!'

Both of the Crocombe boys and Aldous jumped at the scream that followed as Radia launched herself into Patti's arms.

Jowan suggested he deliver the boys back round to their grandmother's for lunch. 'If I don't see you before you leave, Joyce Foley,' he began, in a low voice. 'It has been our pleasure havin' you here. You are the best digital nomad we've ever had. You've done more than you could know for our little bookshop and for our community.'

Joy didn't think she'd done anything at all for the community but didn't like to say so, so she smiled and thanked him.

'Come back, please, anytime,' he said, and the straight-lipped smile beneath his beard made the whiskers on his chin bristle out.

Joy was saved from having to answer him by the commotion of the youngest Crocombe boy attempting to wrestle Aldous out of the T-shirt so he could get it back onto his teddy bear where it belonged.

Meanwhile, Patti was bouncing Radia in her arms and hugging her over and over, while Radia squashed her aunt's cheeks with both hands. They were laughing wildly like nobody else existed.

'We'll be off then,' said Jowan. 'Come along, Aldous. Good luck to you, Miss Foley.'

'Jowan?' she stopped him. 'I made Minty some wedding website templates that she can populate herself. It's easy really. There's instructions printed out by the till. If she does the same for every client, she'll soon get into the rhythm of it, and they'll all be nicely uniform.'

Jowan smiled. 'I think you might be overestimatin' our technical abilities, but I know she'll be grateful to you. Thank you.'

The bewildered little dog, who'd quite enjoyed the cosiness of the T-shirt, shook himself and trotted out the door after his master, and the Crocombe boys trailed behind him, calling, 'Thanks for having us!' and 'See you at school!' to Radia as they left.

That was enough to silence Radia, and she let herself be slipped back down onto her feet.

Joy knew she had seconds to smooth things out. 'They must have just assumed, since you're their age and here in the village, that you'd be going to school with them, I guess?' She tried to make it sound light and breezy, knowing Radia would be reeling with emotions.

Radia said nothing, only looking between her mother and Patti.

'Are you staying?' Radia asked her aunt, somewhat bluntly.

'Um...' Patti appealed to Joy for help.

'Well, we're off to the airport soon, so...' Joy shrugged.

'What about... you know?' Patti said, surreptitiously doing a mime of her dad in his aviators asleep in the car and their mother driving wildly and honking an invisible car horn.

Joy sighed and her shoulders slumped. 'I guess we can stick to our original plan and leave for the airport tomorrow.'

Joy expected Radia to scream and jump around again, and was surprised when she didn't.

'And Mum?' the little girl said, lifting Charley fox from his story-time spot on the floor. 'I'm going to have a nap.'

'Um… OK,' Joy replied, drawing her neck back and narrowing her eyes. 'If that's what you want, sure.'

Radia glanced one more time at Patti, who deftly handed her the Percy Pigs. She skulked wordlessly into her bedroom, slowly and deliberately closing the door behind her, one eye peeping round the frame at the two sisters until the catch clicked shut.

'What was all that about?' Joy asked.

'Overwhelmed, probably,' said Patti. 'It's a lot to process for a kid, isn't it? An auntie just turning up unannounced.'

'It's a lot for a sister to process too,' Joy told her, smiling again. 'Tea?'

'Matcha green tea latte please,' Patti joked, doing a little kick with her heel that was supposed to denote her fancy city ways.

'Builder's it is,' Joy laughed, turning for the café kitchen.

She couldn't have guessed what was going on in the little bedroom at the Borrow-A-Bookshop at that very moment.

Unseen, Radia Pearl, who was always so compliant and easy to read, was sliding open the bedroom window, just a few inches, and burying something in the empty window box outside, where her colourful plastic windmill, planted on their arrival day, still whirled in the breeze.

'There,' she told her accomplice, Charley fox, in a whisper. 'Easy-peasy.'

She wiped the soil from her fingertips until no trace was left. Gingerly, she slid the window shut and turned the lock so it looked exactly as it had seconds ago before Charley fox had whispered in her ear his brilliant idea of hiding her passport where nobody would ever think to look for it.

She high-fived his little paw and took him under the duvet where they conspiratorially ate the whole bag of chewy pigs and practised innocent, unknowing expressions in readiness for the excitement that was bound to come.

Chapter Twenty-eight

In the end, Patti had been quite correct. They heard their mother approaching before they saw her.

It had happened after Radia's unusually long nap, when Patti had grilled them all fish fingers and potato waffles and served them up with baked beans at a little blue table set for three in the bookshop square.

They hadn't opened up the shop all afternoon, letting Radia sleep. Instead the sisters had sat in the closed café and talked about everything that was going on in their lives. Patti was still as single and averse to dating as ever. Joy didn't know what to make of the fact she referred to herself as a 'houseplant parent'.

'You don't just find perfect women online who can fit in with your schedule,' she'd said. 'Hook-ups, yeah, but actual date-after-date stuff? Who's got time for that?' she'd said, draining her tea, and Joy had pretended she got it, even though dating definitely wasn't something she knew anything about these days.

They'd skirted around the topic of Monty of course, and Joy could only hold up her hands in genuine ignorance when Patti asked her what her plans were for Radia's school place. The whole thing was up in the air, she'd told her, but with Sean definitely out of the picture, autumn in London was sounding extremely appealing.

'Oh my god, you can come to mine for Christmas and meet the cacti!' Patti had half-joked, but it was definitely a real, heartfelt invitation.

Joy's heart had expanded at the idea, but what would their mum say about that? She'd want to host Patti, wouldn't she? Since Patti was always in and out of their house, even though she had her own place with her flatmates a few miles down the road? How would she get out of Pamela Foley's Christmas extravaganza? Joy didn't dare imagine a Christmas invitation from her mum would be open to her too.

Patti didn't have any answers, so they'd switched back to the safe topic of their careers, until it was time for tea.

The rain hadn't come back but there was a definite chill in the air which the sisters ignored, wanting to salvage at least one summer's afternoon for themselves after so long apart.

They'd dug about in the freezer for what Patti referred to as 'golden tea' food, and Joy referred to as 'processed beige rubbish', and had fun just acting like sisters trying to pretend this was their kitchen and all of this was perfectly normal.

Pulling on jumpers, they'd called Radia outside into the square and Patti served up their meals with a stupid French accent and a tea towel over her arm.

'Mes-dames,' she said, sitting Radia down. 'And Monsewer!' she nodded at Charley fox, pulling out a chair for him too.

Radia was in seventh heaven, and as they all tucked into their food, the grilling began. *Did Aunt Patti have a girlfriend yet?* Nope. *Did Patti cut her own hair?* Bit rude! *Why was she here?* Just for hugs. And so it went on, until they were setting cutlery down on empty plates and there was a shrill squawking sound that Radia mistook for just another seagull but it had made the sisters stiffen and stare at one another.

'She's here!' Joy said.

'Who is?' Radia wanted to know.

Joy tried to sound as neutral as possible. 'Your grand-mother. And grandad too.'

Radia scraped her chair back awkwardly on the cobbles and wandered through the passageway, Joy following behind, her arms crossed.

There, on the slope, was her mum, looking little and aged in a way Joy didn't remember. She was burdened with overnight bags and groceries, and behind her, like a 1980s nightclub bouncer in a black summer jacket and shades, was her father, placid and wordless as usual.

'This must be it, Mike,' she was saying, ever so loudly, making the evening tourists turn to look at her as they made their way down to the Siren or up from the beach.

More like Patti than Joy, but bottle blonde with big specs and pink lippy, Pam Foley was no shrinking violet, and now she was here, curiously suburban in her spotlessly white Skechers, unselfconsciously causing a scene already.

'Ring her, Mike! Ask where this bleedin' place is!'

'Grandma!'

Radia's cry had her spinning round, dropping all her bags, spreading her arms and welcoming the little girl as if she saw her every day of the week.

Joy felt a pinch of resentment in her chest. She didn't want to feel it. It was ungenerous when she had Radia all to herself all the time… and yet, the prospect of sharing her carefully protected child with her mother didn't feel great. But there was absolutely nothing she could do to prevent it.

She watched her dad, wondering how he'd react when Radia inevitably launched herself at him, once she'd finished roughing up her granny. *He'd better hug her*, she thought unkindly.

She saw the hesitation from him, but then there was a great cry of 'Grandad!' and the silent giant picked up the little girl into the air like she weighed nothing at all. He hugged her close to his chest and kissed her forehead, and Radia didn't even say 'yuck' or wipe it away.

Joy had expected awkwardness between the three of them when there was, evidently, none at all. How the hell had that happened? Is this what they meant when they said that thing about blood being thicker than water? She'd wanted to believe it was nonsense but here they were, strangers who shared DNA, making a child's synapses fire out messages of recognition, telling her she belonged with these people.

And now, everyone was looking at Joy. It was her turn, apparently.

She stepped out towards her parents, not nervous, exactly, but nowhere near calm.

'Hi, Mum,' she heard herself say. That was good. Casual, she thought.

'Oh my god, Joyce! Look at you!' her mother cried, very loudly. The lace curtains at the cottage window overlooking the scene twitched at the commotion. They were being watched.

Pamela stepped towards her daughter and wrapped her in a hug that almost knocked Joy backwards. At first, it felt showy and fake, and then, when her mum didn't let her go and she felt Pam's heart thumping and her tears heaving, it felt the way it was probably supposed to.

Joy let herself be held and rocked and kissed, standing there halfway up the slope at the point where Up-along became Down-along, depending on your perspective and direction of travel.

To her surprise, her dad took off the aviators to reveal crying eyes and stepped in, spreading his long arms in a hug around his wife and eldest daughter, saying nothing at all, but giving away so much.

Radia clapped and danced beside her aunt before stopping everyone in their tracks by wondering out loud whether there might be any prezzies in the bags they'd brought.

Chapter Twenty-nine

Five years, almost six, as if they hadn't already been aware of the fact, is a long time to miss. Radia's whole lifetime to be precise. Suddenly, now that they were here in Devon, the texts Joy had exchanged with her mother, the post-cards and Christmas cards that had criss-crossed the planet, connecting them up on important days, sometimes getting lost, sometimes arriving late, were now exposed as exactly what they had always been: inadequate at best, insulting at worst.

Radia had been brilliant, of course, chattering away and showing her grandparents every inch of the book-shop and dragging them round the back to the garden, announcing that this was where their new friend Monty had barbequed the big fish. Joy had avoided her mum's eyes at that moment and insisted it was too chilly to stand around outside any longer.

Finally, after insisting on reading stories for a long time so everyone could see how clever and grown-up she was, Radia had caved and at last fallen asleep on her little bed beside Joy's father who, no matter how uncomfortable he looked crammed onto the edge of the bed (still in his aviators), was soon snoring contentedly beside his grand-daughter.

That left Joy, Patti and their mother clearing away the coffee mugs and the remains of the Colin the Caterpillar cake (Pamela Foley was, like her youngest daughter, devoted to M&S and couldn't pay a visit to anyone without calling there first).

'So,' Joy said when the cups were put away. 'Bedtime?'

Her mum looked at the clock on the wall, which traitorously said it was only half-seven. *Dammit.*

'I… should probably get to my room at the Siren's Tail, right?' said Patti.

'You're staying the night in the village?' Joy was amazed.

'Couldn't very well sleep in my car. Besides, I've never been in this part of the country before. No point rushing back immediately,' Patti told her.

'Don't you have that fragrance launch on Tuesday?' Pam asked, bringing it home to Joy that her mum knew Patti's work plans for the coming days when she usually didn't even know which hemisphere Joy and Radia were in from one week to the next.

'I brought your shampoo from home,' Pam told her. 'Never use hotel shower gels, girls,' she added wisely. 'Don't I always say that, Patti? Not unless you want to itch all night long.' She was searching through a bag and pulling the bottle out. Patti took it and gave her mum a kiss on the cheek.

'Night, Joy. See you at breakfast, yeah? Come down to the Siren's Tail.'

'Oh, I'm not sure we'll have time,' flustered Joy.

'*We* won't be there,' threw in Pam, in a tone that said, *So don't let us stop you meeting up.* 'We've got a little bed and breakfast about a mile away, lovely looking place. We'll be there in the morning, before we head home.'

'You're leaving tomorrow?' Joy was getting emotional whiplash. One minute she was wishing they hadn't come, then she was reeling, thinking how they'd be going again so soon.

'Aren't you flying off somewhere tomorrow?' her mum asked.

'Yeah,' Joy conceded. 'Lisbon, for a few days.' She didn't add the bit about coming back to London straight after, even though she'd just been hurting at the thought of missing her mum and dad. Nothing about the way she was feeling made sense.

Before Joy could orientate herself further, Patti had kissed her cheek and walked out the door, shouldering her backpack, and with three slices of caterpillar cake, wrapped in a napkin, in her hand. 'Nighty night!' she directed wickedly at Joy.

Her mum only smiled indulgently, watching her go.

Little sister syndrome, thought Joy. Patti could always do as she pleased and get away with it because she was the precious, cute one. Still was, evidently.

'So…' Joy said again, inhaling through her teeth, then clicking her fingers in a weird, awkward gesture she'd literally never made before in her life.

'So…' her mum echoed in a happy kind of chirrup that wasn't fooling either of them.

Nothing about this was comfortable or happy. The whole thing made Joy's chest ache and her cheeks burn. She stood for a long moment, digging the toe of her left shoe into the floor.

'Dad seems well?' Joy tried. 'After the eye thing.' The café clock ticked so loudly Joy wondered if it was faulty.

Pam wasn't having any of this. 'Shall we take a walk?' she said, already on the move and not waiting for an answer.

Joy trailed after her through the shop, picking up her jacket on the way and complaining that it looked like rain out there.

'What harm can a bit of rain do?' Pam called over her shoulder as she stepped out into the evening, then realising what she'd said, grimaced and turned back to her daughter. 'Oops, I don't suppose the local people would like to hear me talking like that, what with the flood and all.'

Joy forced a laugh.

'Which way?' Pam asked, once they were on the slope, looking down in the direction Patti had just walked towards her hotel room.

Joy thought of her sister checking in, getting a drink sent up from the bar and climbing into a nice big bed somewhere in that cosy pub. Lucky cow.

'Up-along,' Joy insisted, not wanting to run the risk of seeing Monty, not now they'd said goodbye, and *definitely not* when she had her mum tagging along.

'See, it's dry,' Pam said, holding up a hand to the cool evening sky, and they turned up the slope.

There followed another strained bout of small talk just like they'd had over coffee, only this time without the distraction of Radia pirouetting on tiptoe while reciting the alphabet. They managed to cover, yet again, what a pretty place this was, how bad for her mum's ankles the steep slope and cobbles were, and how, if Joy wanted to keep her ankles strong, now was the time to do it.

'Pilates, you see?' Pam told her. 'Your cousin Tess is doing it five times a week, which personally, I think is overdoing it, but…'

'Mum,' Joy couldn't take it anymore, 'you haven't come to see us before. Why now?'

It was enough to stop Pam in her tracks. She held onto a gate for a moment, seemingly to catch her breath.

'We never knew where you was, before.'

Joy held her nerve. 'Fair enough.'

'Then, a few days ago, Patti showed me the newspaper report about... him.'

'Oh!'

'And a few things fell into place for me. I'm not too big to admit, mistakes have been made.'

Joy only listened. She knew how to interpret this: mistakes had been made *on both sides*. She was definitely not in the right headspace to consider whether she too shared the Foley stubbornness. Especially not when she realised her mum had stopped to rub at her ankle right at the door of a cottage bearing a sign that read 'Bickleigh', painted on a piece of driftwood and strung all around with decorative fishing net and colourful buoys.

'Let's get off this slope,' Joy told her, and to her surprise her mum offered her an arm.

They climbed in silence until they reached the top of the village where, of course, everything was closed. The visitor centre car park was long since cleared and all the little concession huts shuttered.

'About that newspaper story your sister showed me recently?' Pam ventured once they located a bench and sat facing out over the roofs of Clove Lore to the sea beyond. The sun was sinking into the horizon in a wonderful hazy orange that held their gazes as she spoke. 'Once I read it, things made a lot more sense to me, Joy. I hadn't much of a clue before. Of course, I always thought he was a wrong 'un, but I...'

Joy didn't move, willing her mum to get the words out and quick.

261

'I blamed you. OK. There! I admit it. I thought it was you letting him get away with it.'

Joy shrugged. It had been, in a way, and she couldn't yet be convinced otherwise.

'Do you remember my fiftieth?' Pam asked.

''Course I do.' The guilt of what she'd done that day made Joy's cheeks redden now. This whole thing was too hard. Joy wished herself anywhere but here listening to the shake in her mum's voice.

'I'd booked Valentina's for lunch, just the two of us? Remember?'

Joy took a deep breath and tried to count out for seven slow beats.

'And you rang about an hour before our reservation time and said you weren't coming?'

Oh god. There was nothing Joy could say in her defence.

'You said Sean had taken the car to work unexpectedly, and you weren't feeling well anyway, and maybe we could go to Valentina's another day?'

'I know.' Joy could barely think about it. She'd cried all that afternoon and Sean had sat there watching the football, her car keys in his fist.

'I was going to come,' said Joy, weakly. 'I'd put on that dress you gave me for my birthday, the black one?'

Pam turned to face her daughter, eyes brimming with tears now.

'He wouldn't let me, Mum.' Joy crumpled on the bench, her arms folded across her stomach.

'I know that now,' Pam told her, bursting into loud sobs that scared the sparrows from the gorse. She pulled her daughter to her, holding her close. 'But at the time...' she faltered, guiltily. 'At the time I thought it was you wanting to be with him all the time, cutting me out of your life.'

'I'm sorry,' Joy wept, her head down.

'Don't say sorry. You don't ever need to say that. I knew, deep down. When you first started missing things, parties and Sunday lunches, I knew from your tone in those texts, it wasn't you speaking. It was him. Making excuses. Somehow always making me feel like an inconvenience, like I was asking too much wanting to see my own girl. I knew it was all him.'

Pam rummaged in her handbag for a tissue and offered one to Joy too.

'It *was* him,' Joy said, monotone and exhausted. 'But I let him do it.'

'No, love,' Pam insisted. 'You had no choice. Like those other girls. Only, instead of sending your dad round and throwing him out on his ear, I took it personal. I was angry and hot-headed. Not like me, I know.'

Joy sniffed a laugh that made Pam smile with relief.

'If I could go back, knowing what I know now!' Pam said, ruefully casting her eyes about the sky.

'But we can't go back,' Joy said, shrugging sadly.

'I should have come to the hospital.'

This made Joy sob afresh, thinking what could have been if they had come to get her. If they'd gathered her and baby Radia up in their arms, bundled them into the car, intervened. If they'd taken them to safety then all this loneliness could have been avoided.

'But I didn't call you to let you know I was in hospital. Didn't tell you Radia was here,' Joy said, berating herself.

'Still. If I'd stuck by you. Understood what was going on. *Not* a mistake I would make again.'

263

Joy didn't want to, but she knew she had to say it now, otherwise she'd never say it and the pain would always be there, gnawing at her.

'I didn't reach out because I felt abandoned. Like you dropped us when we needed you.'

Pam pulled her child closer. 'Yes,' she said, the tears making her voice thick. 'I see how you'd see it like that. I can't blame you. I'm so sorry, my Joy.'

A sea breeze whipped Up-along and lifted the words into the air.

'So what now?' Joy said, turning her face to her mum's. 'We start again?'

Pam seemed to hold her breath waiting for Joy's answer.

Joy's hand settled on her mum's. 'OK. We start again.'

The sun at last sank into the sea and the first of the evening stars shone high up in its darkest depths. Mother and daughter sat and watched them shine, their four hands clasped in a soft knot, all of the unsaid words that had kept them apart for so long now released, and along with them, the resentment and sadness had lifted too.

'Beautiful spot you've found here,' said Pam in the peace of the evening, and Joy had to agree.

There was nowhere she'd rather be right now, except maybe in her little flat in London with her family around her table.

'You know, Mum? After Lisbon, I've nothing in my diary.'

Pam turned to her daughter with interest and the pair fell into chatting, planning for autumn, dreaming of winter, until all the lights in Clove Lore were lit.

Joy and Radia were heading home, at long last.

Chapter Thirty

Clove Lore was made for weddings. Its dramatic skies, ever-changing seascape, impressive beach waterfall and the grand vistas of the Big House's sweeping lawns viewed from the rhododendron walk and camellia grove, all offered up the perfect backdrop for the best day of a couple's life.

There had been incredible, lavish weddings in the village's halcyon past. Generations of Clove-Congreves tying the knot had hosted dignitaries, royalty even, in the ballroom, back when it had sparkled under crystal chandeliers and glowed with candlelight, like something from a Julia Quinn novel.

There had been smaller affairs where sweethearts amongst the fisherfolk had exchanged vows in the little chapel that had been destroyed in the Christmas flood last year. The ruined spot, if you are in a fanciful mood and listening hard enough, still echoes with the sound of the choir in their Sunday best, singing for the bride and groom.

Generations of honeymooners have been waved off from the launch in scrubbed-up sailboats, the halyard rope strung with fluttering stubs of white ribbon-like kite strings.

Minty herself, the lady of the manor, had pulled off a long-awaited wedding of her own back in mid-summer.

An admittedly modest affair, all that the estate's diminished funds allowed, it had taken place when the village was approaching something that felt like normality after the flood, when the soil in the flower beds, brought in by truck to replace the stuff that had washed away, was still a rich black and sweet smelling, the camellias just taking root after their spring re-planting. Everyone had stopped in their painting and dehumidifying, repointing and plastering, and swapped wellies and overalls for long-neglected party clothes. It had been a cosy, simple affair, and in Minty's opinion surely the most heartfelt occasion the Clove-Congreve family had ever hosted.

But today, Minty insisted, would be a different thing entirely. Today, Elliot and Jude's wedding day, was her new venture's flagship event. It would be a day of breath-taking, showstopper surprises, a landmark in society occasions that would raise the bar for Devonshire destination weddings. She'd seen to the arrangements with characteristic zealous efficiency and now it was here, her Big Day.

'There'll be no slipping off and no slouching,' she told the waiting staff, assembled before her now, bleary-eyed at nine in the morning.

She couldn't afford to bring professionals in, but now that she'd drilled the two catering college students – home for the summer from Plymouth – and little Samantha Capstan, who lived only a short walk away along the main road and whose mother ran a laundry service in the area washing bedding for B&B owners, Minty was confident they'd not let her down. Even if Sam trembled every time Minty added another thing to the very long list of things she expected her to remember.

'And don't let anyone wander around holding coats or hats. Convey them straight to the cloakroom please,' said Minty walking up and down the little row, casting her eye over their white shirts, black trousers and neat aprons. Sam fidgeted and shuffled. 'Sore feet already?' Minty asked the girl.

Sam pulled herself bolt upright, her eyes fixed on the wall ahead like an army recruit.

Minty smiled with satisfaction. 'And top up every glass that looks to be less than half full. But be mindful that no guest is to become inebriated. Jolly, yes; leery, no. Yes?'

'No. I mean, yes?' Sam replied, her bottom lip wobbling, wishing she'd applied for the summer job at the fudge concession instead.

One of the catering students elbow-nudged the other with a sidelong glance at the poor struggling girl.

'And you two,' Minty rounded on the boys. 'Breaks are fifteen minutes every four hours. Please refer to the schedule.' Tapping her pen on her clipboard, she indicated the thirteen-page document that was also printed out and taped across the kitchen walls to ensure there was no room for confusion today. 'And remember, if in doubt…?' she prompted, fixing a sharp eye on the smaller of the two students.

'Uh, shout?' he said.

'Shout? *Shout?* Good grief, no. If there's even the tiniest hint of trouble, head straight for Jowan. I mean, *Mr* de Marisco Clove-Congreve.' She turned to indicate the gaffer tape cross on the floor like an actor's mark, where Jowan was to be stationed all day. One of the boys took the opportunity to snort a laugh and Minty's head whipped back accusingly. 'He will liaise with me on the…?'

'Talkie-walkie?' Sam threw in, unable to hide the fact she wished this was over. They'd already been through the whole thing the day before and there is such a thing as overkill.

'Close enough,' Minty told her witheringly, not understanding why the young people regarded the black plastic radio strung across her body as a ridiculous relic of a time before even their parents were born. She'd found them in the attics and was delighted they still worked, so why wouldn't she make use of them?

As if to prove their efficacy, the device crackled into life now, making everyone start in fright, even Minty.

'You there, Mint, my love?' asked Jowan who, from the sounds of him, was stationed somewhere near Newfoundland and not, in fact, in the pantry.

Minty dismissed her serving staff, telling them to wipe each champagne glass in the crates before setting them out on the trestle tables, and to *Use the special glass cloths, please.*

She lifted her radio to her face. 'This is Coordinator One. Why aren't you using your call sign? Over.'

'It's me, Mint.'

'Well, I know that, but our guests might overhear and think we're running some kind of amateur operation. *Over.*'

Jowan sighed heavily into the crackling receiver. Guests wouldn't be arriving for at least a couple of hours. 'This is Number Two. Over.'

Minty dropped her shoulders, giving up. 'Is there a problem, Jowan?'

'No, Coordinator One. Only it's time for Aldous's walk. Over.'

Minty looked at her watch, then consulted her schedule. 'Quite right.' And then, thinking again, she added, 'When you return, get him in his spot in Leonid and Izaak's room. We can't have him frisking our guests for cheesy nibbles.'

She thought she heard Jowan chuckling before he delivered a terribly serious, 'Roger that. Number Two. Love you. Over and out.'

Through the high windows, she glimpsed a van pulling up on the lawn outside.

'No, no, no! Round the back!' she called, even though they couldn't hear her.

Marching from the ballroom, she grumbled about how in her day carrying out simple instructions was the *least* a delivery person could manage and hadn't they received their copy of her schedule, for goodness' sake?

–

From the window above, Monty watched the unfortunate florist's delivery guy gaping in wide-mouthed amazement in the face of Minty's dressing down, as she pointed a neat red fingernail at the tyre-trampled grass. Failing to get through to him, she was now exasperatedly showing him the schedule.

'She's going to lose a supplier at this rate,' Monty said, turning from the window to see Elliot brushing his long hair down over the jacket of his dark suit. Jude wasn't going to know what hit her when she found this guy standing at the end of the aisle.

'Ready, mate?' Monty ventured.

Elliot set the brush down and tugged at his collar. 'Ready to marry Jude, definitely. Bit less ready for Minty's wedding circus.' He assessed himself in the full-length mirror, pushing back his sleek black hair. 'Should I do a plait or something?'

'Uh, no, loose is best. More weddingy?'

'Is it?'

Monty shrugged. 'No idea.'

'Might tie it back,' said Elliot, unsure, and worrying at his cuffs now.

'Doesn't Minty have anything to say about the groom's hair in *The Schedule*?' Monty joked, gesturing wryly at the many A4 pages Blu Tacked across the walls of the high-beamed attic apartment which Izaak and Leonid had made their own with every houseplant known to green-fingered man.

Elliot was too busy concentrating on his tie to reply.

'You know, I, uh… I have this list?' Monty said, pulling the book from his back pocket to show Elliot.

'*Best Man Speeches and Wedding Etiquette Guide?*' read the groom.

'Yep, there's a whole checklist thing I'm supposed to go through with you.'

'There is?' Elliot came to sit on the low armchair by the window and set to work polishing a pair of already very shiny shoes on Minty's morning *Telegraph*, hoping she wouldn't mind sacrificing it to the wedding cause. 'Fire away.'

'Uh, OK.' Monty searched the contents page until he found what he was looking for. 'Here we are, OK, number one. Are you absolutely sure you're doing the right thing?' Monty pulled an apologetic grimace.

'It says that?'

'More or less. Is the groom in full understanding that what matters today is the marriage itself and *not* the show of the wedding day.'

'Yup,' Elliot said confidently, brushing polish on leather and scenting the air with the familiar smell of manly marriage preparations that must stretch back decades.

'And does the groom acknowledge and accept his duties to his partner's happiness in the months and years *after* the wedding day?'

'You can skip these ones,' Elliot assured him. 'I know exactly what I'm doing.'

'OK.' Monty turned the pages. 'There's a few like that, actually. Aha! Try this one, number four. The best man must offer the groom his support in perpetuity, especially in lieu of family members who may not support the marriage or who may be detrimental to its success in the future.'

Elliot's boot brush paused, hovering over the shoe in his hand. 'Your support in perpetuity? That's nice.'

'Seriously though, I'm here for you both, and not just for today.'

'Understood.' Elliot started work on the next shoe.

'Even if your folks aren't here.' Monty chose his words as carefully as he was able. 'Even if they never come around. I'm here for you.'

Elliot set this shoe down beside the other on the news-paper. 'Thanks, Mont, I appreciate that.'

'*Mont?*' Monty ventured a smile.

Elliot shrugged. 'It felt like a Mont moment.'

'Fair dos.'

Elliot started work on his shoes with the dry brush and a van door slammed heavily outside. Monty cocked his head at the roar of the engine as the florist tore out of the estate. This was followed by footsteps in the hall below them, then on the staircase. Moments later Minty hammered at their door.

'I won't come in,' she yelled. 'Only it's nine forty-six and I was supposed to bring your boutonnières to you one minute ago.'

Both men suppressed a smirk and glanced from the door to the schedule on the wall.

'The florist had sent white freesias and lavender sprigs instead of sea holly and gorse, and, I ask you, how anyone makes that kind of mistake... oh, hello.'

Monty had pulled the door open.

'You're not dressed,' the lady of the manor told him.

'Getting there,' he assured her. 'Is the bouquet right, at least?'

'The bouquet?' Minty froze. 'The bouquet! I... it's still in the van. I sent the whole lot back until that stupid boy brings the entire order, correctly put together as per my original instructions.'

'Right-o,' Monty told her. 'Thanks, then.' He made to close the door but Minty stopped it.

'Jowan's bringing Aldous up in ten minutes. He is to be locked in this room until his next scheduled walk. Make sure he has fresh water.'

'Will do.' Monty resisted the urge to salute, and he shut the door.

Elliot rolled his eyes, grinning wickedly at his friend. 'Poor Minty. I'm beginning to wonder if she's cut out for all this.'

'What? Organising?'

'Dealing with people.'

'Ah, I think you've a point there,' Monty admitted. He moved back towards the window where the van had indeed left two long green gouges across the lawn in its race to get away. Minty was going to be furious.

Monty put his best man's book in his back pocket, reminded of his duties. 'Elliot?' he ventured gently. 'I'm… I'm sorry they didn't come, your parents. It really is their loss.'

Elliot blew out a breath. 'They were invited. They ignored it. What else could we do?'

'I could have called them? You know, explained things, on your behalf.'

'There's nothing to explain.' Elliot switched to the chamois now and rubbed vigorously, bringing up a glossy sheen. 'I was up in court for disturbing an illegal fox hunt, a guy fell from his horse, nothing to do with me. I told Mum and Dad that all along, but they were too worried about their *standing* amongst their pals and so… they picked a side. I have to accept that.' Elliot laced his gleaming shoes onto his feet and stood to admire them.

'You sure I can't do anything to help smooth things?' tried Monty.

'Mate, I know you want to help, but you need to understand, they cut me off. Every time somebody says I could have done something more to get them back on side, it hurts me, you know?'

Monty wasn't sure he understood.

Elliot tried a different tack. 'It's like saying *I* should be the one to bend, to make amends, when they've made it clear I'm not their priority. They chose to save face with Dad's hunting friends and their cronies who sit with Mum on the council. They were ashamed of me.' Elliot said this last bit slow and emphatic. 'Suggesting that I need to reach out and talk them round makes me feel like *I'm* to blame for their decision not to stick by me when the case fell through and I was cleared. Hell, they should've believed me anyway. How could they think I'd harm another person like that?'

Monty thought hard. 'OK,' he said finally. 'I get it. Sorry. I won't say it again. The whole thing must be horrible for you.'

'Ah, well. I can't be the only one it's happened to. There'll be millions of guys out there whose family members are too proud, or too narcissistic, to say sorry and make amends. What can you do?' Elliot, in front of the mirror again, brushed invisible lint from his jacket. 'Not everyone gets to have a big reunion or to play happy families. And not everyone wants to. Anyways,' he shrugged, 'I have family here. Jude is my family, and Jowan, and you, and... hell, even mad old Minty.' Elliot seemed to gulp down a lump in his throat but he was smiling thinly.

'And all the people at your vet practice?' Monty added. 'And every barking, wagging, scratching, meowing thing within a hundred-mile radius.'

'Exactly.'

Monty turned to the long windows once more, but he wasn't seeing the sky greying over Clove Lore – *not* a good omen on a wedding day. Nor was he seeing his reflection in the draughty old panes where his crisp white shirt was untucked from the darkest blue wool trousers and his tie hung loose from his open collar.

Instead he was seeing himself chattering into the book-shop phone, carelessly giving away Joy's location, not thinking, confident he was doing nothing wrong. Then his brain replayed the way Joy's whole body had tensed up and her expression changed from the dopey, relaxed 'morning after' look to dawning horror and betrayal as she filled him in on what he'd just done. He could see her

274

now, crying big tears she was trying to hide from him. Tears he'd made fall.

He played it all through in his mind. How she'd thrown him out, quite rightly, and then how, days later, she'd come to him on the beach, looking utterly distraught. He'd said sorry, of course, and he'd meant it, but had he fully understood what he'd done until now? He'd jeopardised everything for her, compromising her child's safety, wrecking the privacy that was so important to Joy, no matter how improbable he'd felt it was that she was being hunted down by that ex of hers, or how unlikely it was that the chatty, nervous mother he'd spoken with on the phone really was all that wicked. It was Joy's perception of things that mattered. She was the one who'd been through hell and felt utterly let down. He'd let her down too – and after she'd taken down her walls to let him in.

'Elliot?' said Monty, as his mind ran on, unpacking it all. 'I've done something awful.'

He tried to explain to the groom how he'd assumed everyone was as kind and as straightforward as the Bickleighs. He'd heard that nice woman on the phone saying she was Joy's mum and just assumed they must get on the way he used to get on with his own beloved mum. 'Shit!' said Monty, dragging a hand down his face. 'I didn't get it!'

Elliot told him it was OK, because he got it now, and poured two cups of black coffee, ready for the long wait until Jude's arrival.

'Mate, I have to step out,' Monty replied. 'Just for a minute. We've got a minute, right? Before it all starts?'

'We've got ages. Jude's not arriving for a while yet.'

'I'll be back soon, I promise.'

'What does it say in your book about the groom giving the best man a pep talk, huh?'

Monty tried to laugh but he was already calculating how long it would take to ring her to apologise properly. How long it would take to blurt it all out, to say, *I encouraged you to trust me, I made you feel safe, then I put you in danger, or at least, I could have done. I didn't put myself in your shoes. I intruded, thought I knew best. Thought I knew what family looked like for everyone. And I muscled in where you'd been protecting yourself and Radia for years.*

He'd find a quiet spot, in the gardens maybe, and make the call. But as he laced his shoes and threw on his jacket, a great clatter rose up from the ballroom below.

Glass smashing? Metal collapsing? And an anguished cry of, 'No, no, NO!'

Groom and best man dashed for the door and onto the grand staircase that led down to the ballroom. Pushing through the doors, they watched helplessly as it all unfolded before them and it became more than obvious that the wedding Minty had scheduled so meticulously was very much not going according to plan.

Aldous was snuffling on the floor for the wedding's bite-sized clotted cream and jam scones, which had proven too tantalisingly delicious for the little dog's snout to ignore.

If anyone could have asked the mutt, he'd have explained it was the diet of rice and chicken he'd been on since Elliot saved his life many dog-years ago that had done it! Just *how* was a good boy supposed to live out his dotage without so much as a sniff of his old favourite scones?

But nobody was asking him. Instead they were all shrieking and saying his name in an angry way that made him tuck his skinny tail between his quivering legs and jump straight into Jowan's arms to escape the lake of champagne that was pooling all over the floor.

The college boys were shamefacedly blaming each other.

One had popped the cork that hit the other's silver salver, which made the stupid dog jump onto the table in the first place, and then there'd been the scramble to stop Aldous spoiling the trays of freshly baked canapés, and then somehow the whole thing (two trestle tables, thirty bottles on ice, all the yummy scone bites, and one hundred delicate glass flutes) had gone flying and then, horribly, stupidly, *typically*, tiny little Sam Capstan had stumbled backwards over the frantic Aldous (who had three mini scones safely in his jaws by that point), and she'd fallen right on top of the boxes stacked behind her on the floor and found they gave way beneath her, breaking her fall.

Minty was approaching the flattened boxes, with Sam lying helplessly on the floor beside them.

'No!' she was saying, as though this couldn't possibly be happening. It simply *wasn't* possible. *Not* Jude's wedding cake! And then, as she lifted the bashed-in lid of the smallest box, everyone heard her whimper.

Three layers of the booziest, most fragrant, lovingly made wedding cake (that had been stirred for luck and everything), were hopelessly wrecked in their boxes, crumbs and once-pristine fondant icing everywhere.

Sam rose shakily to her feet, wiped her hands over her marzipan-smeared bottom and left the ballroom crying for her mum. Minty watched her go, her chest heaving heavily.

She lifted her walkie-talkie, even though Jowan was standing a few feet away behind Elliot and Monty in the doorway.

'This is Commander One,' she said weakly, her eyes still fixed on the cake. 'Mop and bucket to the ballroom, please.' She didn't even say 'over' as she turned on her heel to survey the rest of the mess, broken glass crunching beneath her feet.

The catering students, to their credit, weren't finding any of this amusing now. One was already crouching and lifting hopelessly splattered jammy scones from the floor.

'Someone has to tell Jude,' Monty told Elliot. 'About her cake.'

'I'll do it,' Elliot replied, pulling his phone from his pocket and stepping outside.

Suddenly inspired, Monty reached for the best-man book and offered the thunderstruck wedding planner one of its pearls of wisdom.

'Says here, Minty, page nine, that no wedding is without its mishap. It's how it's dealt with that matters. Test of our wedding mettle sort of thing?'

Minty was not feeling philosophical. She fixed him with an incredulous open-mouthed look that had Jowan wisely on the move and inviting Monty to join him outside.

'Come help me find that mop, eh?' he said in a low voice.

Monty was pulled away, knowing his duties had expanded in the face of the disaster to include sweeping broken glass, mopping champagne and binning an entire wedding cake. The possibility of getting away to call Joy was momentarily out of reach.

While carefully shutting the remorseful Aldous in Leonid and Izaak's rooms a few moments later, Monty's phone bleeped a notification that made his heart sink to his shoes.

10.30AM: Gate 8 Exeter to Lisbon departing now

He'd set the live flight departures alert days ago, back when he and Joy were wrapped up under the covers dreaming about him visiting London this September, back when he'd promised to track their flights to and from Lisbon so he'd know when it was time to set off on his own journey across the country to Joy's place.

What was he thinking? Even with a heartfelt apology, telling her he'd learned his lesson and how he'd do better in future, she wouldn't want to talk. She'd left the country, and without phoning or messaging him. If she'd been missing him the way he missed her, she'd have called before getting on her flight. And why on earth would she do that? She had her daughter to consider, and he'd squandered the trust they'd both placed in him. He deleted the alert for their return flight and closed the door on Aldous.

All he could do now was focus on being this wedding's best man. *What a joke*, he told himself. Best at nothing.

Chapter Thirty-one

Jude had taken Elliot's phone call about the fate of her cake pretty well, considering. Her dad had cried, of course. Impossible not to. Not only was he giving away his little girl – he'd only just been rendered totally speechless when she emerged from the bedroom in her mum's beautifully altered wedding dress; he'd had to be fanned with a newspaper – he simply couldn't bear the idea of a Crawley wedding without a Crawley and Son wedding cake.

He'd cried all the harder when he'd packed Jude into his old bakery van, Diane. Jude had driven that old van all the way to Devon, where she was supposed to be holidaying in a bookshop for two weeks but somehow ended up with an English boyfriend and a new home.

Diane's rusty blue paintwork, which still bore the legend 'Crawley and Son' across its side, was now shined up (as far as possible) and decorated with a big white bow and ribbons over its front grille.

Jude clambered in along with her mum and grand-mother, saying they'd better get to the venue and see what exactly was going on. Daniel and Ekon were to follow in a cab behind them.

Jude's gran had confided in everyone that she had some little red pills that might help calm this Araminta woman down, claiming they 'did wonders' for her pals at the New Start Luxury Residential Village. Daniel and Ekon, both very familiar with their hospital's dispensing cupboard, had taken one look at her stash and confiscated them, saying there was no way she'd have been prescribed those. Jude had made a mental note to ring the New Start owners to inform them of a black market in recreational drugs on their premises. Another thing she didn't think she'd be doing on her wedding day.

It wasn't quite the send-off she'd imagined either, but Jude was determined to have the traditional bride's 'poor oot', like in her little Scottish village back home.

Her mum handed her the jangling bag and even though there wasn't a soul on the main road to catch them, Jude threw the coins into the air and her dad watched them fall at his feet, picking up a shiny fifty pence and holding it up proudly.

'Send the taxi back for me,' he shouted weepily. 'And good luck!'

'And you!' Mrs Crawley called back, blowing kisses, as her husband pulled his Crawley and Son apron over his head and marched back inside, determined to make something of his own for his daughter and son-in-law to cut into on their wedding day.

—

The grey sky had done nothing to dampen the mood of Clove Lore's residents as they made their way Up-along to the Big House estate.

Mrs Crocombe had splashed out on a new dress and her daughter had set her perm freshly the night before. Bovis walked ahead of her in his skinny T-shirt and apron, pulling the insulated bags of confetti burst ice cream, fifteen big tubs, behind him on the ice-cream parlour's delivery sled.

Mrs C. had her eye fixed on the top of the slope, where James da Costa had set their rendezvous. Her nerves threatened to get the better of her. After all, weddings were renowned for moving guests to feats of romantic revelation and all week long she'd suspected her dashing beau was planning something big. He'd fallen more reticent and withdrawn each day, busying himself on his phone, tentative, twitchy, and he'd been so shy around her. There might well be another wedding in Clove Lore soon if her suspicions (and hopes) were correct, and they almost always were when it came to this sort of thing.

The nip of whisky she'd taken to calm her nerves was working its magic. She was going to be brave and take the plunge if he asked her. At her age, what was she waiting for? The young ones got their Clove Lore love stories, she saw to that, but did that mean she never would? James had shown her how good rebelliousness and romance could feel. The last fortnight had been a whirlwind of emotion and happiness and, even if the whisky was making her tummy churn a little, she had no intention of going back to her wallflower ways.

On her way to meet him, she greeted Tom and his girlfriend Lou as they left their cottage at the top of the slope. Tom, who was rarely out of waterproofs, looked devilishly handsome today in his suit.

'Seen your brother this morning?' Mrs C. called out.

'He's been up at Wedding Central since first light,' the fisherman told her.

'Shame the computer lady's gone, really,' she said wistfully. 'I had her picked out for Monty.'

Tom, holding Lou's arm as she struggled in heels on the cobbles, shook his head and inhaled through his teeth. 'Bachelor for life, my brother.'

Mrs C. didn't think so and explained at length all the way up to the Big House how, 'Some folk think they're destined to be alone forever but that special someone shows up out of the blue and *poof!* Love happens.'

A few feet ahead of them, Bovis shook his head grumpily at all this.

'I hope you're right,' Tom told her, all the more glad to have Lou on his arm.

Mrs Crocombe broke away from the little party saying she'd better wait for James, and Tom made a very immature '*Wooo!*' that left her chuckling. Once they were gone she turned her face to the village and watched, waiting placidly for her dashing yachtsman, humming a bridal march and thinking of the surprise they were going to give everyone tonight.

Bella and Finan arrived next at the Big House, carrying two cases of emergency Prosecco to replace the expensive champagne that had hit the floor earlier. Minty looked like she wanted to sob in relief as she took the boxes to the fridges, but not without first berating Bovis for dragging his mucky sled up to her doors. He doffed his invisible cap and made for the big freezer in the back kitchen with his ice-cream bags.

The Siren's Tail was closed up for the afternoon, though a very promising-sounding sous chef was on their way to the village to help relieve Monty for the evening service tonight and, if things went well, they'd stay on, if they could be convinced to. It was Monty's moping these last few days that had prompted Finan to at last get him some cover. Their chef really hadn't been himself, padding silently around the kitchens, unshaven and sallow.

Monty, however, had brushed up well for the sake of Elliot and Jude and was waiting at the open doors to the ballroom. He smiled and chatted, shaking hands with each new arrival, as was his duty, though his dull eyes told a very different story of defeat and regret.

Elliot was on florist watch, even though it was dawning on everyone that if they weren't back by now, and they weren't picking up the phone, they probably had no intention of coming back.

Minty clutched her schedule. 'So many things to tick off, Jowan,' she said with hushed urgency in her husband's ear. 'And they're not here! They're simply not here!'

Jowan, in his wedding suit, pulled his wife aside so she could run through the catalogue of failures. Elliot followed.

'No balloon lady! She said she'd been forced to rethink her entire business plan after visiting us and she was jacking it in to try selling Avon! And I've been on the phone begging the harpist to reconsider this last half hour, but she was adamant we *hadn't* actually come to an agreement and that she wouldn't be setting foot in this house.

'That woman used some very *choice* language you wouldn't expect from a classically trained member of the Barnstaple conservatoire! And we've obviously got no flowers now. And not one of the society papers have sent a photographer. Too rural, I suppose! And I'm afraid I didn't think we'd need a run-of-the-mill wedding photographer if the papers were coming, so... there isn't one. And after the scone farrago, the caterer has downed tools and told me I wouldn't get so much as a ham butty out of her.'

'Oh, Mint,' exclaimed Jowan in sympathy.

'Perhaps I could have been a little less insistent she replace all the spoiled food at no extra cost, and well... they've all gone.'

'Gone?' echoed Elliot.

'Even the college boys have left, said it wasn't worth their while, not for five quid an hour.'

'Five quid? Is that even legal?' said Monty, joining them in the corner.

'So, there's nothing?' said Elliot, and Minty quailed.

'*Nothing?*'

The voice behind them sent them spinning out of their huddle and Elliot gasped at the sight of his fiancée, fresh from her bridal bread van and in her white gown. 'Jude!'

Any concern about Minty's disastrous planning dissolved for a moment as Elliot took in his bride. Jude smiled up at him, just as goofily in love as ever.

'Hello,' he said, taking her hand.

Jude smiled back, half in a dream.

'We've hit a few snags,' he told her, but before he could go into details, the celebrant arrived.

'Oh thank the Lord!' cried Minty, scratching a tick onto her clipboard and hurrying the woman through into the ballroom while the celebrant explained once more that the Lord didn't have anything to do with it; this was a humanist ceremony.

'Yes, yes, very good.' Minty bustled her inside.

'I'll, uh, get everyone in their seats,' Monty told the bride and groom. 'You look beautiful, by the way,' he told Jude, before going to help Mrs Crawley and Jude's gran to their spot at the front of the ballroom.

'Yes, you do,' Elliot told her. 'So beautiful.'

Jude grinned back, swishing her dress bashfully, but the chaos at the Big House couldn't be ignored forever. 'So, it doesn't sound like Minty's got a handle on things?'

'Well,' he began. Elliot wanted to break it to her gently. 'Not if you like balloons.'

Jude swept a hand. 'I never wanted balloons. That was all Minty.'

'Or a harpist.'

'Oh, OK.'

'Or catering.'

'*What?*'

'Don't worry, we've got ice cream and Prosecco.'

'Right,' said Jude, grimly, her eyes scanning around, not really seeing anything, as their guests filed past, all of them wondering why the bride was already here.

Leonid and Izaak appeared next, having spent the last hour directing the cars in the visitor centre car park. They were leading Mrs Crocombe inside.

'I'm sure he'll be here any minute,' Izaak was saying to her. 'Try not to worry.'

'It's not like him to be late,' Mrs C. said again.

Izaak however, was looking between Jude and Elliot. 'Things are not OK?'

'Well, not really,' Jude told him. 'Minty's scared the living daylights out of every wedding supplier in the south-west. They've all ditched her. I don't even have a bouquet.'

'Oh dear!' said Mrs Crocombe, her hand to her mouth.

'No bouquet?' said Leonid. 'Impossible. I can make you flowers.' He was already on his way to grab his secateurs. 'Back in a minute.'

'Letitia?' said Bovis, on his return from the kitchens and ready to collect his sled. 'Where's your fella?'

'I don't know,' Mrs Crocombe told him, confused. 'He said he would be here.'

Bovis, never one to shy away from chivalry, pulled his apron over his head to reveal his ice-cream-sundae-embroidered 'Crocombe's Ices' T-shirt and crooked his elbow at her. 'The parlour can stay closed for the afternoon. Will you allow me the honour of 'companying me inside?'

Mrs Crocombe hesitated. 'I shouldn't really. He could arrive at any moment and then what would he think, me on your arm?'

'I knew he was not to be trusted,' Bovis said, overconfident as always. 'That's what I told him last night. I did not hold back. And I was right, wasn't I?'

'You were right? About what? You spoke to him?' The tone of Mrs Crocombe's voice cleared the hallway of everyone except a gulping, suddenly nervous Bovis. 'What did you do, Mr Bovis?'

'Nothing any friend wouldn't do. I told him I didn't like the look of him, not from day one. Sliding around, an oily type. I said if you thinks you're going to get your hands on Letitia's residents' emergency payment, you've got another big think coming your way, mister.'

'What? No, you wouldn't do such a thing?' Her hands shook as she covered her mouth.

'I would and I did. Don't think I didn't see him with his ears flapping every time the till chimed! He wanted your ten thousand pounds, guarantee it. And anything else he could get his hands on!'

'How dare you!' Her voice shook as she slapped a weak hand to Bovis's chest. 'You offended him, accusing him of… what? Being a lothario, only interested in that extra money coming to me?'

'Gone, i'nt he?' said Bovis, not understanding the pain he was causing, thinking as always that he was doing absolutely the right and proper thing. 'I had to protec' my friend, and my boss.'

'Protect me? Mr Bovis, you've scared away the only chance at love I'll ever have!' With this, she burst into silent sobs and hurried away, leaving Bovis red-faced and uncomprehending.

'Not your last chance,' he cried after her, his hand stretched out in useless supplication. She was gone, and once more Bovis had managed to spoil another big occasion for another Clove Lore resident. Tugging at his T-shirt, he plodded in her wake.

Elliot and Jude had listened to the whole exchange with wide eyes and clamped lips, from their spot behind a grand stone column by the vestibule's cloakroom.

'Oh dear,' Jude said, once she was sure they were gone. 'It looks like we're losing wedding guests now too.'

'Poor Mrs C.,' agreed Elliot, just as Daniel and Ekon made their way inside, looking all around them at the dark panelling and stucco ceiling. Daniel delivered a message from her dad back home: he was baking up a storm in her kitchen and not to wait for him, but to get wed on time.

Jude turned to Elliot with panicked eyes and said she most definitely was not going to get married without her dad there.

The next half hour passed in a blur of guests arriving, the murmur in the ballroom growing with whispered rumours about furious caterers and wedding DJs. Someone blamed 'Minty actin' all high and mighty' and another replied, 'What's new 'bout that?' And everyone looked at the time and tutted and turned in their chairs to watch the doors while the sky grew duller with every minute that passed.

The celebrant went out to her car to retrieve her portable speakers and everyone cheered when she connected them to her phone and hit play on her 'pre-celebration'

Spotify list, filling the ballroom with jangly instrumental covers of Taylor Swift and Nick Drake, and even though Tom Bickleigh was cracking jokes about the whole wedding party doing a runner, it definitely helped settle the crowd's nerves.

The first drops of rain pattered gently on the high ballroom windows and nobody wanted to say it, but they were all thinking the same thing; that it didn't bode well at all.

Soon, only Elliot, his best man, and Jude were waiting by the ballroom doors. Minty was on her phone somewhere and only occasional hoots of disbelief and despair could be heard from her as she tried (and failed) to get her suppliers back on side.

Jowan arrived from giving Aldous one final scheduled walk on the lawns pre-ceremony, when Elliot's colleague Anjali rushed past them all, bringing with her a little menagerie of creatures from the surgery.

'Sorry I'm late,' she said, smiling uneasily, and lifting the carry case to show Elliot a sorry-looking kitten with a bandaged ear. 'Couldn't leave Felicity with no one at the practice to watch her.'

Elliot poked a finger through the bars. 'Hello, little one, how are you feeling?'

The cat hissed at Anjali's black Labrador, Terrence, who trotted placidly by her side. He'd at least made an effort and was in a bowtie. 'What's a vet's wedding without a dog?' Anjali added, knowing she was pushing it.

'I'm only glad you didn't bring those ferrets that are in with whooping cough!' said Elliot.

'Did consider it,' quipped Anjali, giving her colleague a squeeze on the arm before she stepped inside the ballroom with her animals to take her seat. Elliot gave Terrence's ears one last scratch before he plodded after his owner.

'Aww, man, it's really special having the animals here,' he said to Jude. Then something made Elliot freeze in thought.

After a long moment where Jude shook her head smilingly, knowing exactly what was about to happen, Elliot said, 'Monty? I saw Mr Moke from the donkey sanctuary heading inside a minute ago. Can you go grab him for me?'

They had time to kill anyway, waiting for Jude's dad, and everyone in the ballroom seemed happy enough gossiping about how Jude's cake had been sat on by one of the waiting staff that morning.

Monty dashed all across the estate following the groom's instructions while Jude fixed her make-up and made herself ready.

Leonid reappeared with the estate garden's last roses of the summer, simple white blooms, one each for the men in the bridal party's buttonholes. For Jude, there was a cluster of waxy greenery that smelled of the rhododendron walk and the camellia grove, and at the centre of the lovely cluster he'd placed long stems of bright pink nerines and bobbing Japanese anemones.

'A touch of early autumn,' he said. 'They won't last long, but they are pretty, yes?'

Jude had to agree that they were prettier than any florist's arrangement and she clutched them to her as her dad arrived in a sweaty panic, carrying with him a tall sponge cake just turned out of its tins, un-iced and not yet cool.

He delivered his daughter a proud kiss and told Elliot it was OK, he could go inside now. It was time.

Of course, Mr Crawley was close to tears again, but Elliot shook his hand and left him outside the ballroom with Jude, although not before asking his soon-to-be father-in-law if he could please catch some pictures on his phone since Minty had ballsed-up booking a photographer too.

The gathering burst into applause as Elliot walked in, followed by a rather solemn, pink-cheeked Monty.

'Ready?' asked Mr Crawley, turning to his daughter at the threshold of the ballroom.

Jude fixed her dad's tie and wiped flour from his jacket cuffs.

'Not quite,' she told him.

They turned at the sound of clopping hooves coming from the reception hall. Mr Crawley's eyes widened in wonder at the sight of Mr Moke leading Mushy Peas, the eldest and best behaved of the Clove Lore sanctuary's donkeys, and the smaller, younger Bon Jovi, who was happily munching the paper flower garland round his neck, as they made their way in through Minty's ballroom doors and up to the celebrant's table where Elliot waited beside his best man, grinning for sheer joy at his wedding venue filled with the animals he cared for year-round.

Jowan and Minty saw to shutting the outer doors and they too passed through into the ballroom, and Aldous, on his very best behaviour, tiptoed along between them. With that, the ballroom was filled. Elliot and Jude were at last getting married.

–

'The couple have prepared vows,' the celebrant announced as the hushed crowd smiled and sniffed away happy tears.

Elliot went first, reading shakily from a piece of paper but lifting his eyes to Jude's as he spoke each line.

'My Jude. I promise you that I'll love you. It's as simple and as profound as that. I'll look after you when you're sick, and I'll be glad with you when you're happy. I'll give you what I can in the way of security and safety. I'll never stray. I promise to want you always. To stick up for us when times are tough. I can't promise not to keep asking for a dog or cat.'

At this, the room laughed and Jude shook her head, knowing she'd never win that battle, certain they'd soon end up with a houseful of rescues.

Elliot continued. 'But, whatever happens, we have each other, and I won't spoil that. I'm yours, for good.'

Monty listened to the whole thing, clasping the rings in his hand, and every word made his heart ache that little bit more as he pictured Joy in her seat on the plane, flying away from him. He wiped his eyes and tried to stand up straight when what he really wanted to do was curl into a ball and mope the day away.

Jude was holding a piece of paper now, with the whole room expectantly watching. She glanced around and seemed to think, making Minty, from her spot at the back, start in panic.

'Is she having second thoughts?' Minty whispered to her husband. 'Has my shambolic wedding planning put her off the whole thing? Is she going to bolt?'

Minty needn't have worried. This was Jude Crawley, after all. The original romantic. The girl who'd come to Clove Lore wanting a fresh start and who'd bravely grasped at it when it came within reach.

Jude screwed up the paper in her hand, and Elliot grinned to see it.

'Elliot,' said Jude. 'I had these things to say, all poetry and that, like they tell you in the wedding mags, but it turns out I don't want to read other people's words. What I want to say is that it doesn't matter if things aren't perfect. If there's always a stinky animal or two hanging about. Sorry, Mushy Peas,' she added with a grimace, looking round at the donkey, and everyone laughed. 'It doesn't matter if there's no dinner, because we'll always have cake. We don't need harps playing or helium balloons, or silver service and champagne. None of that's what makes a marriage. I just want you, and,' she looked around at the faces smiling back at her, 'and all of our friends. I love you, Elliot Desvaux. Let's just be married and love each other.'

She nodded decisively to show she'd made her vows, and Elliot couldn't help but lift her up into his arms and kiss her as the celebrant announced that it was time for the rings.

Hurriedly wiping his eyes, Monty stepped forward, his mind rushing with thoughts of Joy and how she'd talked about grooms lifting their brides as a sign that they'd lift them up from now on, that they'd taken over the job of protecting them, and right at this moment it didn't sound all that out-dated and silly after all. It sounded very much like something that he might like to do.

He did his duty and handed over the rings, watching on as Elliot kissed the slim gold band before slipping it onto Jude's finger and she did the same for her husband, making the whole room erupt with happiness and the donkeys *ee-aww* in surprise at all the noise.

'I pronounce Jude and Elliot legally married and bound to one another in love!' the celebrant said over the cheers.

The celebrant's jangly playlist started up once more. Ekon, Daniel and Jude's granny gave each other the nod that it was time and they all fired the confetti cannons they'd sneaked inside with three loud cracks, sending great bursts of colourful paper streaming into the air and showering over the entire happy scene to yet more applause.

Minty slipped out to bring in the chilled Prosecco, and Monty too made his exit, calling his twin brother and a bemused Mr Moke to follow him.

There was still a wedding reception to rescue, and since that was all he'd be able to fix today, Monty set his mind to the task before him: there would be food and a party that Elliot and Jude would never forget. He could salvage this, at least.

Chapter Thirty-two

'Right, I need you to get Mushy Peas's pannier baskets. The biggest ones,' Monty instructed Mr Moke, who wasn't too pleased about being bossed around by one of the Bickleigh boys, but off he went in the direction of the stables anyway.

'And Tom, can you get as much fresh fish from your place as you have?'

'Right-o,' his brother replied, already understanding what was going on without needing to be told. 'I've some fresh bass, some brown trout and there's plenty mackerel in the freezer. What else do you need?'

'Bring as much of the parsley that's growing in Dad's herb bed, and anything else that looks good and green? The Siren'll have the rest.'

With that Tom turned into his cottage gate and waved Monty off on his way down the slope, where there were lobsters and crabs, mullet and squid, and whatever else there was in the morning's catch waiting in his pub's kitchens, plus all the butter and loaves he'd need.

Bursting through the swing doors of his kitchen, Monty was surprised to find a stranger standing there, all dressed in black chef gear and with their hands pressed together nervously.

'Who are you?'

'I'm the new cook, I think. Kit Keating, they/them,' replied the young person, probably in their early twenties, a little bewildered to have arrived and found nobody to welcome them other than the cleaner and a note telling them the pub was shut for two hours and to make themselves at home if they should happen to arrive before Finan got back from the wedding.

'And not a moment too soon!' Monty shook Kit's hand. 'I'm the other chef. Monty. He and him.'

Kit smiled at that. 'Should I, uh… start preparing anything, Chef?'

Monty had never been treated like the head of a kitchen before. It felt odd. 'You could run up the steak pies? Finan was going to do them ahead of evening service. Twenty of them, individual?'

'OK, you've got it, twenty of my special steak bakes coming up. Can I add my blue-cheese twist, makes them super savoury, very umami?' Kit added.

Monty had to smile at their enthusiasm, something he'd never been able to muster for a steak pie. 'You can add anything you like, my friend. And you don't need to call me "chef". The kitchen's yours too. Only, I'll need to take all the fresh seafood we have, sorry.' Monty hauled open the fridges. 'And ice. Can you help me with the ice, Kit?'

Together, they tipped all the ice bags the kitchen had into trays and Kit said, 'Uh, I should have mentioned, the phone was ringing when I got here? I thought it might be Finan or Bella, so I picked up. Turns out it was somebody already staying here? They wanted to upgrade their single room to a twin with a roll-away? Needs it for another night, apparently. Anyway, I wrote it all down on the pad by the phone, told them someone would call them back later. Hope that's OK?'

'Sure,' Monty shrugged. 'Leave it for Finan to deal with when he gets here.' He had his nose in the fridge, pulling out the ingredients he needed, not thinking one bit about the inn and its guests.

Soon, Monty was on his way up the slope, dragging three lidded polystyrene fish crates on the pub's sled behind him, dripping melting ice as he went. Meanwhile, Kit rolled up their sleeves and turned for the stove with a determined grin.

'Jesus, this slope gets steeper every day,' Monty muttered, glancing up at the sky, clearing a little now, with glimpses of blue behind the rain clouds.

'Next stop, bricks,' he told himself, preparing to make the turn off the slope towards the bookshop.

He kept his head down, not wanting to look at the shut-up shop, not wanting to see the darkness and emptiness there.

All he needed to do was wait for Mr Moke and they'd dismantle the barbeque in the bookshop's backyard and transport the whole thing up the hill.

With a couple of additional grills borrowed from Minty's Aga, they'd be able to reconstruct a decent barbeque. It would be wide enough to cook a decent meal for all the guests. 'Hope they like fish,' he told himself, as he picked his way through the blue café chairs and tables in the square, trying not to let his sadness come for him.

He'd expected it to be quiet, prepared himself for it, in fact. The whole village was up at the wedding. He'd *expected* it to be still and full of happy spectres from days ago. He had *known* it was going to hurt being back here, and he'd steeled himself against it as best he could.

What he hadn't expected was to round the corner into the bookshop's garden to hear a plaintive voice asking itself, 'How exactly do you order a replacement passport, for god's sake?'

Monty stopped in his tracks, dropping the sled ropes at his feet at the sight of her. 'Joy?'

She jumped up from the spot against the back wall where she'd been scrolling on her phone, slumped and muttering.

All she could do was stare back at him now, her mouth open.

'You're still here,' Monty told her, blinking.

'Why aren't you at the wedding?' Joy asked, pointing at Monty's suit.

'Oh,' Monty looked down at himself and then at the sled by his side. 'Been a bit of a wedding disaster, really. I need the, uh… bricks.' He gestured behind her.

'Oh.' Joy looked back at the barbeque, not thinking clearly enough to suppose this was quite an odd thing for Monty to be doing.

'Your flight left at half-ten,' he said.

'I know.' She shrugged, taking the smallest step towards Monty and stopping when she saw him flinch. 'Only, you need a passport to get on a plane, and Radia's has mysteriously vanished.'

'It has, has it?' Monty wanted to smile, but he stopped himself. 'So you're… still here.'

Joy spread her fingers. '*Ta-dah!*' Her awkward smile fell into sheepish shame. 'Listen, I—' she began, cutting off Monty who'd also scrambled for words at the same moment. 'Sorry, you go ahead,' she told him.

'What I was going to say was, uh…' He stopped, just to look at her, letting the amazement strike him full force.

'I can't believe you're still here.' He shook his head. 'I thought I wasn't going to see you again and...'

Joy's smile broke out, but she whisked it away, biting her lips shut.

'I was going to call you this morning,' he went on, 'but then all the glasses smashed and the cake got ruined...'

Joy tipped her head, not understanding.

'I wanted to reach you and say sorry again, make you listen. Beg you, really, to forgive me, but by then I was sure you'd left, so...'

'Stop,' said Joy, and Monty looked like his heart was on its very last beat. He had his hand to his chest. She stepped closer still. 'I'm the one that's sorry,' she told him. 'I expected you to understand what was going on with my folks when I hadn't even explained it to you. I was angry because I was panicking, and I chucked you out when I really didn't want you to go. I wanted to tell you all this down on the beach, but you looked so decided, so tired and hurt, like you were done with me and all my drama.'

Now it was Monty stepping forward, almost in touching distance. He watched Joy's eyes scan over his tie and collar, up to his hair and back to his mouth, where she kept her gaze as he spoke.

'You have every excuse to behave however you want to when all you've had is unkindness and gaslighting and let-downs. And you're right. I *was* decided, down on the beach that day. I'd decided I had no right whatsoever to get involved in your life when you had a child to look after. Not if I couldn't be careful with that child's safety, not if I made their mum unhappy, even for a minute. I decided I'd let you go for your own peace of mind.'

Joy was shaking her head but he pressed on.

'But even though I'd decided, I still wanted to come to you in London *so* badly.' His voice shook at this. 'And I seriously didn't want it to be the end of us, not when we'd only just met, when we were just starting something. A *good* thing, I thought.'

'It *was* good,' Joy broke in. 'I loved it! I want more of it. I want more of you!' She was breathless now and there was a light in her eyes that told Monty it was all true.

He took the last step that closed the gap between them. 'I'm so sorry I made things difficult for you with your family.'

'I'm glad you did,' she told him, and Monty was raising his eyebrows in surprise and taking her hands in his when the sound of footsteps and hoof-clops stopped their words.

They both turned to see Mushy Peas's fuzzy nose poking around the corner followed by Mr Moke, red-faced after hurrying down the slope.

''Ave you got the bricks yet?' the stable man said, not remotely aware he was interrupting the most important moment in Monty Bickleigh's life.

Chapter Thirty-three

It turns out all you need for a wedding to be a big success is people in love and the promises they make; everything else is just the icing on the cake. Which, incidentally, Jude had at last.

Mr Crawley emerged from the kitchen of the Big House carrying his simple sponge cake in a thin coating of fresh butter icing in the 'nude' style he'd seen in Jude's bridal magazines. Leonid had cut a cluster of baby's breath and white alstroemeria from the gardens to top the whole thing off and nobody had minded one bit that there wasn't a fruit cake. Radia Pearl announced that, 'Nobody likes fruit cake anyway!' and was first in line for a slice.

She hadn't waited for a wedding invitation on discovering there was an *actual donkey* in the bookshop garden. It had been all her Aunt Patti could do to get her into her party clothes and jelly shoes with her hair brushed before they all headed up the slope, following in the wake of Mushy Peas, who did a grand job of transporting two pannier baskets full of bricks to the parterre garden behind the Big House, where Monty set up his barbeque.

Izaak had the wood and coals ready for them when they arrived, and by the time the bride and groom were on their second glasses of bubbly and had caught up with all their guests in the ballroom, the fire was lit beneath the grills and Monty was rolling up his sleeves ready to make the biggest seafood barbeque Clove Lore had ever seen.

The sky had cleared over the blue Atlantic as the smoke rose in white curls and the wedding guests spilled out into the gardens. Mr Moke ran donkey rides around the lawns for the little ones and Finan drove off in Minty's Discovery, taking the long way round to the Siren, to bring his speaker system up from the pub's function suite.

Before long, there was music filling the gardens, and everyone had a glass in their hand and a smile on their faces. Elliot and Jude danced under the spreading oaks and kissed and whispered.

Radia found her friends, the Crocombe kids, once more and they were running around the low hedges of the parterre maze and screaming with happiness. Patti and Joy watched them play, sipping Prosecco.

'This is better than installing cables in a Lisbon office block?' Patti remarked.

'Thank goodness Gaz stepped in and took that job,' Joy replied.

'And we have a few days' breathing space staying at the pub?' said Patti.

'Yep, before we go back to London.' There was a hint of something sorrowful in Joy's voice as she watched Monty, very much in his element, turning and brushing, basting and tasting, at his barbeque. 'And you go back to…?' Joy prompted.

'Corporate events, some convention stuff, winter weddings, I suppose.' Patti shrugged.

Minty, who was circulating as unobtrusively as she could manage, overheard this last part, and revealed herself now, holding up a bottle. 'Top up?' she asked, and Patti held out her glass. 'So you do weddings?' Minty asked.

'Sometimes. I'm a corporate and celebration events planner. London mainly.'

'Interesting,' Minty said, filling her up. 'You don't have a card on you, do you? I may wish to pick your brains after, ah… everything that's happened today.'

Minty looked so crestfallen, Patti immediately found the card in her wallet and said she must call her 'any time'. As she handed it over she told her truthfully that in spite of it all, this was the best wedding reception she'd been to in a very long time, and Minty had concealed a blushing smile at that.

That evening, after Monty had fed everyone the most delicious freshly cooked seafood and fish dishes they'd ever tasted, and there'd been (short and rather informal) speeches, and Mr Crawley had grinned and sobbed all the way through his toast to his daughter, and the ice cream was devoured and the cake cut to the sound of cheers and applause, all that was left to do was get the donkeys in their stables and the kids in their beds.

Patti carried Radia down the slope to their room at the Siren.

The remaining grown-ups at the reception, beneath the lights spilling down from the Big House windows, slow-danced in pairs dotted all across the parterre and lawns.

Monty let the coals cool and left his station, where he'd kept the food coming all afternoon, and made his way to Joy, waiting patiently under the sycamore.

'Shall we dance?' he said, his hand outstretched.

Joy let him lead her to a quiet spot where the music still reached them and he spun her once before pulling her close to his body.

'I never get to dance,' she told him.

'Well, that's about to change,' he said, his hand spread across her lower back in a way that made her core soften. She leaned close and let him sway her gently, his cheek against hers.

'You saved the day,' she told him, softly, close to his ear. 'Feeding everyone.'

'And I loved it,' he told her, pulling back so she could see him smiling. 'I want to cook outside every day.'

'You already told me that.'

'I know. And you said, *Why don't you?*'

'That's right. So, why don't you? You don't want to be stuck in a pub kitchen. You're a fisherman who loves to fish and cook his catch in the open air. So do that.'

'As easy as that?' he said.

'Yes. Must everything be hard? Can't we have what we want sometimes?'

Monty thought for a moment and tipped his head, conceding that maybe it was possible after all.

'And what do you want?' he asked.

Joy's feet wouldn't move any more, but she kept Monty close, her head on his shoulder. 'I want to work close to home, with no more planes or hotels or childminders. I want what Radia wants.' She lifted her head to look at him, a note of fear in her voice. 'And I want you.'

'Well then, you can have me,' he said, his eyes falling to her lips. 'And you must have all the other things you want and need too. I wouldn't stop you.'

He waited for her to lift her mouth to his and as their lips touched he closed his eyes like he might swoon away entirely.

They kissed and swayed as the sun set on Jude and Elliot's showstopper wedding and the stars rose in the early-September sky.

Chapter Thirty-four

They hadn't talked about it. Not all the way down to the Siren that evening and into Monty's rooms behind the kitchens. Not while they kissed the whole night away and woke up on the first crisp, dewy morning of the year. Not even when Joy was telling him goodbye and Monty was heading bleary-eyed to the kitchens.

Instead they'd said, 'We'll see each other soon, in London, yeah?' And they'd shrugged like that was the easiest thing in the world to manage. 'Yeah, it'll work. Occasional weekends and quiet times at the Siren.'

It had been enough to comfort them for now, even though home was calling and Joy, Patti and Radia were behind the pub, shoving their luggage into the boot of Patti's car and getting ready to set off, Patti remarking how it was funny how they had never found Radia's passport.

While Monty and Kit started on the fried breakfast orders, Joy asked her sister for a few minutes alone and stepped out onto the harbour wall, just to breathe Clove Lore in one last time.

There were no boats moored by the sea wall today. The *Peter's Bounty* was out dropping its nets already. Seagulls, terns and oystercatchers turned over shells on what was exposed of the beach and scouted around the benches looking for food. The tide was still in, covering much of the sand and the long chains that crossed the bay.

Not one person was about. The holidaymakers, she supposed, were heading home, ready for the beginning of the school term, something she'd have to get her head around. September was a time for settling down to a long stretch of work before the homemaking of autumn and the cosiness of the dark nights really set in.

Radia was excited for school, of course. She'd have a lovely time with her grandparents and her aunt Patti, and there was Christmas to look forward to too. It was going to be good, Joy told herself.

Only, out on the sea wall, looking at the shimmer on top of the gentle waves, and the watery blue of the sky, London didn't have the same appeal as it had a few days ago. She knew why too. The idea of not being within touching distance of Monty felt like an impossibility somehow, especially after last night when there'd been nothing whatsoever withheld between them, no secrets, no half-told stories, nothing sad or hurting at all – nothing but the thought of today and her departure, that is, and it had been perfect, the happiest Joy had felt in years.

She took one last look down towards the great lantern at the end of the harbour wall and drew in a deep breath, one that would have to last her for many weeks, months even, until she could get back here. This couldn't be her last visit to Clove Lore, not when there was still so much to see here, so much to feel.

As she turned to leave, a woeful sound met her ears, carried on the breeze. A woman, crying, she thought.

There, at the end of the harbour wall, someone was looking out to sea, and Joy recognised her. She picked up her feet and ran to meet her.

'Mrs Crocombe, what's the matter?' she cried, as she got closer.

'Oh, Joyce, dear,' Mrs C. replied, wiping her eyes on a tissue that she hurriedly concealed up her sleeve.

'You're crying. What's wrong?'

'I've been a fool,' she said, weakly. 'His boat's gone. He's gone.' She turned to face the sea again and Joy's brain caught up.

'The Captain? He wasn't at the wedding, was he?'

'No, dear. He left without saying goodbye. Mr Bovis thinks he was after my recovery-fund money, and after a lot of thought, I think he might be right. After all, why on earth would a man like that want me for myself?'

'You got played,' Joy said, thinking hard.

'Played?'

'Taken in. Happens all the time.'

'Not to me it doesn't. Well, I'm glad he's gone.'

'Yeah?'

'All that excitement, not knowing what I was imagining, what was real? Feeling old and silly one minute, then young and hopeful the next. It wasn't as enjoyable as I thought. I'm too old for that kind of companionship.'

Looking back along the sea wall over Mrs C.'s shoulder, Joy had to disagree. 'I'm not so sure about that. There's still plenty people who won't make you feel like that. Solid, dependable people.'

'Hmm?' Mrs Crocombe turned, following Joy's eyeline to where, in the middle of the sea wall, in his skinny T-shirt and holding two mini tubs of mint choc chip, stood Bovis, his lips hidden away in a sorry smile.

'Oh!' exclaimed Mrs C.

'Peace offering,' he said, as he approached, holding up two pink plastic spoons. 'An' I thought you might like to know my ideas for a nice rhubarb and cinnamon winter gelato?'

'I'll leave you to it,' Joy said, squeezing Mrs C.'s shoulder gently, winking at Bovis as she went. 'Look after her,' she told him.

'I'll do my best,' he promised, before taking the last few steps towards Letitia Crocombe who, despite having won a cool ten bob on Monty and Joy this summer, would never, not over the course of a million summer love matches, at least not until today, have thought about putting her name in her betting book alongside the glowing-cheeked, earnest Mr Bovis.

—

'So that's it then,' Monty asked the top of Joy's head as he bear-hugged her outside the Siren. 'Breezed into town, cruelly made me fall for you, re-established Jowan's business, and now you're off.'

Joy laughed into his chest. 'That's the long and the short of it.'

Radia clung to Patti a few feet away, acting up and not wanting to leave at all now that it was happening, even with the prospect of Granny and Grandad waiting for them in London.

'I... uh... I bought something for Radia,' said Monty, unsure of himself suddenly. 'I ordered it online after hearing her talk about it. Do you think I should give it to her? I don't want to interfere.'

'Go ahead,' said Joy, breaking out of the hug to watch Monty pulling the gift from his back pocket.

'I didn't have time to wrap it. Sorry, Radia.'

'You can still call me Rads,' the little girl reminded him, taking the gift with huge eyes.

'It's a pencil case that's a calculator *and* a notebook,' Monty said, 'like you wanted.'

'It's Hello Kitty!' Radia screeched, jumping at Monty for a hug. 'Thank you!' She was gone again in an instant, asking her aunt to take off the cellophane so she could play with it, and Monty was left holding the spot where the little girl had ferociously kissed his cheek.

'You didn't have to get her anything,' Joy told him.

'I wanted to. I want her to be happy.'

Joy looked to her daughter. 'That's all I want.'

Monty sighed hard. 'OK. Time to go. I'll be seeing you?' he said, trying to sound casual, like this was fine, like there wasn't something else he desperately wanted to say, something enormous.

Joy's feet seemed stuck to the sea wall.

'Call me when you get home?' he asked.

'I'll call you from the Services when Radia needs her first wee. Reckon that'll be,' she checked her wrist, 'in about twenty minutes.'

Monty smiled and delivered one last swift kiss to her lips. Anything else and he'd fall down at her feet.

Joy watched him pull away, her chest heaving and she tried to take the first step away from him.

'Right,' she said.

'OK,' he nodded.

But her feet still wouldn't move and her heart wouldn't budge.

'Mummy, are we going?' shouted Radia, and Joy turned to look at her daughter, dark hair against the blue of the water in the harbour, the September sunlight making her eyes shine.

'Do you *want* to go, Radia?' Joy heard herself say, and Patti's head turned.

'Do *you*?' Radia asked back, and all three sets of eyes peered intently at the breathless, gasping Joyce Foley as she turned between Monty Bickleigh and the gleaming, bustling village of Clove Lore clinging to the valley above them.

Chapter Thirty-five

'I'll be right here, waiting for you.'

'Two o'clock?' said Radia, her hair done in the stubby pigtails she'd insisted upon, clutching at the hem of the blue-and-white-checked dress that she'd been so proud to put on that morning.

'Two o'clock,' said Joy, kissing her yet again. 'Have a lovely, *lovely* day.' The words came out shakily and the teaching assistant, sensing tears, swiftly intervened, whisking Radia inside.

Seeing her now amongst her classmates, it was obvious Radia was taller than the lot of them, but the fearless girl didn't seem to mind. She was grinning unselfconsciously.

Joy heard the TA telling Radia she'd show her to her peg – 'It's got your name on it!' And before Joy could steel herself for it, Radia, not once looking back, disappeared out of sight.

Joy's chest heaved in a great terrified, proud, heart-broken convulsion that she hid behind a pained smile like all the other mums saying goodbye to their babies, who somehow, miraculously, had transformed in the blink of an eye into a school child.

'Right, grown-ups,' said the head teacher, 'off you go. Cup of tea and deep breaths. We'll look after them, I promise.'

Joy clasped her coat shut at the neck and turned to where Patti was waiting, leaning on the railings and holding up her phone. 'I got some lovely pictures,' she said weepily.

Joy wiped her eyes on the back of her hand. 'What now, then?' she asked her sister, who only turned and gestured with a bob of her head a little way down the road to where Monty was standing, hands in his pockets, still wary of over-interfering in family stuff.

The school bell rang to indicate it really was the start of the day and the classroom doors closed upon the emotional families. Joy wandered towards Monty, slowly, trying to remain as present as she could on this important day. She wanted to remember every detail, even though it hurt.

'Patti has calls to make, what should we do?' Joy asked Monty with a lopsided smile, pushing her glasses onto her nose, and the pair walked out along the main road above Clove Lore, which looked even prettier today in the September sun than it had all summer long, leaving the little primary school behind them for a few hours.

'How about a spot of house hunting? Or you can help me set up my new grill stall? The gas tanks and the widget-things are arriving today.' He put his arm around her shoulder as they walked.

Patti took a loud call some way behind them on the footpath.

Joy wiped at her eyes once more and sniffed. 'Widget-things, you say?'

'That's what we say in the biz,' Monty tugged at her arm, good humouredly.

'In the fisherman and seafood grill business?'

'Yep,' he told her proudly. He'd come to an arrangement with Bella and Finan: they'd let him have the prime grilling spot outside the Siren by the picnic tables and he'd help his brother bring in the catch of a morning, and in the afternoons and evenings, he'd cook whatever had been drawn from the sea in their nets for the tourists and locals alike. He could even store his catch in the pub's fridges. And Kit had received the fastest promotion in chefing, becoming the head of the Siren's kitchens within days of their arrival.

'You didn't have to come straight off the boat,' Joy told him. 'You must be tired.'

'What? And miss Rad's first day at school? No way. Besides, I knew you'd need the hug.'

'I do,' Joy said, 'oh, I really do,' and she pulled him closer to her side as they walked through the very first of the falling leaves.

'I guess I should get on the phone too,' she told him. 'Get some contracts settled for the winter, local stuff, or remote connections, things I can do from a home office. Gaz'll have some ideas too.'

'No regrets?' he asked.

'No regrets,' she told him.

It had taken her a second or two to decide that day on the sea wall, when faced with the option of starting over again in London with her parents close by and Monty nowhere near, or beginning afresh in Clove Lore, the place that had stolen her and Radia's hearts.

She'd made the right decision, she knew. Even though Pamela Foley had taken a bit of convincing that this was really what she wanted. She'd told her daughter she'd support her no matter what and they'd spoken on the phone every day since. There were plans already being made for a half-term holiday in Clove Lore, and Christmas too, and even her dad had said he couldn't wait to come back to the seaside to visit them.

Patti had offered to stick around for a week or so to help them settle into their rooms at the Siren, though it was becoming increasingly obvious to everyone except Patti that she was showing very little sign of wanting to get back to the event-planning rat race in London.

'It's going to be a lot of adjusting,' Monty said, gently, as they took the turning off the main road down towards the visitor centre car park that led to Down-along.

'It is, I know,' said Joy, but she was smiling nonetheless, her eyes fixed on the sloping seaside village where her future lay.

Only yesterday, the latest Borrowers had taken possession of Borrow-A-Bookshop, finding on their arrival a display of children's books on the table by the door, to be kept in place throughout their stay, as was Jowan's tradition. And beside copies of *Oi Frog!*, *Mog the Forgetful Cat*, *Topsy and Tim*, *The Tiger Who Came to Tea*, *The Brilliant World of Tom Gates*, and rather a lot of books about pirates because Radia couldn't narrow them down at all, as well as, of course, a well-thumbed copy of *The Borrowers*, was a note making sure the new people understood that there was to be a children's story time *every Friday afternoon*. The note had been signed off with these words: 'I will let all my school friends know to come along. Please remember the strawberry squash and scones, Love Radia Foley, from the Siren's Tail.'

Monty and Joy decided not to call in at the bookshop as they made their way Down-along.

'Let them settle in, poor things. It's a shock to the system, getting your very own bookshop to play in,' said Joy.

'Good idea,' Monty told her, 'and they won't want locals interfering too much.'

'Definitely not.' Joy faked a shudder. 'Shall we go and check on Mrs Crocombe?' she said as they drew level with the Ice Cream Cottage.

Monty peered in through the glass where the old matchmaker could be seen perched on a stool behind the counter, watching Mr Bovis present her with a tall pumpkin-spice latte from the machine, topped with expertly swirled whipped cream.

'He's getting better at those,' Monty said.

'Just in time for autumn,' Joy added, as Mrs C. spotted them through the glass and lifted her hand in a friendly wave.

She was still pale and tired-looking, Joy noted, but that was to be expected after the last few days. It went without saying that Mrs Crocombe would need time to get over the Lucky Boy she'd thought she'd been falling for.

Through the glass, Bovis was sprinkling a dusting of cinnamon over his latest creation and coming to join his friend on a stool by her side.

Monty and Joy watched the pair lift their cups to one another and take smiling sips, and Joy recognised the warm spark of companionship and kindness she was sure would be the cure for Mrs C.'s broken heart.

'Let's leave them to it, eh?' she said, walking on.

'Good thinking,' Monty said. 'Besides, I *did* think we might pop in here today?'

Joy squinted askance at him in the low morning sun, not understanding what he was on about. Not until they came to Jowan's cottage, with its owner and Aldous standing by the gate, the 'For Sale' sign conspicuously absent.

'Just in time,' said Jowan, holding out the key.

'Do you want to take a look? See if you like it? Zero expectations, of course,' asked Monty, cautiously. 'You don't have to, honestly. It has to be your decision.'

Joy lifted herself to kiss Monty's cheek. 'Can't hurt to look,' she said.

Grinning all the while, she took the key from Jowan's hand and then made her way through the little white gate, past the seed heads setting amidst the fading summer bedding, and slipped the key in the lock.

'Hurry up, Pats!' she called, looking back at her sister, still quite a way up the slope and talking to a colleague, explaining how she might not be taking on any London jobs for a while, and how she fancied an extended family holiday by the sea. Patti waved a hand that told her sister to go on inside without her, she'd be there in a while.

And so, with her heart in her mouth and the strangest feeling that she was finally home before she had even stepped inside, Joy turned the key on her new life in Clove Lore. Monty slipped his hand into hers to let her know he was right here for her, by her side, no matter what she wanted to do, and he always would be.

A Letter from Kiley

This, and I can't quite believe I'm saying this, is the third instalment in the *Borrow-A-Bookshop* series! The first was *The Borrow a Bookshop Holiday* (2021) in which Elliot and Jude fall in love, and the second was *Christmas at the Borrow a Bookshop* (2022) where a wandering Viking and a runaway mermaid find each other (it makes sense in the book, OK?) before an almighty flood threatens their 'insta-love' connection.

While reading these two braw books first would definitely help you feel your way into *Something New at the Borrow a Bookshop*, you can still read this story as a standalone.

Anyway, I'm just so glad you picked up my book. I really hope you enjoy it, and if you do like Joy and Monty's story, please consider popping a review on any online place you like. I appreciate any and all cheerleading and encouragement!

This series is set in Clove Lore, which bears a striking resemblance to picturesque, historic Clovelly in Devon. You might have been there yourself, in which case you'll already be besotted with the place, or you might have seen it on the telly, including the movie adaptation of *The Guernsey Literary and Potato Peel Pie Society*. It's not hard to see why I'd set a book about gladly losing your heart in such a breathtaking spot. However, the bookshop, the local characters, their quirky eccentricities and the romantic magic in the air, they're all my invention.

If Joy's story of escaping coercive control strikes a chord with you, I'm here to hold your hand and point you towards Women's Aid UK for advice and assistance.

Some of you will recognise the pain that Elliot is in too, estranged from his family. They don't get a reunion. It was important to include this aspect of family relationships in one of my stories as all the happy families in fiction can leave some folk feeling unseen. Elliot knows what it feels like to be 'cut off' and is proof that sometimes extremely loveable people are let down by the people who are supposed to love them most and it's OK to set boundaries to protect yourself from them.

Oh, and one last thing, just in case you're wondering: Joy's decision to educate Radia herself? Hats off to her. She's been doing a difficult, noble thing and even though Radia longs to go to a school in this story, I'm in no way disparaging anyone who chooses 'education other than at school'. Goodness knows, so many children need home-schooling or its many alternatives to thrive, and plenty Local Authorities force children out of the school system whether they want to be out or not. Three cheers for all the EOTAS grown-ups, their supporters and their amazing young people!

Now for the thank yous. Thank you to Lotte who suggested Radia's birth hospital and named Charley fox. Thank you, Keshini, Jennie, Dan, Hannah, Vicki, and everyone at Hera Books who read, edited, proofread, typeset and did all the technical jiggery-pokery to get this book into your hands. Diane Meacham designed this stunning cover; thank you so much, Diane.

Thank you to my little family for pottering away on your own and letting Mummy write in peace, or at least trying *very* hard to let that happen. I love you all. Mouse, I love you so much. Thank you for being my best friend.

Lisa, thank you for listening and always knowing what to do.

An especial thank you goes out to Catherine Wilcox for her kindness and mentorship.

Lisa and Vicky, and the dream team, you're amazing. Thank you for everything.

Finally, thank you, lovely readers, reviewers, bloggers and booksellers. I will continue to try to write uplifting books with your support.

Don't forget to come say 'hello' over on Instagram @kileydunbarauthor or on Twitter @kileydunbar I'd love to meet you there!

See you again soon for another Borrow-A-Bookshop story.

Love, Kiley x